ST. MARTIN'S

MINOTAUR
MYSTERIES

Other titles from St. Martin's **Minotaur** Mysteries

Minotaur is also proud to present these mystery classics
by Ngaio Marsh

THE ROOM WAS STILL . . .

. . . with the mustiness that takes over old houses when the dusting-powder smell of female occupancy is removed. I flipped the wall switch inside the door, testing to see if the power was still on. The overhead light popped on and the sluggish ceiling fan revved up to a whir, punctuated by the click of a bearing in need of oil. The faded carpet was matted in a few spots, suggesting heavy furniture recently uprooted.

I stepped back. A steely flash swept the corner of my eye, whipping down toward my shoulder. A rush of adrenaline surged through me, and I threw up my right hand. Pain sliced across my forearm. I snatched at the knife and snagged a wrist with my left hand. I jerked hard and heaved my weight to the left, slamming the attacker against the wall. The wood-handled steak knife clattered across the floor. I lunged for it, rolled and jumped to my feet. I spun. I raised the knife . . .

It was Barb, sprawled on the floor against the wall, her mouth opening and closing like a fish on a boat deck gasping for breath . . .

BIG EASY
BACKROAD

MARTIN
HEGWOOD

St. Martin's Paperbacks

Disclaimer: *Big Easy Backroad* is a work of fiction. Names, places, characters, and incidents are products of the author's imagination or are used fictitiously. Although Bay Saint Louis, Mississippi, and Waveland, Mississippi, are real cities, I have taken certain liberties in changing the landscape and have combined the two cities (under the name Bay St. Louis) to prevent confusion on the part of the reader. There is no Bayou Pitasa in Bay St. Louis or Waveland; that is the bayou that runs in front of my family home in Pascagoula, on the eastern end of the Mississippi Gulf Coast. Any resemblance to actual events at any of the locales depicted in this book is coincidental. Any resemblance to any person, living or dead, is coincidental.

BIG EASY BACKROAD

Copyright © 1999 by Martin Hegwood.
Excerpt from *A Green-Eyed Hurricane* copyright © 2000 by Martin Hegwood.

Library of Congress Catalog Card Number: 99-22040

ISBN: 0-312-97141-9

Printed in the United States of America

St. Martin's Press hardcover edition / July 1999
St. Martin's Paperbacks edition / July 2000

10 9 8 7 6 5 4 3 2 1

With love to Linda, Eliza, and William, for never doubting and never complaining; and to my parents, Tommy and Jean Hegwood, for a lifetime of support and encouragement.

ACKNOWLEDGMENTS

I thank these friends and family members for their assistance: Susan Anthony, Judy Berry, Margaret Bretz, Oliver and Jennifer Diaz, Andrea Dukes, Tommy Furby, Neal and Katherine Graham, Elsie Hammett, Paulette Holahan, Kay Jerome, Bill and Julie Kehoe, Richard Lucas, Harry Moran, Liz Hegwood Smith, and Jan Warner. I also want to express my appreciation to fellow writers Neil McGaughey and Charles Wilson for their encouragement. Special thanks go to the following: Kenn Davis, for helping me get the manuscript into shape; Jimmy Vines, my agent and the one who saw something there; Joe Veltre, the editor who took a chance on me; and Erika Fad, Joe's assistant who has walked me through each step.

BIG EASY
BACKROAD

ONE

"It ain't seeing the body that made me throw up, Jack. I seen plenty of stiffs before."

"Tony," I said, "that was no slasher movie out there. That was real."

"Real bodies is what I'm talkin' about. I seen 'em. Lots of 'em."

"Lots of bodies?"

"Like at funerals and stuff."

I nodded as I laid my cinnamon roll beside the Newport display and poured myself the darkest dregs from the coffeepot. Hell, the stuff even smelled like it was scorched. Felt hot right through the Styrofoam. Three weeks I had stopped by the TimeSaver on my way to the docks, and I had never managed to catch a fresh pot despite the fact that I always got there before sunrise.

"You gotta admit those are bodies," he said.

"Sure they are."

"Of course they are. And I seen lots of them. So, see, it wasn't walking up on that man all dead and everything that made me sick. It was that rat."

"What rat?"

"You think a rat would eat a dead man?"

"It's possible," I said.

"Just before I got to him, I shined my flashlight on the biggest rat in Orleans Parish haulin' ass outta there. I could just see that rat eatin' a chunk outta his neck. That's what made me sick." It sounded like an apology. Nineteen-year-old boys, especially Eighth Ward kids like Tony, kids with daggers tattooed on their biceps, feel like they have to apologize for such things.

"Sounds bad," I said. "You see anything else?"

"Like I told you. His throat was slit wide open, all the way down to the bone. Oh, yeah, and he was laid out on a sheet."

"Did you say a sheet?" That made my heart beat a little quicker.

"And this box was right beside him," he said. "Had two candles on it. Little white ones like they use in church. Wax had dripped all over the box."

Through the burglar bars inside the plate glass of the storefront I saw a fifth police cruiser pulling into the lot. It was still dark, not quite dawn, and the flashing light bars painted everything blue. Two policemen, one scribbling on a notepad, towered above a gray and hollow-cheeked man in a sweat-stained shirt squatting on the curb in front of the door. The few teeth he had were yellow and broken, and he had a three-day stubble on his face. He also had a bad case of the shakes.

"This box, was it long?" I held my hands up two feet apart. "Was it shaped like maybe a little coffin?"

"I didn't look too good." He shuddered as he hunched his shoulders. "You don't reckon that rat . . ."

"It was in those weeds minding its own business and you scared it. That's all. What about the box?"

"I guess you could say it looked like a coffin," he said, "for a rat or something . . ."

"Forget the damn rat."

"It was like one of them boxes whiskey bottles come in."

So, six years after killing Big Jim he comes to the surface again. I swirled my coffee around, and a few scalding drops sloshed on my hand. "Why did you go over there?" I asked.

"That wino out there busted in here yelling about how he had stumbled over this dead guy in that empty lot." He stepped toward the coffee machine, shaking down a foil pack of Dark Roast Luzianne. "I figured he was having the DTs and told him to beat it. But he kept pulling at my arm and everything so I locked up and went to take a look."

"Tony, son, I've told you a million times not to come out from behind that counter."

"Hey, I carried my pistol." He patted the chrome-plated .38 holstered above his back pocket.

A white station wagon with the *Channel Six News* logo whipped into the parking lot, and from the passenger side a woman stepped out, tall as I am, her blonde hair shining under the yellow glow of the streetlights.

"What did the dead man look like?" I asked.

"He was sorta black, looked Puerto Rican. Pretty young. I'd say mid-twenties. About your height. Six feet, six one. Hard to tell with him laid out on the ground."

The two cops who had been standing beside the wino walked inside. One looked Tony's age, too young to be a cop. But when you turn forty, you see doctors and judges who look like they could go to the prom. And every morning I see a new gray hair where there was a dishwater blond one the day before.

The other cop had some years on him. His gut pushed hard against his belt and he had deep crinkles around his eyes. They brushed past me to the counter and waited for the new coffee to brew. The young cop lifted the pot and the last few drops sizzled on the warmer.

"The Undertaker at it again?" I asked the older cop.

His eyes narrowed as he stared through the steam over the rim of his cup. "You know something about this?"

"Nothing but what I just heard. Sounds like the Undertaker to me."

"We got all the investigators we need, mister. Don't be talking about no Undertaker, 'specially around that TV reporter out there."

He rubbed his eye with his knuckle and turned toward the blue lights. He sipped his coffee in short, loud slurps and kept looking outside as I glared at the side of his face. If these cops were half as good as they thought they were, they would have made a case six years ago. And nobody would ever have had any need to hire guys like me. But he did have a point. Bringing up the Undertaker was the last thing the NOPD needed.

"C'mon," he said to the young cop, "let's wrap this up."

As they walked out the door, Tony said something I didn't hear. Some grim work was going on outside. Six cops in a knee-high ground fog shone flashlights across the lot, flattening the brown weeds as they kicked around, looking for the knife they knew wasn't there. A camera flashed as an investigator on one knee chalked a line around the body. An ambulance down the street, flickering red and white, inched toward the store. Had it looked like this when Big Jim was killed?

"Hello?" Tony said. "Anybody home?"

"Huh? Oh . . . yeah. I was just thinking about something."

"Well? Who is he?"

"Who?"

"Who else? The King of Mexico," he said. "That Undertaker dude. Who is he?"

I sipped some coffee. "This stuff is burned up, Tony."

"You say that every day. Who is he?"

The ambulance eased into the lot and parked beside the Channel Six station wagon. The driver killed the white strobe but left the red lights flashing.

"It was too far back for you to remember," I said. "Several years ago they found two bodies one night over on the banks of the Harvey Canal. Found another one the next week under the I-10 overpass. They all had their throats slit, just like that guy out there."

"They have them whiskey boxes, too?"

"They're miniature coffins. That's why the newspaper started calling the guy who did it the Undertaker."

"Oh, man. They ever catch him?"

I shook my head. "Word got out about the coffins so everybody figured they were voodoo sacrifices or something."

"Voodoo? Cool!"

"They were drug killings, Tony. The dead guys were all street pushers. But naturally the press played up the voodoo angle. Made national news for a month and embarrased the hell out of the cops."

"Hey, this makes national news, maybe they'll put me on that *Dateline* show."

"I'm sure they'd love to hear all about that rat."

A cop shooed the reporter away from the body. I sipped the remaining bitter drops of my coffee, chewed the last bite of my cinnamon roll, crumpled the wrapper, and tossed it, along with the coffee cup, into the trash can by the door.

"Hey, Jack! Got one for you. How can you tell a male chromosome from a female chromosome?"

"You pull down its genes," I said. "You told me that one last week."

"Hey, it's hard to get fresh material, you know?"

"Yeah," I said. "See you later, Tony. Stay behind that counter, you hear?"

The air was thick with exhaust fumes from the idling police cruisers. The blonde reporter called out and trotted over to me as I walked to my truck. The cameraman, a chubby kid with oily, shoulder-length hair, grunted as he hoisted the camera to his shoulder. "Do you know anything about this?" she said.

I glanced past her, over her shoulder, and saw the two cops who had been in the store. They leaned against their cruiser with their arms folded, watching as she stuck her portable microphone near my face.

"Just drove up," I said. "Don't know a thing."

She wheeled around without a word and dashed over toward the cops at the edge of the weeded lot. The cameraman jogged after her, panting and cursing in low tones. Under the glare of the television camera, the EMTs lugged the body toward the ambulance. I drifted away from the curb and coasted to the street with my window rolled down, the morning quiet broken only by the deep horns of the tugs on the Mississippi River and an occasional crackle from a police car radio.

I pulled out into the street and headed uptown toward the Celeste Street Wharf, on my way to unload ships for the last time. My side mirror reflected darkness, except for the gleam of the TV camera's light on the faces of the older cop and the blonde reporter.

She had only been in New Orleans for two or three years. She wouldn't make the connection. But some city editor, or some longtime reporter who had been around back then, would be asking NOPD about it, and soon.

Because everybody who was in the city when they found those bodies remembers the Undertaker, and they know he's still around.

They even know who he is.

TWO

On a moonless night three weeks earlier, somebody had backed a truck up to Celeste Street Loading Dock 16-A leased by Oriental Jade Imports and lifted two crates of rugs from Singapore worth three hundred grand. That got the attention of Bayou Casualty Insurance Company and they decided to send in an investigator. None of their in-house guys are worth a damn at undercover, so, as usual, they gave me a call. It was a perfect time; my cash supply had run way too low.

For eight years I have been the owner and only employee of Jack Delmas Investigations, Incorporated, of Bay Saint Louis, Mississippi. I can't take credit for any part of that name. "Delmas" came from France in 1699 when my ancestors landed with d'Iberville on what is now the Bay of Saint Louis. "Jack" is short for Andrew Jackson, who led my third great-grandfather in the Battle of New Orleans and for whom I am named. My brother made me throw in the "Incorporated" part. And "Investigations" I owe to Big Jim Brannan, the man who brought me into the business.

I do freelance investigations for insurance companies, the kind their in-house agents won't, or can't, do. That usually means undercover, like it did this time. My working conditions aren't normally as good as what the in-house guys have. And the work's not always steady—not that I mind that so much—but the pay is better and I don't have to go to any office parties.

My ex-wife didn't understand why I hated office parties. I finally got her to see that it wasn't so much the party I couldn't take, it was the office. She didn't understand that either.

Any rookie could see it was an inside job, and I pegged two suspects within the first week: Bob Blair, a complaining sort, a four-year employee going nowhere; and Randy Wallace, a twenty-year-old dropout, whose rap sheet included a breaking and entering. The next two weeks I learned enough about them to nail down that they had acted alone. When I decided to make my move, I set up a dummy shipment, a wooden crate six feet high with markings from a cabinet maker in Bombay. I also set up a video camera.

For the hell of it, I got an army buddy who'd cut his teeth on booby traps in the Mekong Delta to rig the crate with a green dye bomb, the kind the banks use. The video was enough, but I figured the thieves couldn't resist sneaking a peek and getting a paint job in the process. I also figured the boys at Bayou Casualty would get a kick out of seeing it on film. Turns out I was right on both counts. I like to give my clients a little extra.

When I reached the riverfront on that last day, the sun had broken the horizon and had started to burn off the fog. The heat of the sun stirred breezes from the river, smelling of mud and diesel fuel. Up on the loading ramp Billy and Frank sprayed garden hoses, splattering water across the concrete and pushing a pool of green water toward the edge.

"What happened?" I asked.

"A booby trap," Frank said.

"A what?"

"You remember, I told you 'bout that shipment got stoled a few weeks ago? All them rugs? Well, they set a trap last night to see if them thieves would come back. One of them paint bombs." He laughed. "They come back all right."

"Guess who it was," Billy said.

"I would have guessed you two."

"It was Bob and Randy. The cops arrested them last night."

"I'm not surprised," I said.

I grabbed a push broom and started sweeping water. Soon the full crew arrived—except for Bob and Randy—and we set up for a freighter that had radioed in an hour earlier from twelve miles downriver. I kept my cover and operated a forklift, as I had done for the past three weeks, in case some follow-up work needed to be done.

I had gotten pretty good with that forklift. At times the breeze from the river, the sweet smell of the blue exhaust, and the vibrations of the seat called up sensations from summers long ago when I'd mowed lawns with my father's little red Wheel Horse tractor all day for a ten dollar bill, my ticket to a night of cruising the beach and hanging around the drive-in. Even though every day for the past three weeks I'd sweated like a fat roofer in July, I decided there are worse jobs than being a forklift driver. I've suffered through a few of them.

The ship docked at nine o'clock. Three hours later the whole crew walked over to a po'boy stand down the street, except for Frank and me. Frank was the foreman, fifty years old, but the gray hair and deep sun creases on his face and neck added fifteen more. He brought his lunch everyday and I usually did, too. The air hung still and hot, and the glare bouncing off the concrete around the warehouse made us squint. We sat outside on a bench under a sheet metal awning on the river side of the warehouse, looking out at the passing freighters and tugs.

"You won't believe what I saw this morning," I said. "I drove up on a bunch of police cars over on Chef Menteur. They'd found a body in a vacant lot next to that TimeSaver."

Frank turned his head and made a spitting sound. "Back when I come here to these docks, it weren't nowhere near as bad as it is now. I'm tellin' my kids they better get out while the gettin's good."

"How many kids you got?" I asked.

"Three. Ain't but one of 'em still at home. How 'bout you?"

"I've got one," I said. "A little girl. She lives with her mama up in Memphis."

"Tell her to stay there. New Orleans was alright when I come here thirty years ago, but it ain't the same nowadays."

"Thirty years," I said. "You must remember the Undertaker."

"I remember him." Frank poured tea into the cap of his thermos.

"Somebody had slit this guy's throat. They found a little box beside the body with some candles melted on it."

"Sounds like him."

"You think it's André Mouton?" I asked.

"Hell, everybody does. But they'll never pin anything on Mouton. He done paid off the cops and the DA, too. Been doin' it for years. They got cops who take home twice as much from Mouton every month as they do from the city."

"They got a different DA now," I said.

"It don't matter," he said. "They're all on the take."

Frank finished his lunch, lit a cigarette, and rested his leathery forearms on his knees. His bronze eyes followed a fast-moving pilot boat on a downriver run, off to guide another freighter to one of the wharfs.

"I told them they could take a long lunch today," he said, glancing at his watch. "No use killin' ourselves in this heat. We ain't got that much more to unload."

When the crew returned I climbed back on the forklift. We knocked off around four o'clock and everybody scattered. I didn't have any more work to do on the case, at least not on the docks, so I told Frank I'd be out of town for a while starting the next day. He nodded and grunted, tired of hearing that old story; he knew he wouldn't see me again.

Squiggling waves of heat rose from the concrete as I walked to my truck. My undershirt was soaked and clinging to my back, and the faded denim workshirt had half-moons of sweat at the armpits. The air in the cab was searing hot. I rolled down the windows and drove east a few blocks heading back to my room at the Alamo Plaza. Around the corner, up ahead on the left, sat the Comus Bar. I hadn't been there in years.

It had a new coat of dark red paint, but it still had the same old sign hanging over the door with the same old slogan . . . COMUS BAR—COLDEST BEER IN TOWN.

I've always been a sucker for a slick advertising campaign.

THREE

I paused to let my eyes adjust to the dark. The only light in the Comus comes from the television behind the bar, from beer signs mounted on the walls, and from a lamp over the pool table, an elongated Tiffany suspended by two chains and topped off by a team of Clydesdales pulling a beer wagon under a clear plastic cover.

The air was chilled and had a pool hall smell of cigarette smoke and beer. I groped my way toward the bar, chair by chair, moving along by memory as much as anything. It was like I was scuba diving in dark water. By the time I sat down I could almost see.

The place looked the same. Booths along the far wall with four or five Formica-topped tables in the center of the room. Cinder-block walls, bumper stickers, Mardi Gras posters, and ten years' worth of Saints' football schedules.

The cold, vinyl-coated padding of the bar stool felt good, like a damp cloth on my back. Behind the bar, toward the other end, a man with a shaved head and a jutting brow was fussing at a blonde barmaid. He had a tiny gold loop in his left earlobe. I figured him to be the new owner; I'd heard old Jimmy had died last year. I grabbed a handful of roasted peanuts from a bowl on the bar, cracked a few, and threw the shells on the floor. An old Comus tradition.

The blonde at the other end of the bar walked toward me. In the dark and at a distance she looked better than other barmaids I had seen in there, but that's not saying much. When she emerged from the shadows, I saw she knocked the top out of the Comus average.

Her healthy, outdoor look was out of place in the smoky haze. The pink crop-top and Esprit jeans cleaved tight to her cheerleader's build. She had a delicate face. Small nose turned up just a bit. Green eyes, wide set, giving her a girlish look. Hair streaked by sunlight, skin fine-grained and flawless, with a light caramel summer tone. She gave me a smile that was lively, direct, and unrestrained, a smile that transformed her from pretty to beautiful. A smile that promptly sent me into a zone.

I swear I started hearing waves lapping on soft sand. Maybe it was the lights, maybe it was the soothing coolness of the room after a day in a blast furnace. Whatever it was, I became transfixed and would have, at that minute, followed that smile over a cliff.

"Could I get you something?" she asked.

Thank God I wasn't directly in front of the mirror behind the bar so I couldn't see the goofy-assed grin I must have had.

"Would you like something to drink?"

"Yeah," I said cleverly.

She waited.

"You want to tell me what that would be?" she asked.

"Uh . . . draft." I was having trouble with more than one word at a time.

She turned and reached into the chest freezer behind the bar, into the frosty cloud for an icy mug, while I reminded myself that I was a forty-year-old professional man and twenty years removed from the moonstruck fraternity boy who had apparently possessed my ass. In one practiced and expert move she held the mug under the spigot with her left hand and pulled down hard on the tap with her right, and that cold Dixie beer filled the glass, leaving no more than an inch of foam.

"That'll be a dollar-fifty." She had a midwestern accent, I guessed Chicago. I laid a five on the bar and took a long draw off my beer.

"You don't sound like you're from here." More cleverness, I admit. But, hey, I was working up to multiword sentences.

"I've been in New Orleans about a year," she said, "but I've only worked here like five or six weeks." She glanced downward like a shy girl. Then she slowly raised those emerald eyes and I locked in on them like a hypnotist's watch. I had the sensation that they were pulling me toward her.

"I'm Jack Delmas." I held out my hand.

"Nice to meet you, Jack. I'm Barbara." She shook my hand with a light grasp. "Most people call me Barb."

I nodded as I felt that silly-assed grin slipping up on me again.

"It's short for Barbara," she said.

"Right." I became even more self-conscious. I took another drink and glanced around the room. "It's been a long time since I was here," I said. "Where's the bowling machine?"

She laughed. "It finally broke down. Nate says you can't buy them anymore. All the old-timers ask about it . . ." She caught herself and her mouth dropped. "Not that you're old. I mean . . ."

"I understand."

She blushed. "I think Nate's going to put in a video poker machine."

I tilted my head toward the guy who had been fussing at her. "Who's the new guy?"

"That's Nate. He's the owner." Her frown told me that Nate was not one of her favorites.

"I haven't seen him before."

"So you come in here some?" she asked.

"Been coming in off and on for years. But not lately."

"Well, you'll have to start coming more often." She patted my wrist. Her hand felt warm and soft as velour. "You know, tomorrow's ladies' night."

"Let me guess. Half price on strawberry daiquiris."

"Nice try," she said. "It's frozen margaritas."

"I'm probably too old for ladies' night."

"Don't sell yourself short," she said. "The guy I've been dating is about the same age as you."

I wondered what she could possibly see in this guy I had never laid eyes on.

"I'll be right back," she said.

Barb scooped a bowl of peanuts from the barrel behind her, stepped around the bar, and carried them to a table of gym rats in tank tops, still glistening from their afternoon workout and drinking beer like it was Gatorade.

I recognized a voice from the television set mounted on a rack near the ceiling. It was the blonde reporter I'd talked with that morning at the TimeSaver.

> In our top story, Channel Six has learned that New Orleans homicide investigators are looking for clues to the identity of a body found early this morning in a vacant lot on Chef Menteur Highway.

The scene from that morning came on. EMTs hauling a lumpy body bag across a grown-over lot under a camera's spotlight as red and blue lights swept across them in syncopated pulses. The camera zoomed in on the body bag. Barb came back, lifted my beer, and wiped the water off the counter.

> The body is that of a black man who appears to be in his twenties. The victim was six feet tall and weighed one hundred and seventy pounds. His throat had been cut. It is the city's one-hundred-and-eighty-third recorded homicide this year.

That grabbed her attention. "Oh, my God!" she said softly. She bit on two fingers, still staring up at the screen. The beautiful smile faded.

> There is evidence that the body may have been moved. Police speculate that the victim may have been murdered in a ritualistic fashion.

A blank-faced police spokesman back at Headquarters said, "We can't say at this time if this is a cult or ritualistic killing. There is some evidence that would indicate a ritual murder, but nothing points to any particular suspects."

The reporter didn't mention the miniature coffin or the candles. The older cop had been smart enough to hide that stuff before the press got there.

Barb gazed at the television. Her hand quivered as she chewed on a fingernail.

"That's bad, huh?" I said.

She had gone off somewhere a long way from the Comus. Without a word, she stepped to the sink and, looking down, washed a few glasses with quick, hard strokes. I drained the last of my beer.

"Barb, can I get another?"

"Sure." Her voice broke. She drew a fresh beer and handed it to me. She tried a smile but her eyes were moist and there were teardrops on her eyelashes. She swept them away with the back of her hand.

"A dollar-fifty," she said.

"Barbara, what's wrong?"

Barb pointed the remote and switched over to the Channel Four news.

"Are you alright?" I asked.

She took a deep, shaking breath. "Look, I'll be right back, okay?" She turned and disappeared into the back room.

I sat there, deflated, and trying to figure out what the hell had happened. I'm talking with this beauty queen who dates guys my age and I'm in this euphoria, and the next minute that news story comes on and it evaporates. I tried to recover the feeling, but it was like trying to recapture an interrupted dream. I propped my elbows on the bar and sipped on my beer, a tactic that usually helps me think through these things.

While I was talking with Barb, the place had been filling up. Now that I had come back down to the planet, I noticed that the front doors were opening regularly, each time sending in shafts of blinding light. I swiveled and surveyed the room. A different crowd from what the Comus had twenty years ago when we used to drive over when we were home on breaks from college.

A waitress I hadn't noticed earlier served cocktails at a table full of pinstriped and buttoned-down young men, fledgling bankers swapping war stories from their first three months on the job. Another group of briefcases sat in the booth near the back of the room, and six or seven Tulane students crowded around a small, round table, sharing a couple of pitchers of Dixie and a big bowl of peanuts. There was only one group of hard hats, sunburned and menacing, and they sat huddled in a booth near the front door drinking longnecks.

The beers started to run through me, so I walked toward the mailbox-style, glow-in-the-dark letters nailed to the back wall and spelling out 4 U 2 P. Ol' Jimmy had thought that up himself and been real proud of it. Garth Brooks boomed out from the jukebox, and from under the Clydesdales I heard the occasional crack of pool balls as two kids in cutoffs and T-shirts shot a game of eight ball with a lot more force than finesse.

Two black men, one thin and narrow faced and the other thick necked and solid, sat at a table outside the door of the men's room. Both wore sport coats, both wore sunglasses. An emaciated woman sat with them, New Orleans black, not much darker than I am. Leather miniskirt, high heels, and a silver satin Oakland Raiders jacket. A kid who looked as if he may have skateboarded to the Comus stood beside the table talking to the narrow-faced man.

As I approached them, the thin man got up and he and the kid stepped into the men's room. The big guy rose and blocked my path. His cologne reeked, strong and syrupy. I tried to walk around him, but he moved to the side and cut me off.

"You gotta wait," he said.

"I've been in there before. There's plenty of room."

He crossed his arms and I noticed the bulge of a pistol under his coat.

"I'd suggest you get out of the way," I said, watching to see that his arms stayed crossed. "That is, unless you want me to piss on your foot."

"Oooo. A tough guy."

"Tough enough," I said.

The narrow-faced man and the kid emerged from the men's room. The kid slipped past us, stuffing something into his front pocket. The man snapped a rubber band wrapped around a roll of bills and put it in the breast pocket of his coat. He slid his chair out from the table, scuffing it across the rough, wooden floor. The big dude sneered at me and stepped back and to the side.

"Didn't mean to interrupt any business transactions," I said, as I eased by him.

Most definitely a different crowd at the Comus these days.

When I finished, all three of the dealers were seated around the table and a red-haired girl in a Phi Mu jersey was standing beside them. By the time I reached my seat at the bar, the two women had gone into the ladies' room. The big guy leaned his chair back against the wall and popped open a can of beer, keeping his sunshade-covered eyes trained on me.

Barb stepped back into the room. Her face had a light sheen of perspiration and her color had returned, but she no longer smiled. I didn't hear those ocean waves anymore.

"You ready for another one?" she asked.

"Who's the guy they found in that vacant lot?"

"I don't know."

"Then why were you crying?"

"I thought it might be Toulouse. He's a friend of mine. But they said that man's black, right? Toulouse isn't black. He's half-Haitian, okay? So it can't be him."

"Who is Toulouse?"

"Are you a cop or something?" She had an edge to her voice.

"I'm sorry, Barb. It's none of my business."

She took a quick breath and blew it out. "I didn't mean to be short with you. I'm just worried about him. He went out on a run a few days ago and I haven't heard from him."

"A run?"

"He's a truck driver for Coastliner Ice Company."

"Coastliner?" I asked. "Out of Bay Saint Louis?"

"You've heard of it?"

"I live in Bay Saint Louis," I said. "I know the man who used to own Coastliner, but he sold it."

"Look, I hate to ask you, but would you mind going by there to see if he's around?"

"Why don't you call them?"

"They don't . . . uh . . . they don't tell people where their drivers are over the phone."

"Why?"

"I don't know. Security or something."

"Security? For an ice truck?"

"I don't know why. They just won't." She leaned forward.

"Please? Go and see and let me know if he's there. Okay?"

"Why do you think it's so strange not to see this Toulouse for four days?"

"He comes in a lot, that's all."

"But you've only worked here a few weeks. Maybe he goes out of town sometimes."

"I used to see him in here all the time before I started working here, I mean like every other day . . ." She glanced down the bar. "I'll be right back, okay? I've got to take care of these other customers before Nate gets his panties in a wad." She walked to the other end of the bar to the service rail and drew a pitcher of draft for the waitress.

I killed my beer and set the mug on the counter. I needed to type a report for Bayou Casualty, but after a few beers I knew I could forget paperwork until the morning. Even with rush-hour traffic, I still had time to clear my stuff out of the Alamo Plaza and drive back to Bay Saint Louis before dark.

"You ready for another?" Barb had come back to my end of the bar.

"I've got to go," I said. "You say Toulouse comes in here pretty often?"

"Almost every day. That's why I'm worried."

"And you met him here?"

"Yeah." She stared past me. "A few months ago."

I pushed my stool away from the bar and stood. "I'll ask around about Toulouse," I said.

"Oh, great! Thanks, uh—" she fumbled for my name.

"Jack," I said.

"Yeah. Call me if you find out anything, okay?"

"Anything you want me to tell him?"

She fiddled with a strand of hair and ran the tip of her tongue across her lips. Her face had a tinge of red and a beading of sweat above her eyes. "I guess not. I just want to know where he is."

I turned and walked through what had become a good-size crowd. The table at the rear was still doing business, going through the routine with some thirty-year-old lawyer type looking to buy a short furlough from his pinstriped jail. I had been in that jail myself once, but I had made a more permanent escape.

Behind the bar, Barb looked up at the television, pointing the remote and scanning the local news shows.

I'd be seeing her again soon. If I found her friend at Coastliner and she considered that a big favor . . . Well, you figure it out. I've found that doing big favors for beautiful women is always worthwhile.

But if her missing friend was the one who had met up with the Undertaker, then I'd have an even better reason to see her again. Maybe she would know something that would give me a chance to bust André Mouton in the chops.

And I had been waiting for that chance for six years.

FOUR

The next morning, after I typed my report, I stepped out to the front deck to taste the salt air I had missed in New Orleans. The low tide exposed little wet sandbars, which trapped a dozen tidal pools and pushed the surf line out three hundred feet from the seawall. Twenty killdees, their heads bobbing back and forth like pigeons on a sidewalk, foraged the ankle-deep pools for minnows.

The soft breaking of the waves set up an easy rhythm that I fell into as I walked down the twelve wooden steps to what passes for my front yard and picked through the sandspurs and cordgrass for a month's worth of beer bottles and soft drink cans tossed from the passing cars of the kids who cruise Beach Boulveard every night of every summer. I admit we used to throw stuff into people's yards years ago when we were riding around. But, dammit, we only trashed the yards of the jerks who really deserved it.

When I finished cleaning up the yard, I crossed over to the beach and jogged east toward town. At the one-mile mark, I stopped to watch a man working his cast net. He held the balled-up net behind him and, with a smooth twist of his torso, launched it high and forward. Like an arial burst of fireworks, it flared into a circle and floated down to the water.

The first mile hurt; I didn't run in New Orleans. Push-ups and sit-ups in the motel room kept my muscles toned, but I missed my daily run and my twice weekly judo sessions. The ability to defend myself in a fight and to put a pistol shot damn near anywhere I want to are two job skills I picked up in the army MP unit back when I was being "all that I could be." I hardly ever have to resort to either. But I work at both, and I'm damn good at them. Big Jim always said if they only save your life once, they're worth the effort.

After a shower I rode my bike to town to visit my brother, Neal, and see what I had missed the past three weeks. Neal's law office is on Main Street, a turn-of-the-century red brick building that used to be a Masonic Lodge. He's on the second floor; his office looks out over the street. Twelve-foot ceilings, creaky hardwood floors, tongue-and-groove dark oak wainscot four feet up the walls. Breezes from the Gulf and ceiling fans keep it cool enough in the summer that he seldom runs the window air conditioner.

His shirt collar was open, the knot in his tie pulled six inches below his neck. His feet were propped on his desk and he was stretched out so far that his head touched the rear wall. Neal's six-five, 260 pounds, and lettered two years as weakside tackle up at Southern Mississippi. He was gabbing on the phone, always gabs on the damn phone. Naturally, he has one in his car. He's also got a PC, a pager, a fax, a cellular phone, and an answering machine. Anybody can find him. Anywhere, anytime. And to think he pays good money for that.

Once I borrowed Neal's car phone to use on a case. I ended up using it to call in pizza orders from the road. I'm not dead set against them, but when I feel like I may need one I borrow one of his. Most of the time it suits me fine if nobody can find me. I'm not too crazy about computers either, but I'll probably get one soon. From what I hear, this Internet is a skip tracer's dream. But I'll never fall in love with any filing cabinet, electronic or otherwise.

Neal waved me to a side chair and held up one finger to let me know he'd be off in one minute. Fifteen minutes later he put down the phone. "Well, how are things at the loading dock?" he asked.

"It's over. It was those two guys I told you about. I'm glad to wrap it up, but I'm going to miss that forklift."

"You should have stayed in law school."

Twenty years later, Neal, and everybody else in town, still can't believe I quit after three semesters. The prospect of spending my life in a law library just didn't feel right. There's a line that's absolutely true that you hear every week in law school: "The law is a jealous mistress."

And that's exactly why I told the bitch to hit the road.

"Let's not start with the law school lecture," I said. "I just finished a job. I feel good. I've got a few days off . . ."

"But you're living from day to day. You're at an age when . . ."

"I'm at a great age," I said. "Just wait. When you turn forty you're too old to join the Jaycees and the life insurance salesmen move you down to their B list."

"You need to start building up some assets."

"I paid cash for my house."

"Camp house," he said.

"My truck's paid for."

"Remind me to get you one of those DON'T LAUGH—IT'S PAID FOR bumper stickers," he said. He took a big sip of coffee. "I'm sorry I brought it up. But you could spend six months a year in law school instead of on your sailboat and be out in no time."

"I couldn't handle all the excitement of a law practice," I said. "I've got a place with the best view on the Gulf. I've got a truck that runs great and as big a sailboat as I can handle by myself. I'm good to Mama and Daddy, and I've got money in the bank. If everybody in town thinks I'm a bum because I don't bust my butt to pay a mortgage and a car note, that's their problem."

Neal grinned and shook his head. We go through this routine every so often. He's the only person besides Mama who's allowed to nag me, and that's only because I know he doesn't mean it. We both know that if I went back into law or banking it would bore him to death before it did me.

"You in town for a while?" he asked.

"Until Monday. Bayou Casualty's had a couple of fires in Biloxi they want me to check on. But no undercover stuff. I'll come home every night."

I slid back my chair and stepped over to the coffeepot in the corner. The half a cup still in there had been thickening all morning, had the color of road tar, and smelled like it had been scorched. I poured it out and got some water from the Kentwood cooler; three weeks of burnt coffee was enough.

"What do you know about Coastliner Ice Company?" I asked.

"I know Mr. Compretta sold it to some group out of Memphis."

"What's the group?"

He frowned and looked out the window. "What have you heard?"

"Nothing. That's why I'm asking."

"It's headed up by a guy named Rickey Dee McCoy," he said.

"McCoy? You mean that redneck who bought the old Fidoli home and painted it pink?"

"That 'redneck,' as you call him, has pumped a lot of money into this little town," he said. "He's bought the icehouse here, one outside of New Orleans, and one down at Grande Isle. All three are on the water and they put ice on an awful lot of shrimp boats. They've also started servicing bagged ice machines at quick stop stores."

"I've never even seen this guy," I said, "but I've heard some stuff about him. I heard he's in the Dixie Mafia."

"Don't believe everything they say at the truck stop. He's an upstanding citizen as far as I can tell."

"Oh, come on," I said. "I'm not in the Rotary Club, remember? I've got free rein to talk bad about somebody, whether he's a big taxpayer or not. What do you know about him?"

"Nothing. It's none of my business."

"Ho! Ho! That's a good one!" I slapped my knees and smiled at him. He was trying to keep a straight face. Neal's every bit as nosy as I am, but he won't admit it.

"All I know about Rickey Dee McCoy," he said, "is that he's created over twenty jobs, he sponsors a Dixie League baseball team, and he built a new playground for the kindergarten at Saint Stanislaus. Sister Mary Teresa thinks he's a blessing sent straight from heaven. Yeah, I hear the same stuff you've heard. But in a town this size, people talk. You ought to hear what they say about you."

"How would you like it if I gave you an excuse to look into Coastliner?" I said.

"Like what?"

"I need to find a driver who works for them. His name is Toulouse."

"I can ask around," he said. "You know his last name?"

"Toulouse is all I know."

"What do you want to know about him?"

"His last name, where he is, and whether he's got a record."

"Are you the one who's looking for him?"

"I'm doing it for this girl I met in New Orleans."

"Did she put you on retainer?" Lawyers love that word.

"I don't plan to spend much time on this. She found out I live here and asked me to check on him."

"And no money changed hands? Just how good-looking is this girl?"

I hate it when Neal's right. But this time he was only half right.

"It's more than that," I said.

"I'm sure."

"She might be able to tell me something I can use to get at André Mouton."

Neal's smile vanished. The big, boyish face darkened and the blue in his eyes deepened.

"It's an outside shot," I said, "but this girl . . ."

"Forget it, Jack."

"What do you mean?" I said.

Neal swung his feet down to the floor and leaned forward. "Forget it. Let it drop. Stay away. How many ways do you want me to say it?"

"Keep trying," I said, "because I'm not buying what you've said so far."

"Big Jim was in the wrong place."

"Yeah, and at the wrong friggin' time. I'm not buying that either."

Neal pinched his lower lip. "He was my friend, too. I knew him before you did. But there's nothing you or I can do about it now."

"Jim got me into this business," I said. "He pulled my cookies out of the fire more times than I care to think about. Don't you think I owe it to Pam and his kids to at least take a shot at busting the son of a bitch who killed him?"

"He came on something he shouldn't have seen," Neal said.

"Does that make it Big Jim's fault? Mouton's got some kind of right to pop a slug into somebody's brain and then kill anybody who happens to walk up and see it?"

"Of course not, but . . ."

"Big Jim was running away."

"I know the damn story, Jack! One bullet in the back, long range. Another to the head, close enough for powder burns. I know all about the cops dropping the charges . . ."

"They never *filed* any charges!"

"And they never will! That case is closed no matter what that girl knows," he said. "Hell, what does she know anyway?"

Now that was a good question, and the first one I should have asked myself if that smile of hers hadn't gotten me all distracted. I fell back in the chair and looked up at the ceiling. Suddenly it sounded like a hell of a stretch even to me. It grew so quiet I could hear the ticks of the clock on the wall behind me.

"Okay, okay. I'll let it go for now," I said. "But I still want to get some background on Toulouse."

"Has this got something to do with Mouton?"

"It's got something to do with an attractive young lady in New Orleans I promised a favor to."

He wrote "Toulouse" and "Coastliner" on a Post-it note and slapped it on the side of his computer screen. "I'll check it out," he said. "Are we still on for Saturday?"

I had forgotten all about Saturday. "I'm glad you reminded me. I'll be ready."

"Tricia won't mind?"

"Gee, Andy, I swear I don't go down to the diner to see Juanita unless Thelma Lou's out of town." I took a long sip of my now lukewarm water. "You know Tricia and I don't have any commitments. She wants it that way even more than I do. She's got a lot more to lose, what with me being a bum and all. Why am I the only person in town who's not upset that I'm not married?"

"For the last four years, ever since you got your divorce, you've been chasing a different woman every month."

"Tried monogamy one time," I said. "Didn't work."

"Well, you might want to zero in on one of them. Sandy's not coming back."

"I think she made that pretty clear."

Neal tapped the ends of his fingers against each other and stared at them. "Kathy talked with her on the phone the other day. Looks like she's getting pretty serious about that man she's been seeing."

"You mean that damned X-ray reader?"

"Radiologist," he said. "Sandy thinks he'll give her an engagement ring any day now."

A sinking feeling started in my chest and crept down to the pit of my stomach. "Every woman's dream," I said. "Mercedes, two-story house in Germantown, membership at the Colonial Country Club. What's the son of a bitch's golf handicap? Two strokes? Maybe three?"

"From what I hear he sounds like a pretty decent guy."

"Join the Junior League. Try to one-up the other doctors' wives at the supper club. Golly, what fun!"

"Jack, what you said about that kind of stuff being every woman's dream? You were right. You can't fault Sandy for how she was raised. Living her life like some Jimmy Buffett song was just not in the cards."

It took four blocks of bust-ass pedaling on my bike to get my heart rate up—this time because I wanted it to be. The rivulets of sweat and the heavy breathing were cleaning out my system, and the Gulf air was clearing my head.

Should have known it would be a freakin' doctor. Hell, if it was just the money; she's in Memphis for pity's sake. She could have at least snagged a rock'n'roll producer. Maybe a big-time cotton planter. For that matter, a professional wrestler. But a doctor. It's so cliché.

I heard a car coming up behind me, slowing down. It sounded like it was moving only a little faster than I was, so I snugged near the curb to let it pass. When it got ten feet behind me, a blast from a woofer siren nearly knocked me over. I flinched, jerked the bike hard to the right, bounced over the curb onto the sidewalk, and spun my head hard around.

Roger Partridge was laughing so hard his forehead bumped against the steering wheel of his patrol car.

"How old are you now, Roger?" I yelled. "Forty? Forty-one? Real funny!"

"Man, you nearly went airborne." He was still laughing. "Come on and get in."

Roger was two months on the force and hadn't yet broken in his uniform. Despite his square jaw and deep-set brown eyes, he still looked like a civilian in costume. I left my bike in the rack at the city library across the street, and we rode under the summer canopy of live oaks and pecan trees that covers downtown, breaking up the sunshine and providing a dappled shade to cool the streets. We left the windows down.

"How does it feel to ride up and down these streets and get paid for it?" I asked.

"Like it did when we were in high school, except for the part about getting paid."

"You mean they let you try to pick up girls and play the radio real loud and drink beer? That kind of stuff?"

"This job hasn't been *that* good, but it's alright," he said. "I was lucky to get it."

"You were lucky? You're an army-trained firearms instructor. How many of those have we got running around this town?"

We drove down a few more streets and I asked him if he knew a driver for Coastliner named Toulouse.

"Yeah, I know that smartass. Pulled him over once to warn him about his turn signal. He starts smarting off about how I ought to be out chasing real criminals—like we got some big crime problem around here. So I wrote him out a ticket and don't you know that pain in the ass contested it in court. Contested a busted turn signal! I had to go to court on my day off to testify, and then he don't even show up. Why do you want to know about that punk?"

"I was talking to this girl over at the old Comus Bar. Toulouse is her friend but she hasn't seen him around. She's worried about him."

Roger snorted. "I guess there's not a son of a bitch on this earth who's so sorry that some woman somewhere doesn't worry about him."

"You seen him around lately?"

"Let's go find his bogus ass," he said.

We drove past the gabled and turreted houses of the old part of town, set far back from the beach on broad lawns. Past several hurricane-ruined piers, some stretching two hundred feet into the Gulf, their parallel rows of pilings serving as perches for a dozen brown pelicans facing into the wind with their beaks tucked snug against their long necks.

"They're adding on some at Coastliner," he said. "They made the boat dock bigger and dredged the Bayou."

"Do you know the guy who bought it?"

"His name's Rickey Dee McCoy. You got to see this character. Looking at his face is like reading a rap sheet." Roger shook his head. "I think he's running drugs out of that place, but I can't prove it."

"It ought to be easy enough to bust a drug dealer around here," I said.

"He doesn't sell here in town. He's keeping this place as sort of a safe and quiet harbor."

"This is as good a place as any for that."

Roger slowed to let a kid in a swimsuit cross in front of us from his car to the beach. The kid was carrying an ice chest that appeared to be heavy and he hopped from foot to foot as the baked pavement singed the soles of his bare feet.

"Rickey Dee's got most of the town thinking he's a legit businessman," Roger said. "I don't believe it for a minute. He comes in here and buys Coastliner, right on a bayou near the Gulf. The only way in or out is a one-lane shell road, and the first thing he does is put a gate across the road. They close it and lock it every night."

"All that was true when Compretta had it, except for the gate."

"Compretta didn't have a fleet of trucks to distribute whatever came into that ice house all over the coast," he said. "And he didn't import a bunch of Haitians to run the place."

"Haitians?"

"Yeah. Like your buddy Toulouse. When we had our run-in I could hear his island accent. Not real strong, you see, but I could tell he was trying to keep it under control. When he stepped out of that truck, he said, 'Why you hassle me, mon?' Just like that."

"If he's Haitian, what's he doing here?" I asked. "Is he a citizen?"

"I called Immigration and Naturalization in New Orleans. He's here on a green card."

"I thought a foreigner had to have some kind of special skill to come in on a work visa."

"According to INS, Toulouse is a marine diesel mechanic," Roger said.

"What's he doing driving a truck?"

"That's what I asked Immigration. They said they'd send somebody to investigate. But since they've only got one man to cover Louisiana and Mississippi both, they couldn't say when they'd get around to it."

"What else you know about him?" I asked.

"His last name is Caron. Rhymes with Capone. Oh, and this guy's a truck driver—excuse me, marine diesel mechanic—right? The day I stopped him he had on this gold Rolex watch and this medallion with an emerald on it. A big one."

"Could have been counterfeit."

"Looked real to me."

A breeze whipped through the car's open window, smelling of brine and the faint decay of dead fish washed up on the sand. Five miles out, the black outline of a fast-moving boat sliced through the sparkling dance of sunlight on the Gulf. Soon we left the sandy portion of the beachfront and got into the marshy flats, where little bayous trickle into the Gulf through bulrushes and skinny pines and bushy shrubs.

The concrete pavement ran out and we bounced along a one-lane oyster shell trail flanked on both sides by a thick bank of cane. A freckled marsh rabbit darted across our path. The drive soon spilled out into the acre and a half of shell-covered lot in front of the Coastliner Ice Company.

"Looks about the same," I said, "but they've got more trucks."

The building is on Bayou Pitasa, a hundred yards upstream from the beach. It's a concrete block icehouse painted aqua blue. There's a loading dock across the front, chest high and running from end to end. That's the one for the public. The company trucks load at a separate dock at the north end of the building.

Behind the building, out of sight, is a dock built out over the water, where shrimp boats take on six or eight hundred pounds of crushed ice so they can stay out on the Gulf for three days at a time.

"They've got a dozen trucks. Compretta used to have three," Roger said. "They're turning out some ice, my friend. These trucks burn up the road between Mobile and New Orleans."

The grinding of the tires on the dry oyster shells kicked up a white dust, and I could taste a fine grit. Four company trucks, royal blue on white, were parked over near the bayou. A pile driver was moored behind them, but was not operating. A rotten-egg smell of bayou mud from recent dredging hung in the air.

"By that pile driver," Roger said, "that's where the new warehouse will go."

We made a big turn in front of the trucks and spooked a tall, gray heron that had been standing montionless at the bayou's edge. We drove up close to the icehouse, where a couple of teen-aged boys stood beside a pickup truck backed up to the loading dock. One of them waved at Roger. Up on the platform a broad, muscular man, glossy black, stood and waited for them. Another man, tall and light brown, leaned back against the wall, his arms crossed. He chewed gum with his mouth open and followed us with his eyes.

"Those are two of the ones I told you about. The shorter one I don't know . . ."

"He's built like a barrel," I said.

"Yeah, a forty-gallon barrel. Straight from Haiti or somewhere down there. I don't think he can speak English. The other one, that tall one, that's Bruno. A real badass. He's the foreman."

"Is he from Haiti, too?"

"He talks like it."

Each of Bruno's muscles stood out, and his narrow waist flared up to a big set of shoulders. His eyes were yellow-brown with just a tinge of green, a western Caribbean blend of Carib, Nigerian, Spanish, and French. They were eyes that showed challenge without a hint of backing down.

"Bruno likes to fight," Roger said. "Broke some guy's jaw two weeks ago over at the Rocket Club. Son of a bitch beats up women, too. He's got this big scar across his shoulder. Slapped some ol' gal and she pulled out a straight razor and went after his ass. But mainly he goes to the strip joints in New Orleans. I hear he and some stripper are into S and M on a regular basis."

"If he's the foreman, wouldn't he be the one to ask about Toulouse?"

"You just read my mind." Roger turned in and almost touched the bumper against the loading dock.

"Wait here," he said, "this won't take a second."

Barrelman handed a fifty-pound sack down to the kids as Roger walked to the far end of the dock and up the steps to where Bruno stood. As they talked, Bruno kept his thumbs hitched in the front pockets of his jeans. After two or three minutes, Roger came back to the car.

"They say they haven't heard from Toulouse in three days."

"Are they looking for him?"

"They know where he is; they're just not telling," Roger said. "He's on a damn drug run down to Miami. I heard the other day that Coastliner was sending trucks to Florida, so I called Tallahassee to see if they had records on them."

"You mean some kind of interstate permit?"

"Ice company truck hauling their own ice don't have to get one. I'm telling you, Jack, this is a great setup."

"So Florida didn't have any records?"

"They had a speeding ticket issued to your buddy Toulouse. And guess where it was issued."

"Pensacola?"

"Not even close. He was in Boca Raton. That's down around Cuba someplace." Roger looked straight ahead and didn't say anything else.

"Am I missing something?" I asked.

"You're smarter than I am. You tell me how you can ship a load of ice from Bay Saint Louis, Mississippi, to Boca Raton, Florida, and make any money."

A shrimp boat, its diesel engine purring, eased up the bayou toward the dock. One man stood at the bow, one at the stern, both holding coiled spring lines and ready to hop onto the pier and tie off. Sunlight glistened out on the water, and I watched a seagull hovering on a wind current, looking for the flash of any fish that might stray too near the surface. Roger backed up, eased into drive, and rolled across the shells, his engine at idle, watching the icehouse in his rearview mirror.

At the driveway's midpoint, a chain-link gate—ten feet high, its posts set in concrete—sat a little past a culvert that channeled a shallow freshet under the drive. Water and foul-smelling marsh mud filled the ditches on both sides of the gate. No way for a car or truck to get around it.

"They lock it up at night," he said.

"I see why you're suspicious, but I didn't see anything that hasn't always been there, except for two Haitians and a few trucks."

"And the gate."

"Yeah," I said, "but with those trucks sitting there all night, I can see why they'd want that, too."

Roger got quiet for a few seconds, working the muscles of his jaws, as the tires clicked along at each expansion joint of the concrete road. "Hell, maybe there's nothing there." His chestnut eyes gazed down the road.

We drove along without saying much, listening to the ten o'clock news on the radio. We passed an old man sitting on the wide concrete railing of the seawall, casting with a spinning reel. The railing was pocked from years of erosion from the salt wind and air, and rust from the interior support rods seeped through where the surface was broken or cracked. The road got smoother the closer we got to town, and soon we were back where we'd started. Roger stopped in front of the library where I had left my bike.

"What does Sheriff Wade say about all of this?" I asked.

"He says to leave them alone because there's not enough to go on."

"I never thought I'd say this, but I believe Wade is right. From what I see, Rickey Dee is keeping his nose clean."

"Maybe so," he said, "but it wouldn't take much poking around to shake something loose. Wade says not to mess with them at all."

"I'll see what I can find out from that girl in New Orleans;

maybe Toulouse has told her something," I said. "But I'm wondering if there's any particular reason the sheriff's backing off Coastliner."

Roger shifted forward in his seat and looked straight ahead. He blew out a short breath and turned back toward me. "What is it with you and Artis Wade, Jack?"

"I don't like bullies, especially when they've got a badge on," I said. "You remember that Crawford kid?"

"The kid was drunk and disorderly and he back-sassed Wade."

"The only thing that kid did was make the mistake of being half Wade's size. You asked me what it was with him and me. Fifteen years ago I had to pull him off this guy up at the Broke Spoke. All the guy had done was bump into Wade on the dance floor."

"He's got a temper. That's all."

"He would have beaten this guy to death," I said. "When I pulled him off, he tried to come after me."

"You and Artis got into it?"

"No. But only because three guys held him back. We've kind of avoided each other since then," I said. "But forget all that. You never told me why Coastliner's off-limits."

"Wade says we don't need to harrass any business owners without some kinda proof they're breaking the law. And I gotta admit I can't prove a thing," he said. "Look, Jack, you know me. I'd tell you if there was anything crooked going on with the sheriff's office. I think Artis is only playing it by the book. I get proof on Coastliner, I'll take it to him. But this is just not a good time, I guess. I think he's under a lot of pressure right now."

"What kind of pressure?"

"Job's getting to him. I think it's sinking in with him that being sheriff is more like being a manager than a cop."

"I heard he joined the Yacht Club," I said.

"He did."

"Maybe he enjoys that white-collar work more than you think."

"He was raised poor up in those pine thickets, and he's trying to break into high society. That ain't exactly a new story."

"If Artis Wade goes from slapping around drunks to hosting

benefits for the Gulf Coast Symphony it'll be the story of the decade," I said. "Is that why he's started wearing suits instead of a uniform?"

"He still wears his uniform sometimes," Roger said. "But you're right. I think he's trying to step up into the beach crowd."

"You remember when we used to spend every penny we had on those alligator shirts? Remember how much good that did? It's going to take more than any suit."

"But I guess people will always be trying," Roger said. "I think that's why Wade gives Rickey Dee such a wide berth. He ain't ruffling nobody's feathers on Beach Boulevard."

"Rickey Dee McCoy's not high society," I said.

"He drives a Jag, he belongs to the Yacht Club, and he lives in a big house. That's high society enough for Artis Wade."

It was too early for lunch, but since I had skipped breakfast to jog I microwaved the Styrofoam take-out bowl of gumbo I had brought home from New Orleans and ate on the front deck. Near the horizon, ten miles away, the sun flashed off a white sail as a boat came about. The wind blew steady, five knots according to my anemometer, probably eight or ten knots out on the water, with only light, see-through wisps of high clouds, not a drop of rain in them.

I called Tricia at the Style Shoppe and talked her into taking the afternoon off for a sail to Cat Island and dinner that evening at Chappy's over in Long Beach. I packed a basket of grapes, crackers, and cheese. I put in a bottle of chablis blush for Tricia and a six-pack of Millers for me. I had everything I needed except for some ice.

Business had picked up. Two men were loading a refrigerated truck at the north end of the building, and Bruno and Barrelman were still handling the drive-ups. I drove in close to the building, wheeled around in a 180-degree turn, and backed up to the loading dock between two cars. I stepped out, walked to the rear of the truck, and laid my hands up on the wet concrete floor.

Barrelman wore a sleeveless T-shirt, faded jeans, and white rubber shrimper boots. Broad face, flat nose, wide lips. A solid man, not tall, with stubby, powerful hands and forearms. I doubt that I could have reached around his chest.

"I need a hundred pounds, crushed," I said.

He crossed his arms, dangled a pair of ice tongs from his right hand, and tilted his giant head down at me with an ebony-eyed stare.

Bruno walked over and stood beside him. "Get something for you, mon?"

"Yeah, I need a hundred pounds of crushed ice." I lifted the ice chest out of the truck and laid it up on the dock.

"*Cent poids de glace, dans la boîte,*" Bruno said. Barrelman slung the chest over his shoulder and walked into the freezer.

"He be bock in a minute."

A crunching roar came from a fast-moving car racing down the shell drive. A silver convertible, Jaguar X-12, sped toward us, fifty yards away and kicking up a cloud of white dust from the powdered shells. It approached the icehouse too fast, and when it braked, it slid a foot or two across the shells into one of the slots in front of the office on the building's south end. Some country song I had never heard before wailed on the Jag's stereo. When the white dust cleared, I knew I was looking at Rickey Dee McCoy.

A weight lifter's chest. Hair bleached blond. Capped teeth, white against tanning-booth skin. Rickey Dee wore a lot of gold— chains, watches, rings—a snug coral shirt, and blue wraparound sunglasses. I couldn't tell how old he was, but I was sure it was older than he looked. He turned off the motor, pulled the rearview mirror around, and patted a lacquered patch of wind-blown hair back into place. He got out, pointed his finger pistol-style at Bruno, and walked into the office.

"Five dollars," Bruno said.

I walked in my door as the phone started ringing.

"Toulouse Caron," Neal said. "His last name's Caron. He's Haitian and, get this, a green-card immigrant. Oh, and that rumor about Coastliner being owned by the Dixie Mafia? Looks like you were right for once; my source says it's true. Says they're running cocaine and crack through there."

"Are you sure about your source?" Neal and I don't ask each other for names.

"Very."

"Do you know where Toulouse is?"

"Not right now. He's been over in New Orleans trying to gain a toehold in the Desire Housing Project."

I let out a low whistle. "Do they know who they're trying to move in on?"

"Don't get any ideas," he said. "They're jacking around with André Mouton because they're stupid. They're not smart enough to leave him alone like you're going to do."

"That explains the Haitians," I said. "A white dealer on a street corner in the projects would tend to draw some attention."

"Using Haitians only means André found out in thirty minutes instead of ten," Neal said. "That Caribbean group might sell some, but I'd guess they've got more to do with smuggling than selling."

"Thanks for checking . . ."

"My man also says Toulouse has been ripping off his boss, Rickey Dee, and dealing on his own on the side."

"Toulouse works without a net, doesn't he?" I said. "Has anybody taken any of this to the cops?"

"The guy who told me about it wouldn't go to a grand jury at gunpoint."

"They could send in undercover narcs. They've got to make their own case; it's not going to fall into their laps."

"That's an expensive proposition. If they're running drugs, it'll come out sooner or later," Neal said. "Besides, I can't believe you're so ready to send in the marines. I thought you were all for legalizing drugs."

"First, I was talking about marijuana. Second, I also think Prohibition was a terrible idea. That doesn't mean I consider Al Capone a role model."

"Well, at this point we'd better let it drop."

"I saw Rickey Dee McCoy today at the icehouse, and you were right: he looks like a mobster. A group nobody knows anything about comes into town and starts throwing money around. And now you tell me your source says they're running drugs."

"You just made a case that couldn't get you into Judge Judy's

TV court. We still don't know anything except what one guy has told me."

"I'll bet that girl in New Orleans I told you about knows something," I said. "I could ask her."

"For what? This is a snake pit and it involves forces a lot bigger than you and me. If the Dixie Mafia is trying to muscle in on André Mouton, things'll break soon enough, with or without you."

"Aren't you at least curious? Don't you want to know if the Dixie Mafia has set up shop down the street from you?"

"Right now I'm more cautious than curious," he said. "I know you, Jack. You always get knee-deep into this kind of stuff, whether it has anything to do with you or not. You tell that girl that you looked for Toulouse and couldn't find him. End of story. You *are* going to stay out of it, right?"

An eight-knot breeze blew from the west on the sail out to Cat Island. But on the way back in, it died at sundown and we got back to the dock late. Instead of going to Chappy's, we rented a movie and went to my place to boil some shrimp. While we watched the movie, Tricia fell asleep on the couch with her head on my lap. The phone rang at ten minutes after ten.

"We've found Toulouse Caron." It was Roger.

"Where did you find him?"

"I didn't. The New Orleans police did."

"Is he in jail?"

"He's in the morgue. Didn't you see the ten o'clock news? That body they found Tuesday in that vacant lot in New Orleans . . . it was Toulouse."

FIVE

The next morning, Friday, I wanted to turn in my report and my bill before Bayou Casualty closed for the weekend, so I drove the forty miles back to New Orleans. The Oriental Jade job ran for twenty-two days straight, weekends and all, and at three hundred per day plus meals and housing, the company owed me eighty-five hundred. That, plus a job in Biloxi starting Monday, would give me fourteen grand, enough to carry me until winter. It would also buy me two months to sail to Key West, something I had done four years earlier and had promised myself I'd do again.

I work no more than six months a year and turn down more jobs than I accept. If I need more money, I raise my daily rate. I'm good enough at what I do to get away with it so far.

I got into investigation as I do most things, by accident. Right after Sandy and I got married, her father, T. W (Buddy) Donovan III, gave me a job in his bank in Memphis. I mean, it's not really his bank, but he's the president. Back then he was senior vice president.

I had been Buddy's third choice for son-in-law because there were only two others in the running. After my discharge, I bummed around Oxford for two years taking a few judo classes at Ole Miss on the GI Bill, tending bar at the Gin part-time and dating Sandy Donovan full-time. Sometimes we'd go to Memphis to visit her parents. Buddy would mention MBA to me, and, for all I knew, he was talking about the Mississippi Bowhunters and Archery Association. But at least I was ex-military police, ex–Ole Miss centerfielder, and I had worked up to third-degree black belt.

That kind of stuff made me a little easier for Buddy to take.

They put me in as assistant manager of the Correspondent Banks section: I dealt with other banks. I did that for a year and then they put me in the Trust Department for another year. Bigger title, a little more money. Another year, and they put me in the Commercial Properties section.

I say "put" because that's what they did. They didn't ask. They'd come in one day and tell me that starting the next week I'd be stepping up to whatever position at such-and-such an increase in salary and then sit back and wait for my reaction, which was supposed to be something like that of a nine-year-old who gets a pony for Christmas. And it was, the first time. Buddy had it all mapped out to where one day—and I guaran-damn-tee you he knew the exact day—I'd be president of the bank and have a position his daughter could be proud of.

Nice of him. Just didn't sound like my idea of fun.

When I told Sandy that going back home to the shrimping-and-boat-repair business would be my next career step, she was delighted. We were young enough to think that love by itself would hold us together. And it was rebellious enough to make Sandy the talk of East Memphis for the entire tennis season, and that opportunity didn't come along every day. So Buddy put the Plan on hold for a year or two or however long it was supposed to take Sandy and me to get over our Bohemian urges. Took Sandy three years; I'm still working on mine.

One day—when the shrimping season was closed, the repair business was slow, and our daughter, Peyton, had just been born—Neal offered me a few days' work. He was suing this condo developer out of Ocean Springs and Big Jim Brannan, the investigator he always used, was working up a report on the guy. Big Jim needed somebody to do some legwork on the case.

Jim Brannan was a redheaded giant from the Irish Channel who loved to drink Bushmills and tell jokes, the dirtier the better. He had a constant gap-toothed grin that drew people, especially women, like gravity. Jim was a tender-hearted barroom brawler who would cry over sad songs and was a sucker for a every hard luck story he ever heard. Yet he had the best investigative instincts I ever saw.

The developer we were investigating had sold this beachfront dream house to a retired couple out of Hattiesburg, but a squall I could have ridden out in a pup tent had taken their roof clean off. Jim sent me to the newspaper morgue on one of his legendary hunches. On the third day of searching, I found a five-year-old story about this same developer and some cheap-assed wiring in one of his condominiums in Corpus Christi. Big fire, three deaths, hell of a lawsuit, and a bankruptcy. He hadn't surfaced again until he'd shown up here.

When I found that story my heart rose like I had discovered sunken treasure. Any hopes Buddy—and Sandy—still held for my banking career ended right there. I didn't know it then, but so did my marriage.

After I dropped off the paperwork at Bayou Casualty, it was time to stop by the Comus to check out what Barb knew about Toulouse's murder. But it was only eleven o'clock and I figured she wouldn't get there until midafternoon. I had some time to kill and I needed some andouille sausage and cayenne pepper for a gumbo, so I drove into the Quarter, past Jackson Square, toward the Progress Grocery on Decatur. I got lucky and found a parking spot beside the French Market, a one-block walk from the Progress.

The sweet smell of ripe cantaloupes and peaches drifted from the fruit stands under the market's long canopy and drew me in for a quick side trip down the center aisle. A shipment of butterbeans and some good-looking collard greens had come in that morning. The lunchtime shoppers hadn't arrived yet, so I had my pick.

When I stopped to inspect a tomato, I spotted Maurice on the other side of the street, walking fast, weaving his skinny body through the sidewalk crowd, heading to Jackson Square. Maurice could tell me the score, but it would cost me.

It took me a full block to catch him and I was trotting. When I got close enough, I grabbed his arm at the elbow and he turned around.

"Buster! What it is, my man?" Maurice always calls me Buster.

It's an alias I used when I worked a case in the Quarter two years back. That's when I first met him.

"Maurice, why are you walking so fast? You looking for something?"

"Same thing I be looking for on these streets every day since I was eight years old—my next meal. You buying?"

"How much information would a meal buy me?"

"Not much."

"Well, let's call this lunch a down payment and if I need more we'll negotiate."

A street washer passed by and the pavement hissed and the smell of steamy asphalt hovered over the sidewalk. We stepped along briskly toward the square.

"What you doing these days?" I asked. "You still reading Tarot cards?"

"Sometime. It's good money but it gets old. I be doin' my magic mostly."

"Same act?"

"Changed it up some. Gotta stay fresh."

Soon we reached the Pontalba, an open-air corner bar and café with French doors all around that open at sidewalk level to the promenade in front of Saint Louis Cathedral. That's where Tarot card readers, jugglers, balloon twisters, and other street performers set up, and Maurice likes to scout his competition. We sat at a two-chair table—half inside the bar, half on the sidewalk—and ordered shrimp po'boys. The ceiling fans moved the hot air around but only enough to melt the ice in our tea glasses.

"You know this lunch only buys background," he said.

"I know the deal. What happened to the dreadlocks?"

"Scared off too many customers. Had to go."

"The beard?"

"Same thing. Hard to draw tourists if they be wondering whether they gon' see a magic act or get they ass robbed. I noticed you ain't got that ponytail no more."

"We both do what we got to do."

Maurice really did look like a new person. His athletic build and roughishly handsome face—especially his perfect teeth and almond eyes—were accented by his even, deep black complexion and his white Christian Dior knit.

"What you know about André Mouton?" I asked.

Maurice bit into his po'boy and chewed it awhile, thinking before he answered. "I guess you know who he is."

"Yeah. He's the boss of the New Orleans cocaine trade. In his sixties. Tough, mean, and dangerous."

"Thought you needed background."

"You think I'm buying lunch for that? What's he been doing lately?"

Maurice gave me a long, searching look. "Why you aksin' about Mouton, Buster? You got business with him?"

"I don't know yet."

"Sometime he not too good to have as a partner."

"I'm not exactly planning to sign any contract with him," I said.

"You better go outta your way to stay outta his way."

"Come on, Maurice. Since when did you start asking for reasons when people buy information?"

He nodded as he followed a passing halter top for a second. "Mouton a regular customer at Brooks Brothers nowadays. He lookin' like he be president of the Whitney National Bank. He going legit. I hear he buying up a lot of repossessed property. Laundered money."

"Who's laundering it?"

"That don't come with the lunch. That cost extra."

"Then save it. How about the cocaine trade?"

"Ol' dude still control it, but word is he be getting out. Competition already be trying to move in."

"What's he doing about it?"

"Just hear rumors. Don't do the drug scene no more."

Maurice waved at a young man with a wispy goatee walking down the other side of the alley toward the river. A saxophone on a cord hung around his neck, and he carried a painted coffee can with TIPS written on the side.

"Did Mouton dust that guy they found in that vacant lot the other day?" I asked.

He nodded his head yes. "When they gonna bring us some more tea?"

"I hear that Mouton, by himself, has killed a dozen men," I said.

"At least."

"But there were only three Undertaker killings."

Maurice laughed. "I guess Mouton jus' like me, Buster. He gotta change his act up from time to time. Them Undertaker murders, he got reasons for doing it that way; they just reasons you people don't know about. Let me guess . . . the dude who just got smoked, he was from the islands. Ain't that right?"

"You already knew that," I said.

"Only thing the news said was that he was black. I was right about the islands, wasn't I?"

"He was from Haiti."

His smile was positively condescending. "What you know about those first three the Undertaker took out?"

"I heard they were three punks who'd ripped him off and he set an example," I said.

"And they was all three from the islands. Check it out."

"So it was . . ."

"Only thing is," he said, "Mouton didn't order those hits; his mama did."

"His *mama?*"

"*Mère* Marie. She call all the shots."

I put both elbows up on the table. "Are you telling me that André Mouton's mother is running his drug operations?"

"Done it for years. She the one who made Mouton, and she the one telling him to go legit."

"His mother tells him what to do?"

"Mouton, he was born here," he said, "but his mama and daddy, they come from Haiti. His daddy die right after Mouton was born. His mama—*Mère* Marie—she been a voodooine since she got here."

"What's a voodooine?"

"She the high priestess; she control the spells."

"How old is she?"

"She be at least eighty-five, maybe ninety."

"And she runs the New Orleans cocaine trade?"

"She getting out of it," he said.

"Why?"

"She losing her power."

"I guess so! She's ninety years old."

"No, man, I mean her voodoo power. She be losing her voodoo power."

"Aw, bull!" I snatched a bite of my po'boy. "Is that what this is all about? Mouton's empire is built on his mama's voodoo power?"

"Not all of it. Mouton use a lot of muscle, but his mama call the shots."

I took a long sip of tea.

"You don't believe it, do you, Buster?"

I looked at him and took another bite of my po'boy.

"Listen to me. André Mouton be history in a year, maybe less."

"You're the only person I've heard say anything like that," I said.

"Other people don't know what I know." He slapped his palm on the table. "Look, a year from now, you tell everybody I call that shot. Be good for business."

"Okay. You're calling the shot. Tell me about *Mère* Marie."

"She been voodooine of New Orleans for fifty years, but she practice bad voodoo. People be scared of her because her spells are e-vil."

I rolled my eyes up to the ceiling.

"Some things you white people don't know about. The power she has, it come and it go. When it be time for it to go, somebody come along and take it."

"Why doesn't André take it?"

Maurice chuckled and shook his head. "Buster, you got any idea how foolish you sound?"

I rubbed my eyes.

"This ain't like giving somebody the keys to some big ride," he said. "The power chooses you, man. You don't choose the power."

"Well, who's going to take it when *Mère* Marie loses it?"

"I hear they's a young woman name Olivia with rising power, but I don't know."

"Is she a good one or a bad one?" I asked.

"She good, I hear."

I finished my po'boy. The waiter came by and refilled our glasses, pouring both ice and tea over the side of the pitcher. Maurice had half his sandwich left; he had done most of the talking.

"Like you said, this is stuff I don't know about. Tell me about this latest Undertaker murder. Did Mouton do it?"

"Like I said, they a good chance," he said. "Dude come in town from Mississippi and start selling rock in the projects. That's Mouton's turf."

"Say the guy who got killed had some friends in town. Would they be in danger?"

"What you mean 'friends'?"

"Like a girlfriend. Somebody who hung around with him. Would Mouton go after them?"

"Prob'ly not. But if he think they be selling, he might. Mouton just scares the hell out of people. *Mère* Marie she know that everybody be talking about this murder. Maybe that's enough. She'll decide."

"And not Mouton?"

"André Mouton do what his mama tell him to do."

"You make it sound like Mouton's weak," I said. "Everybody else thinks he's stronger than ever."

"Didn't say he be weak. Just 'cause he join the Chamber of Commerce don't mean he not still dangerous. But people who know see a new power coming on."

"A new voodooine?"

"Like I say, they some things you people don't know nothin' about."

SIX

S he don't start her shift until three. We ain't busy before then. 'Course yesterday she didn't show up at all."

I had seen him in the bar a couple of days earlier when I met Barb. She'd called him Nate.

"Did she call in sick?" I asked.

"Ain't called in at all. I tried to call her but her phone's been disconnected." He looked down at the bar, shaking his shaved head. "You want something to drink?"

"Give me a cream soda," I said. "Are you the new owner?"

"I'm the manager." He set the bottle on the counter, no glass. The word LOVE was tatooed on the ridge of his knuckles, one letter per knuckle. "That'll be a dollar."

"Do you know how I can get in touch with Barb?"

"Look, man, I done told that other cop everything I know about Barb. Like I said, I can't find her myself."

"I'm not a cop. Why were the cops asking about her?"

"They checking out that murder over by Chef Menteur and Barb knew the guy."

"I need to talk to her, too. You got an address or some other phone number?"

He frowned, cocked his head to the side, and looked me up and down. "I don't give out stuff like that on my workers."

Nate walked to the other end of the bar where a white-haired man with a two-day beard and a wrinkled suit drank Jim Beam doubles on the rocks and chased them with draft beer. Back in the kitchen a tray of silverware crashed to the floor, and Nate started cursing and stomped off through the service door.

Behind the bar, next to the phone, a sheet of paper was taped to the wall. It had five names and telephone numbers, written in felt-tip pen—the bar's employees. I memorized Barb's number, finished my cream soda, and walked back to the pay phone near where the three coke dealers had set up shop a couple of nights before.

But I didn't call Barb. I punched in a different phone number, a number I hadn't called often enough lately.

He answered on the third ring.

"Detective Bureau. Broussard."

I'd met Cotton Broussard at Fort McClellan when we were both fresh out of college and both in MP training. We shipped out together to the 793rd in Bamberg, Germany, the same month Khomeini sacked the embassy in Tehran. Within a week, the C-5s and C-141s landed thousands of troops at staging areas around Europe, ready to sweep into Iran and kick some serious ass. But they were put on hold for what turned out to be over a year. They'd watch Koppel every night and get mad at the Ayatolla one night and Jimmy Carter the next. Within two weeks they were good and worked up; and since it didn't look like they'd be pounding on the Iranians anytime soon, they started pounding on each other. For 444 days our job was to hold down the lid on a boiling pot, using our bare hands. It was in some German bars long past midnight that I fashioned the blend of judo and bar-room brawling that I use today. It was in those same bars that I learned that when the tables start flying and I hear the beer bottles breaking, there is no one on earth I'd rather have beside me than Cotton Broussard.

Cotton is Cajun to the bone—dark complexion, black hair, broad build. Once in a honky-tonk in Lafayette I saw him lift an upright piano off the ground on a bet. In true Cajun fashion, he's married to the girl he started going with when he was in the ninth grade and she was in the eighth. I spend a few days with them each summer at their camp down at Grand Isle, but it didn't look like we would be doing that this year.

"Cotton, my friend. This is your long lost buddy, Jack."

"I'm sorry, I don't know any Jack."

"I'm hurt, Lieutenant."

"Jack . . . hmmmm . . . I remember there was this Mississippi redneck named Jack—I think it was Jack Bob or something like that—used to try to pass hisself off as an investigator. Last I heard, they ran his ass outta town."

"Jack Bob, huh? You coonasses are getting a little more sophisticated in your humor. Television finally spread to Lafourche Parish?"

"Good to hear from you, Cap."

"You too, Cotton. How's Janelle?"

"She's responding to that chemotherapy real good. Doc says we gotta good chance to beat it, but we ain't outta the woods yet."

"Is she up to having visitors yet?"

"Won't be long, Cap. I'll let you know."

"Are you making it alright?"

"All except for the money. Those treatments ain't cheap."

"Doesn't your group insurance cover it?"

"Covers most of it. But some of the stuff they doing is experimental, least that's what the insurance calls it. They don't pay experimental, and that's thousands of bucks. But, hey, enough about that. What can I do you for?"

"I'm trying to find this woman I need to talk to. Her phone's disconnected and I don't have her address. All I've got is a first name and a phone number. Can you run it for me?"

"You got it. What's the number?"

"Six-two-one-four-two-oh-six."

"First name?"

"Barbara. Goes by Barb. It's probably listed by initials."

A minute later Cotton said, "I show a B. D. Novak: N-O-V-A-K. Probably Barbara like you said. Four thirty-two Jasmine Street. Hey, how you investigators gonna stay in business with these computers around? They gonna put you all outta work."

"When they come up with one that can look somebody in the eye and tell if they're lying, then I'll start worrying."

"That's the truth, cuz," he said. "You need anything else?"

"I hear NOPD is looking for this woman in connection with that murder over on Chef Menteur. Victim's name was Toulouse Caron. Can you find out why they want to talk to her?"

"What you mean?"

"Are they looking for background?" I asked. "Or is she a suspect?"

The neighborhood is uptown, several blocks out of the Garden District toward the river. It must have been some place in its day. But its day had passed by some time ago.

Down both sides of Jasmine Street are rows of turn-of-the-century raised cottages, each ten feet apart and set back from the sidewalk exactly the same distance, maybe fifteen feet. Low, wrought-iron fences set off the postage-stamp yards.

The houses are yellow, watermelon red, mint green, and pink, with only an occasional unimaginative white, but they're faded and weathered and need repainting. Weeds have taken over the Saint Augustine grass, and wild vines have covered the fences. Junk cars, some with flat tires, were set along the curbs; and beer cans and broken bottles were scattered along the sidewalks. FOR SALE and HUD repossession signs were interspersed along the block, and two of the houses were boarded up.

Four thirty-two was in the center of the block, a white clapboard row house with a dusty wooden porch across the front. A sad Boston fern drooped from a hook under the eave, and a yellow Chinese wind sock fluttered at the porch's far end. Silver duct tape held an irregular cardboard cutout over a broken pane in the window by the door. In front of that window sat a dollar-store aluminum lawn chair with frayed webbing.

I parked by the curb across the street. The smell of cooking collard greens hovered in the air as I walked toward Barb's house. The sagging wooden steps and the faded boards of the porch groaned when I stepped to the front door.

Four knocks, no answer.

I knocked again, a bit harder, and called through the door, "Barb? You in there?"

The door was in the middle of the house. I tested the knob; it was unlocked. I pushed lightly and the door creaked open to my right, to a hallway with no foyer that ran straight through the house to a back door. The rooms were off to either side and all those doors were open.

"Barb?"

I stepped inside, edging down the left wall to the first door off the hallway. I eased it farther open, stood in the hall, and peered into the room. A cheap and threadbare plaid couch with matching chair, a coffee table, a TV stand but no TV, and a beanbag in the corner. No pictures, no posters, no rugs.

The room was still, with the mustiness that takes over old houses when the dusting-powder smell of female occupancy is removed. I flipped the wall switch inside the door, testing to see if the power was still on. The overhead light popped on and the sluggish ceiling fan revved up to a whir, punctuated by the click of a bearing in need of oil. The faded carpet was matted in a few spots, suggesting heavy furniture recently uprooted.

I stepped back. A steely flash swept the corner of my eye, whipping down toward my shoulder. A rush of adreneline surged through me, and I threw up my right hand. Pain sliced across my forearm. I snatched at the knife and snagged a wrist with my left hand. I jerked hard and heaved my weight to the left, slamming the attacker against the wall. The wood-handled steak knife clattered across the floor. I lunged for it, rolled, and jumped to my feet. I spun. I raised the knife . . .

It was Barb, sprawled on the floor against the wall, her mouth opening and closing like a fish on a boat deck gasping for breath.

I threw the knife to the floor, handle first.

"Damn, Barb! What are you trying to do?"

I plopped on the floor beside her, my heart still racing, pressing my hand against the cut on my forearm. She struggled with shallow gulps of air, each breath a labor, as she tried to prime her flattened lungs. It took several minutes.

"Are you alright?" she asked, her voice small and shaky.

"I'm fine! Other than this cut and the fact that my damn heart's about to explode, everything's just great! What the hell were you trying to do?"

She pushed herself up and leaned back against the wall. She forced down a breath. "I didn't remember your voice. You didn't give the password."

"Password? Hell! You in the habit of trying to knife everybody who doesn't give you some password?"

"Don't get mad . . . please . . ." Her chin quivered and tears welled in her eyes.

I slid across the floor, reached around her shoulders, pulled her near, and she started crying silent tears. And damned if *I* wasn't the one who started feeling guilty.

"It's alright Barb. I'm sorry I yelled at you."

She sniffed and wiped the tears from her eyes with her little finger. "I am so embarrassed."

"Forget it. It was an easy mistake. I should have identified myself."

"No, what I mean is . . . I can't remember your name."

I had to laugh despite myself. "It's Jack. Jack Delmas."

She grinned, pleased with herself for making me laugh.

"I'm sorry about Toulouse," I said.

The smile left her face.

"Have the cops come by here yet?"

Her mouth dropped open and she shook her head. "Why would they come here?"

"You ought to know."

"I don't have any idea."

"What do you know about the murder, Barb?"

"You don't think I had anything to do with it, do you?"

"I don't know what I think."

"Why would the cops be looking for me?"

"They'll question all his friends," I said.

"You don't think I . . . ?"

"Like I said, I don't know what to believe."

"Toulouse was my friend."

"I know that, but I've heard some bad things about him."

"He was nice to me," she whispered.

There was a childlike appeal in her voice, her eyes. Please, somebody, just be nice to me, just make these scary people go away. Her lips parted as her breathing became rapid and shallow, and she cleared her throat several times in quick succession.

"I heard that Toulouse was selling drugs," I said, "that Coast-liner Ice Company sells drugs. I heard he was selling in André Mouton's territory. And you know what?"

"What?"

"I believe every word of it. What do you know about all of this?"

"Nothing."

"You went into the Comus for months before you started working there, right?"

"Yeah." She looked away.

"And that's where you met Toulouse?"

She nodded.

"Was he selling drugs at the Comus?"

"Selling? They don't sell drugs at . . ."

"Wait a minute. I've only *heard* things about Coastliner, but I've *seen* them selling drugs at the Comus. That's why you went there in the first place, isn't it?"

She paused, pulled her legs in close, and laid her head on her knees. The faint hum and soft tapping of the ceiling fan in the next room echoed through the empty hallway.

"That's why you were sweating so much the other day after you went to the back room, isn't it?" I grabbed her wrist and pulled her arm toward me, turning it upward. No needle marks. "At least you're not shooting up yet. I'm not your mama or daddy, so no lectures. But I know who you're dealing with. Toulouse was a pusher who tried to muscle in on the wrong territory, right?"

"Probably." She wiped her nose with the handkerchief.

"My guess is he was ripping off Coastliner and selling for himself. Maybe on the street, maybe at the Comus. Right so far?"

She nodded.

"And you started buying from him a few months ago."

She tilted her head back and closed her eyes.

"So what's all this password crap? Who are you afraid of?"

She gave me an incredulous look. "Why, Mouton, of course."

"What do you know about Mouton?"

"Only what Toulouse told me."

"Which was?"

"About what you said, Jack. Toulouse was trying to muscle in on the wrong territory."

"What else?"

"That's all," she said.

"If Mouton killed Toulouse, wouldn't you want to see him charged with murder?"

"Oh, please. Get real."

"I'll go to the police. But I've got to have something to make a case against him. Did Toulouse tell you anything else?"

"I'm scared," she said.

"You know something, don't you?"

She shook her head.

"If that's all you know, what makes you think Mouton would come after you?"

Barb gazed at the floor. She pushed her hair back over her ear. She sniffed a few times and swallowed hard.

"Everybody thinks I was Toulouse's girl. We hung around together a lot. I'd ride around with him in his truck sometimes."

"Do you know how dangerous that was? You're lucky Mouton's goons didn't hijack the truck and chop you up for crab bait."

"He always said he was in danger. I never believed him. I thought he was trying to impress me," she said. "You hear a lot of that kind of stuff in a bar. One guy told me the CIA had hired him to assassinate Saddam Hussein. When Toulouse and I would ride around in his truck, after the first joint he'd tell me all kinds of stuff. I thought he was funny."

"Did he sell any drugs when you were with him?"

"Never. See, Toulouse didn't sell . . ."

"Come on, Barb."

"What I mean is, he didn't sell on the street. He had somebody else who did that."

"Who was it?"

"Toulouse called him 'Little Boy,' 'Little Man,' something like that."

"But you weren't ever with him when he sold?"

"All we'd do was smoke some pot and listen to some CDs. I wasn't Toulouse's girl or anything. His boss is the one I've been seeing."

Damn! I thought. *Not Rickey Dee McCoy.*

"His boss is sending somebody to get me. They're supposed to knock and say 'Coastliner Ice Company.' When you didn't, I thought you were one of Mouton's guys."

"What's his boss's name?"

"Rickey Dee. He's moving me to his place. It's a mansion."

I rubbed my hand across my mouth. "Barb, he's jerking you around. He's probably not coming."

"Yes, he is! I was going to move over there anyway. I stayed at his place once for a few days, but his old girlfriend came back so I left. She's a real bitch. It's over between them. He's trying to move her out, but he doesn't want to hurt her. He's so nice. As soon as he moves her out, I'm moving in."

"He's kicking his old girlfriend out. What makes you think he won't do the same thing to you?"

"She's a bitch. You wouldn't believe some of the things she's done."

"When did you meet this guy?"

"I went to Bay Saint Louis with Toulouse one day. Rickey Dee took me for a ride in his car. He's got this really great Jaguar convertible. And then we went to dinner at the Yacht Club in Gulfport. He's got this really neat yacht. Rickey Dee's a lot of fun; he really is."

"You see him a lot?"

"Yeah. Well . . . sometimes. He comes over to see me all the time. He's really good to me."

My forearm was still bleeding and I needed more than tissue to stop it, so we walked back to the kitchen to get a dish towel. The apartment was sparse, nothing on the walls and little furniture. A square kitchen table, metal frame and Formica top, with two straight-back chairs. The shelves and countertops were empty.

"You know Rickey Dee McCoy is a big-time dealer," I said. "You know he's going to end up like Toulouse or at least in prison."

"How do you know his last name?"

"Bay Saint Louis is a small town."

"He owns an ice company. He's rich."

"He also deals drugs. He'll get caught."

She shook her head no. "He's safe over there."

"What do you mean 'safe'?"

"He's got protection. A few weeks ago I went over there with Toulouse. We got really messed up, you know, and Toulouse thought it would be funny if we surprised Rickey Dee. I swear, poor Toulouse. He was such a fool. We tiptoed up to Rickey Dee's office and Toulouse throws the door open and we go 'Surprise!' real loud. There was this *big* guy in there, and Rickey Dee was sitting behind his desk counting out a big stack of hundred-dollar bills."

"So? Where's the protection?"

"Rickey Dee told me later that the guy had connections or something."

"Who was he?"

"Rickey Dee didn't say."

"What did the big guy do when you and Toulouse broke in?"

"He pulled a gun on us. And Rickey Dee goes, 'Don't shoot! Don't shoot!' Then the guy snatches that money up and stomps out of there. He just glares at us, you know?"

"This guy had a gun?"

"He was wearing it on a holster. The kind you wear across your chest."

"You think you'd recognize him if you saw him again?"

"I doubt it. Like I said, we were really messed up. I remember he had real dark hair. And he was big. Strong-looking, you know?"

"Did he say anything?"

"No, he just walked out. But, see, it's safe for Rickey Dee over there."

"You almost got shot; you call that safe?"

"It's safe . . ." Her voice was muted.

"If you lie down with dogs, you're going to get fleas."

She smiled. "That's southern, isn't it?"

"I don't know if they say it up North or not, but it's true. Where are you from?"

"Grand Rapids, Michigan."

"I'll take you right now and put you on a plane to Grand Rapids. I'll lend you the money for the ticket."

Her eyes withdrew. "I can't go there . . ." So quiet I could barely hear her. "They kicked me out."

"They'll take you back."

"You shouldn't be here when Rickey Dee comes."

"Can you stay with some friend for a few days? Maybe some relative?"

"I've got a sister . . ." She looked at the wall in front of her. Her eyes were empty and so was her voice.

"Go visit her. Stay there until things cool down."

"No!" She perked up. "You've got to leave. You can't be here when they come."

"Why not?"

"Rickey Dee told me not to talk to anybody. And he meant it."

"I'll give you a ride to Bay Saint Louis."

"I'll be alright, okay?"

"Barb, you didn't have the front door locked."

"I had just got here when you came. I was going to lock it."

"You can't play around with these people."

"I'll be alright."

She laced her fingers behind her neck and bent her head forward, shutting out me and the rest of the world. Whatever else she knew about Toulouse and Mouton would have to come later. It was over for today.

I left her knowing she wouldn't go home. I also knew that, as bad as it was, at least for a few days she'd be safe at Rickey Dee's.

SEVEN

Neal's always telling me I've got a bad habit of picking up strays. He's right; I admit it. But how could I know that Barb would be the type to hang around with scum like Toulouse and Rickey Dee? I mean, if you could have seen that smile. But, hey, it wasn't the first time it's happened to me.

The next morning I decided to forget the whole thing. Just stay out of it. If Mouton went down, he went down. There was nothing I could do about it this time. And it didn't matter how pitiful she looked sitting on that floor.

What I was going to do was get the boat ready so Neal, Kathy, my blind date and I could take it out that afternoon. I had a few days off and, by gosh, I was going to enjoy them. If Barb wanted any of my help, she could find me easily enough. I had done all I was going to do. To heck with Toulouse and Mouton and Rickey Dee and all the rest of them.

It was a pretty day, make that a gorgeous day, and I had a date to go sailing. The rest of it was none of my business, and I was going to do what Neal said.

Stay out of it.

Yes, sir. That's what I was going to do.

As soon as I made sure Barb had gotten to Rickey Dee's all right.

I turned in from Beach Boulevard and eased along the washed gravel driveway, which was flanked on both sides by sprawling live oaks, their limbs draped in Spanish moss. A Lincoln Town Car, gold, and a Cadillac Coupe deVille, dark blue, were parked up where the drive loops back on itself and forms an oval in front of the house's entrance. The Continental had Louisiana plates. There were also a pair of twelve-passenger vans parked around the loop. Since Rickey Dee had moved in, there were often a lot of cars in the drive—usually expensive cars, usually from out of state—and some stayed for days at a time. God knows who was in there this time.

The house has no front door; it's a front gate. Vertical wrought-iron bars across an archway that leads to a terrazzo courtyard, onto which the rooms of the house open. There's a high brick wall around the backyard where the pool is. I rang the doorbell and stood in the strong breeze that was drawn through the archway. It had been cooled by the yard's deep shade and smelled of the blooming wisteria and honeysuckle that covered the trellis Mr. Fidoli had set out in the loop of the driveway.

Shortly after I'd rung the doorbell a second time, a hairy, olive-skinned man in swim trunks and a Cozumel T-shirt walked through the courtyard to the gate.

"Yeah?" His voice had a breathiness that sounded practiced.

"My name's Jack Delmas. I need to see Mr. McCoy."

"You with the group?"

"I'm with Immigration." I figured it would get me in.

"Wait here."

Two minutes later he came back. He opened the gate without saying a word, wheeled around, and walked off ahead of me. The late morning sun shone hard and bright on the courtyard. A dancing reflection of sunlight off pool water flashed against the walls of the second arch and a strong chlorine smell drifted through the passageway.

When I walked through the second arch, I nearly bumped into the nun.

"Excuse us, dear," she said.

She wore the black habit and long, gray skirt of Saint Stanislaus School downtown. Behind her, in single file, walked four waist-high children, dripping wet and wrapped in beach towels. They were all licking Fudgesicles. Down at the covered poolside bar, Rickey Dee McCoy and a young woman in a red-and-yellow cotton sundress were giving Popsicles and Fudgesicles to four more kids, as two nuns dried off the remaining little swimmers as they came out of the pool. The olive-skinned man stood behind the bar retrieving the frosty treats from the freezer and handing them to Rickey Dee and the woman.

"This has been so nice, Mr. McCoy," one of the nuns said. "The children don't get to swim very often."

"Any time, Sister," he said. "You let me know when they want to come."

The woman in the red-and-yellow dress gave Rickey Dee a sweet smile as she handed out some more Fudgesicles. She patted the head of a little boy standing beside her.

He turned to the kids. "How'd y'all like to go to Slippery Sam's sometimes?"

"YAAAAH!" they squealed.

"Oh, Mr. McCoy," the nun said, "you're so good to us."

"My pleasure, Sister," he said.

"You've been such a blessing since you moved to town."

At the far end of the pool, Bruno from the icehouse was sitting with his feet in the water. A tall woman in a pair of cutoff jeans and a Nike T-shirt, her white-blonde hair pulled up in a bun, stepped out of the house and walked toward him. She sat on the edge of a chaise longue near the diving board. They both watched the children and the nuns. The woman waved at them.

Barb was nowhere to be seen.

The man who had met me at the door walked the two nuns up the concrete steps leading away from the pool, the towel-wrapped children trailing behind, each with a quickly melting Fudgesicle. The young woman in the sundress eased behind the bar as she and Rickey Dee waved and called out good-bye to them. I stepped to the side as the nuns, the children, and their olive-skinned escort walked past me and through the archway.

As soon as the last nun was out of sight, the woman in the sundress lifted a bottle of José Cuervo Gold from behind the bar and set it on the counter. Rickey Dee lit a cigarette, sat at a round metal table, and pulled a deck of cards out of a beach bag. At the far end of the pool, the peroxide-blonde woman stepped out of the cutoffs and pulled the T-shirt over her head. Her bare breasts plopped out, and she began slathering them with sunscreen.

The olive man came back through the arch and walked in my direction. "C'mon," he said, as he gestured toward Rickey Dee with his head and walked ahead of me toward the pool.

She had shed the sundress. With her bleached hair and pumped-up breasts straining against her bikini top, she could have passed for the twin of the bimbo doing the nude sunbathing over by Bruno. She gave Rickey Dee some orange drink in a tall glass, and he gulped down two big swallows. He dealt three poker hands as he followed my approach through blue wraparound sunshades, crunching ice with his teeth. Over at the pool, Bruno pushed himself up and walked to a director's chair, drying his feet off with a white Seagram's 7 Crown beach towel, his eyes trained on me.

"If you're from Immigration, come back Monday to the office. You guys done tied up my foreman over there all day yesterday. Next time bring your own damn interpreter." Rickey Dee arranged the cards in his hand and took another big gulp of his orange drink.

"I'm looking for Barb Novak," I said.

He looked up at me. "Yeah?"

"She ain't here," the woman said.

"Shut up! I'll handle this." He glared at her; then he turned to me. "She ain't here."

"She told me she was coming over yesterday."

"How come Immigration's looking for her?" he said.

"It's a personal matter."

"You got any ID?"

"I'm not from Immigration. I'm looking for Barb Novak."

"You not with Immigration?"

"I'm checking on her. My name's Delmas."

"You a cop?"

"No."

"He ain't a cop?" the woman asked.

"You deaf or somethin'?" Rickey Dee said. "No, he ain't no cop."

She reached into the yellow, straw beach bag beside her chair, pulled out a fat joint from a Ziploc bag, and grabbed Rickey Dee's lighter from the table.

"So what you doin' here, Delmas?" He glanced at his poker hand. "How many cards y'all need?"

"If you're interested," I said, "you might try looking for Barb at 432 Jasmine Street over in New Orleans. She's probably still waiting for you to come."

"Who said I was going over there?"

"She did."

Rickey Dee's eyes hardened. I bit lightly on the corner of my mouth. I had not meant to tell him that.

"I told her you wouldn't show. Looks like you've got plenty of company already."

"Hey, Delmas, she's the one who didn't show. I sent somebody for her."

"Maybe you need to hire better help. If you wanted to find her, it's easy enough. She's there on Jasmine Street, scared to death and naïve enough to think you'll protect her."

"Hey, first of all, she ain't there. The place was locked up and nobody answered the door. Second, you talking protection? Anybody messes with Barb, they answer to me. I ain't got to answer any questions from you. If you don't have no business here, it's time for you to haul ass."

With that the olive-skinned man stood and stepped in my direction. He brought his hands down on both my shoulders, gripping hard. "You heard the man."

I grabbed both straps of his tank top. I threw my weight backward as I planted my foot in his stomach. He lurched forward and flipped, yelling and kicking, high into the air. He splashed into the pool on his back. The woman started screaming and Bruno raced over from the pool. When he got close, I crouched into the ready stance.

"Hold it!" Rickey Dee shouted. Bruno put on the brakes. Then he jerked into his best high-school-bully pose, jaw tilted upward, chest out, arms dangling at his side.

"Hey! What's your problem, Delmas?" Rickey Dee never stood up. "You come into my place without no invitation. You start asking questions. You rough up one of my guests. Who the hell you think you are?"

I stepped back to get a better angle to watch Bruno. The olive-skinned man flailed away in the pool, coughing up a lungful of water.

"Listen, McCoy," I said, "it looks like you got all the gash around here you can handle. Barb's not even close to being in this league. You leave her alone."

"Get the hell outta here, Delmas!"

I backed to the steps and scooted through the courtyard, looking over my shoulder. I started my truck and lurched around the Town Car and the Coupe deVille. I gunned it and my tires squealed as I wheeled around the tight loop of the driveway. When I reached the street, I spotted Bruno in my rearview mirror. He was leaning against the Lincoln, one arm resting on its roof, studying me without heat or hurry.

Burning me into his memory.

EIGHT

Downtown stood Saturday-empty except for two pickups at the hardware store and a sliver Grand Prix at the drug store. The predators that have drained the blood from Main Street—giant supermarkets, cut-rate discount chains, and out-of-state department stores—are at strip malls out on the highway.

Neal, Kathy, and their two kids were coming over at one o'clock with my blind date. We planned to cook out and then go sailing around three. The boat was still in a mess from two days earlier when Tricia and I had gone out on it, so I threw on my cutoffs and an Ole Miss T-shirt and tossed a bucket, a bottle of ammonia, a mop, and some sponges into the bed of my truck.

I drove through town, across the four lanes and the median of Highway 90, and headed to the marina, north a quarter of a mile on the banks of a cove scooped out of the main bay. When I cleared the highway, I noticed the flashing blue light in my rear-view mirror.

I don't know how long he had been behind me; there was no siren. I pulled onto the wide gravel shoulder and the sky blue, unmarked squad car of Sheriff Artis Wade pulled in behind me, its single flashing light at the end of a wire, sitting on the roof above the driver's side on a magnetic base.

I climbed out, stepped toward the rear, and sat on the bumper. The sheriff was saying something into his radio mike, his meaty fist hiding it from view. He put on his coat when he got out of the car and ran his fingers straight back through his black hair. He walked toward me, slapping a ticket book against his left palm.

Wade's head is huge and so is every feature—nose, ears, jaws, and neck. He's only an inch or so taller than I am, he might be six-two, but he's got 60, maybe 70, pounds on me—probably tops 250. A lot of it's gut, but he's still got arms as big as my legs.

He stopped ten feet away and stared at me from behind mirrored sunglasses. He stuck his ticket book into the breast pocket of his coat.

"Was I speeding, Sheriff?"

"Let me see your license."

He could see I didn't have a wallet, but I walked to the cab and got it from under the seat. I held it out to him. "Still got another year to go on it."

"That tag expires next month."

"Appreciate the reminder, Sheriff. I didn't think you made traffic stops any more."

He swaggered past me to the driver's side and ran his finger across the inspection sticker in the lower left corner of the windshield; it was only a month old. He stuck his head in the open window.

"Sheriff, I don't have any beer, whiskey, pot, or anything else that would interest you. You plan to write me a ticket for something, go ahead. You got a search warrant, show it to me. Otherwise, I'd appreciate it if you'd let me go about my business."

He straightened up and turned to me. "I had a complaint called in on you, Delmas."

"You want to tell me what it's about?"

"You went up to the McCoy place a little while ago and assaulted a man. They said you was trespassing at the time."

"Anybody file papers?"

"They might."

"If they decide to, I'm sure you can show them where Judge Mosby has his office."

"Don't get smart, Jackie Boy. I'll run your ass down to the station in a New York minute."

"Not very professional language," I said. "Tell me, which charges would you run me in on?"

"Trespass and assault." His jaw was clenched tight enough to crack a tooth.

"Assault? You mean felony assault?"

"Damn right."

"Tell you what, Artis, you do that. Take me in and get those sleaze balls to sign felony charges. Then I'll get the DA to let me go to the grand jury under oath and tell everything I know, or even suspect, about them and their whole operation."

Wade circled around me back to his car. He stopped, squared his shoulders toward me, and hitched his thumb in his belt. "You stay away from there," he said.

"When did you start delivering messages for Rickey Dee Mc-Coy?"

Wade raised his thumb from his belt and pulled back his coat, exposing his shoulder holster. "Mr. McCoy hires twenty-three men. Twenty-three jobs, Delmas. Somebody comes into town and sinks that kinda money into a business, he don't need some sorry-ass beach bum gettin' into his face. You keep your ass away from him."

My face grew hot. "Go back to that pimp Rickey Dee and tell him if he's got a problem with me, tell me to my face. He's in my town now and I ain't about to deal with his damned errand boy."

Wade reddened and his hand twitched toward his pistol. But a man was mowing his yard across the street, and we were in view of cars on the highway. I turned on my heel and walked to the cab of my pickup. I felt the bull's-eye between my shoulder blades as I fought the urge to run. A tingle ran along my back like two roaches were racing up my spine. That son of a bitch was just hot-tempered enough to shoot.

Perspiration beaded on my forehead and trickled down from my armpits. I got into the cab and, with the back of my hand, wiped the stinging sweat from my eyes. I started the engine and checked the side mirror.

Wade sprayed gravel and kicked up a cloud of dust as he floored the baby blue Ford into a hard U-turn. The tires yelped as they hit the pavement, and he laid down black strips of burned rubber for twenty feet. He flipped on the light bar, cranked up the siren, and raced through the red light at the highway.

NINE

"How many hamburger patties will we need?" I asked.

"Two for me," Neal said, "two for you. I know Kathy won't eat more than one, and I'm sure Laura won't either."

"How do you know that?"

"It's your first date. She's not about to pig out on a first date."

"I'll pat out a couple of extras in case she hasn't seen *Gone With the Wind* lately."

It was bright outside and ninety-three degrees. The offshore afternoon sun had sucked into the sky enough saltwater to make clouds and cool the water's surface and stir the Gulf air. When the clouds got heavy and black, usually around three o'clock, the lightning would start and the winds would pick up, and sometimes the storms would come on shore. But on that afternoon it looked like the wind was going to push them on by to the east.

Out on the deck, Kathy and Laura, my blind date, were drinking Miller Lites as Kathy kept one eye on Billy, my nine-year-old nephew, and Lisa, his sister who had just turned seven. They were climbing in the low branches of the live oak in my backyard and gathering gray strands of moss.

The music of Lisa's laughter drifted across the yard. It made me miss my daughter, Peyton. She would be coming down from Memphis for a two-week stay around the Fourth of July. A vision flashed through my mind of Peyton, Sandy, and the X-ray reader. They were at the swimming pool of the Colonial Country Club up in Memphis and Peyton was jumping off the side of the pool into his arms.

God Almighty!

Neal sliced into a baseball-sized onion that was green at both ends. It was a strong one and it made his eyes water.

"Where did Kathy find her?" I asked.

"She's a freelance court reporter out of Gulfport. She was taking a deposition for us one day when Kathy stopped by the office. Kathy found out Laura wasn't married. You can fill in the rest of the story."

"Kathy's never going to give up, is she?"

"Not until she gets you married off."

He laid the onion slices on a plate and set it on the counter. He rinsed his hands and splashed water into his eyes.

"Man, I've got to get out of here. These onions are killing me." He walked through the sliding door and over toward the grill. I popped B. B. King into the CD player, picked up the platter of hot dogs and hamburger patties, and stepped outside.

They had started gossiping about two deputy clerks at the courthouse, a pair of old maid sisters who had been there for thirty years and had claimed ownership of the chancery clerk's office, Miss Katie and Miss Irene Denley. The Denley sisters were currently in what sounded like the third stage of their breaking-in-the-new-kid procedure with Laura. Kathy and Neal laughed at Laura's stories, told a few of their own, and predicted what Miss Katie and Miss Irene would do next.

Laura was probably thirty years old, a pretty brunette with brown eyes. Been in Shreveport all her life before she came down to the coast after she broke off her engagement. She had friends down here and wanted a change of scene.

The coals were gray and ready, and I set down the platter and walked back into the kitchen for the barbecue sauce. As I washed my hands, five hard and quick raps rang through the front door. I walked toward the front, drying my hands with a dish towel, and five more impatient knocks came, RAP-RAP-RAP-RAP-RAP!

I gave the knob a half twist. The door burst open and two deputies rushed in, knocking me backward. I sprawled on the coffee table and rolled off face down to the floor. One clamped my arm and planted his knee between my shoulder blades while the other one cuffed my wrists behind my back. The first deputy got off, gripped my upper arm, and, with the help of the other one, jerked me to my feet.

"You have the right to remain silent. Anything you say can and will be used against you . . ." It came from behind me. I knew the voice.

"What the hell's going on?" I yelled.

Neal ran into the room. A deputy stepped in front of him and put his hand on his .357.

"Hold it, Neal," the deputy said.

"Cooper, what the hell you mean busting in here like this?" Neal shouted.

"This man's under arrest."

"No shit, Sherlock! I got eyes! What's the charge?"

"He's under arrest for the murder of Barbara Denise Novak."

TEN

I think the deputy kept talking. I remember something about a lawyer being provided. I'm almost sure Neal continued to shout at them.

Sound blended into a jumble, whirred around until it became background buzz. Everything went into slow motion. I was seeing a collage with no distinct images. I felt weightless.

Why did I leave her there?

I must have sunk to the coffee table. I felt a tug on my arm and it snapped me back into focus. I pulled away. The deputy jerked my arm again, trying to lift me off the table. I swung around hard, crashing my elbow into his soft belly, bending him over. He raised his right hand high to chop down on me, but Neal lurched past Cooper and blocked the deputy's downward swing, moving his 260 pounds between us, grabbing the deputy's arm.

"Pitalo!" Neal screamed. "You call off these goons right now or I'll have your ass—and you know I can."

Pitalo, the voice from the doorway, walked toward us. "Aw right. Knock it off . . ."

"But, Sarge, he hit me." The deputy I didn't know turned toward me. "You don't hit no cop! Never!"

"Hey!" Neal shouted. "We got four witnesses who saw you roughing up a man in cuffs in his own damn house . . ."

"Quit yelling at him!" Pitalo said.

"I'll yell as much as I damn well please! You got a warrant?"

"Extradition papers!"

Neal got six inches from Pitalo's face. "This the way you serve extradition papers?"

"On a murder charge? Damn right!"

They screamed at each other, Pitalo and Neal, their noses almost touching, the two deputies flanking them, one on either side. Looked like an argument around home plate. With all the wrangling and close-quarter screaming, they forgot I was sitting on the coffee table. Nobody noticed when I stood up. "What happened?" I asked.

All four of them looked at me like I had just walked into the room.

"What the hell happened?"

"Hush, Jack." Neal walked away from the deputies to where I sat. "Don't say anything."

"They're talking about Barb. That's the girl I . . ."

"Shut up!" he whispered. "Shut up right now or *I'll* beat the crap out of you."

I nodded and he went back to arguing with Pitalo. A deputy grabbed me at the elbow and pulled me backward toward the door. Outside on the back deck, behind the glass, Laura stood gaping in stunned silence, frozen still, a Miller Lite loose in her hand. She looked as if she had been shot and was ready to fall.

I'm usually a little smoother on first dates.

One deputy walked in front, another in back, down the tall flight of wooden steps. Out by the curb, Artis Wade leaned against his sky blue Ford, arms folded high and resting on his belly, chewing gum in deliberate bites. When we were halfway down, he got in his car, flipped on his light bar, and waited for us to get into ours. I wondered if the bastard was going to turn on his siren.

They patted me down and put me in the backseat. Pitalo and the unknown deputy got in up front. Cooper had his own car, two New Orleans cops were there in an NOPD squad car, and Neal followed in his Lincoln—a five-car parade headed downtown. A crowd of neighbors, eight or ten of them, stood on the seawall, drawn by the blue flashes from the squad cars. They looked like they were trying to decide whether they should go ahead and call the real estate agent right then. Lisa and Billy were in the group, hiding behind a tall man, peeking around his legs with wide child eyes.

As we rode I closed my eyes and called up in my mind that old house on Jasmine Street. Barb was sitting in the hallway, arms wrapped around her knees, waiting for Rickey Dee to rescue her.

And I was walking out the front door.

Pitalo removed the handcuffs and led me to the desk against the back wall for booking. They arrested me on a Louisiana request for extradition, which the two New Orleans cops had brought with them that morning. They stood around the coffee machine waiting for me to decide if I would waive or fight it in court.

Neal pressed his finger to his lips from time to time to keep me quiet as the desk sergeant took my prints, made mug shots, filled out forms, and turned me over to old Mr. Pate, the jailer. Maybe because they knew me, maybe because they didn't know any better, they didn't take my belt or the stuff in my pockets.

Pitalo followed Mr. Pate and me to my cell, the one on the right. Milky gray paint flaked from the concrete walls and the floor needed sweeping. I could feel the sand grinding under my shoes. The barred windows to the outside were open; they seldom used the A/C in the cells. A fan at the end of the hall pulled in fresh, warm air from the courthouse lawn, smelling of newly mown grass and lawnmower exhaust, evoking that feeling of freedom from summers long ago. The door clanked shut behind me, they walked back up front, and I sat on the cot and waited for Neal.

Thirty minutes later, the main door to the lockup slid open, its heavy echo rumbling down the walk. Mr. Pate walked beside Neal to my cell. Neal sat on the other end of the bunk, a hard expression on his face.

"Looks bad," he said.

"I feel like I've been blindsided." I propped my elbows on my knees and pressed my palms against my temples. "What happened?"

"The New Orleans cops got a phone tip. They found a body that has been preliminarily identified as Barbara Novak in a house she had been renting on Jasmine Street. She was stabbed once in the chest. Died instantly."

"Who identified her?"

"I think they said it was her boss," he said. "Anyway, Forensics said she had been dead two hours when they found her. That was yesterday afternoon around three."

"I didn't know NOPD worked this fast," I said.

"Pitalo told me some bigwig on the force is pushing it. Guy named Guidry."

"Is this Guidry some kind of deputy chief or something?"

"Pitalo didn't say. But he did say that the New Orleans cops think this case might be related to the murder of Toulouse Caron. It's got their attention."

I leaned back on my elbows. "Where did they find her, Neal?"

"In the kitchen, in the back of the house. It's one of those old row houses over near . . ."

"I know what the house looks like."

"How?"

"I was there. I was there yesterday around noon." I sat up and looked at my brother. His jaw was slack and his eyes narrowed with one eyebrow cocked, like he wanted to ask a question, but he didn't.

"What else do they have?" I said.

"There was a lot of blood in the kitchen, but they also found some up front near the door in the hall. It's a different type."

The fresh scar on my forearm glowed. I glanced down at it. Neal looked at it, too.

"A neighbor across the street saw a man go into the house around noon and leave around twelve-thirty. She got a good look at him. Her description fits you."

I sighed, bent forward, and rested my forehead on my hands.

"She also described the vehicle. Old blue Ford pickup with a dent on the rear fender, driver's side, and a Saints bumper sticker."

He stopped.

"I've been meaning to get that dent fixed," I said. Neal didn't smile. "Is that all?"

"Two more things," he said. "They lifted some prints and they're doing a match on yours. Also, they found what looks like the murder weapon in your truck thirty minutes ago."

Neal leaned back and rubbed his eyes with the tips of his fingers. I stood and started pacing.

"I went in the Comus last week and started talking to her," I said. "When the story about the Undertaker killing came on TV I could tell she thought it might be Toulouse. She found out I was from Bay Saint Louis and asked me to check with Coastliner and see if he was okay."

"So you took it on yourself to start poking around."

"She was afraid that Mouton had killed him."

"She told you this?"

"Not exactly."

"Well, what exactly did she say that made you think she'd ever even heard of André Mouton?"

"For one thing, the way she looked when she saw the TV story."

"The way she looked? You cooked up some plan to bring in André Mouton based on the way some stranger reacted to a television news story?"

I reached over my head and gripped the bars of my cell with both hands. "The point is, I was right. She did know the guy in the story. It did turn out to be Toulouse."

The ancient central air conditioner on the roof above us kicked on and started roaring, and one of its belts set up a steady squeak. Out the window it looked like a light rain as the old unit spit drops of water on the cars below. I rested my head against the bars. Neal sat silent behind me.

"When they identified Toulouse, I went back to find out if Barb knew anything about Mouton. I figured if she knows some guy who gets murdered by the Undertaker, she might know the Undertaker."

"And you decide to do NOPD's job, and you're the one who ends up in jail," he said. "We'll worry about André Mouton later. Right now we've got to get you out. Was there anything you saw that day that would give you any idea what happened to her?"

"Nothing."

"And you didn't see anybody else?"

"She was alone when I left the house."

"So the murder took place after you left?"

"That's good, Neal. *Of course it did!* She was scared to death that Mouton had killed Toulouse and was coming after her. She was waiting for Rickey Dee McCoy to send somebody to get her."

"Rickey Dee McCoy? Why would she be waiting for him?"

"She was his girlfriend."

"I thought it was this Toulouse character."

"Toulouse was just a friend of hers. She said Rickey Dee was going to bring her over here to his house."

Neal tapped his fingertips against each other.

"I was set up," I said. "Whoever called in that tip set me up."

He blew out a big breath. "You think they saw you coming out of her house?"

"They had to."

"Well, unless they knew who you were, how could they have found you this fast?"

"They could have traced the tag through a computer," I said.

"But wouldn't it take a cop to do that?"

"Believe me, Mouton or Rickey Dee, either one, could get that information faster than a cop on the beat could. They could have tracked me to my house and planted that knife within an hour."

Neal stood and put his hand on my shoulder. He squeezed gently and then patted me twice. "I'll get you the best criminal defense lawyer in New Orleans, Josh Hallman. You need to waive extradition and go on back to New Orleans with those two cops. I'll call and see if I can get Hallman to meet you at the jail. You don't want to spend any more time in that place than you have to."

Mr. Pate came and let Neal out. I flopped back onto the cot and looked at the ceiling, running the scene at Barb's house over and over in my mind—potholes, broken beer bottles, seedy houses—trying to remember any cars that were on the street, trying to recall anyone on the street who could have seen me going into the house—or coming out.

Neal came back in a few minutes and said Josh Hallman would be waiting for me, and if we hurried we could make the evening session of court and get a bond set. He would get my dark suit and run it over for the court appearance.

The deputy with Neal was a kid I used to coach in tee ball

down at the church at a time that I swear seemed no more than three or four years earlier. We all decided there was no need for cuffs. We walked down the hall and the deputy looked to be as embarrassed as I was, so we started talking about baseball and it helped both of us.

When we reached the squad room up front, the two New Orleans cops were standing beside Pitalo's desk as he wrote on a form. Neal pulled me aside while we waited.

"This lawyer I called, you do what he says. He's the best, but he takes some getting used to."

"Criminal defense lawyers are all a little crazy. No problem."

Neal rubbed his chin with the back of his hand. "Josh isn't crazy. He's just kind of . . ." He reached for the right word.

"Flamboyant?" I asked. "I can handle that."

"Oh, he's flamboyant alright. But he's . . ."

"Okay, Delmas, let's go." It was the deputy I didn't know. He grasped the back of my arm above the elbow and steered me toward Pitalo's desk. I signed some papers and then the New Orleans cops took over.

They cuffed me, led me outside, put me in the backseat, and we started the short drive to the New Orleans lockup.

I had heard Neal speak of Hallman before. Said most prosecutors were scared to go up against him. Any lawyer who could command that kind of respect in that snake pit they call the New Orleans criminal justice system had to be smart and tough. I also figured he had to be as mean as a stepped-on hornet in clover.

But nothing Neal said—and nothing I thought—prepared me in any way for my first encounter with Josh Hallman.

ELEVEN

During the ride, the shorter officer riding shotgun spoke only once. That was when we passed a covey of six bikers, decked out in their colors, turning off at the French Quarter exit.

"We'll see that pond scum again before midnight."

Two-man patrols are like marriages; no two are alike. Some crack jokes all day. Some talk sports. Some curse the general state of the world and most of its inhabitants. These two used words like each one cost money.

We whipped down the interstate at cop speed, eighty or eighty-five, and pulled into Central Lockup at Tulane and Broad in forty-five minutes.

In the booking room, six banged-up desks were set in a row, each of them behind the counter and perpendicular to it. The counter ran the width of the room, with a gate at the far end. Telephones rang constantly, uniformed officers walked hand-cuffed prisoners from desk to desk, intake officers typed in the blue glow of computer screens. There were more people smoking in there than I have seen in any public building in years, and the smell had permanently settled in the air-conditioning. In the middle of the back wall an iron door led to central lockup.

They led me to a cold, gray steel chair at the end of a gunmetal desk, the domain of a pudgy, bald, black sergeant named Simpson. He was a twenty-five-year cop with a face that was bland, imperturbable. They dropped the papers from Bay Saint Louis on the desk.

"He's clean. Here's the paperwork."

They walked away, one to the coffeemaker in the corner, the other to the men's room.

"They usually talk this much?" I asked.

Simpson snorted and grunted what I guess was a laugh, "Humphf!" He studied the papers, holding them out at arm's length trying to focus, then giving up and putting on a pair of glasses. "Alright, uh, Delmas. Empty your pockets, take off your belt and shoestrings, put 'em in the tray. Murder, huh?"

"They've got the wrong man, Sergeant."

"Uh-huh."

Simpson marked off each item on a printed list, a record of my belongings: canvas belt, leather shoelaces from my Top-Siders, eighty-seven cents in change, twenty-six dollars in currency, a wallet, a set of keys, and the Case pocketknife my grandfather had given me. No watch, no jewelry. He couldn't have checked it faster with a supermarket scanner.

"Sign here."

A young officer came to the desk. "Is this Delmas?" He didn't look at me.

"That's him."

"That guy's got something for him." He pointed his thumb toward the front counter. Neal, still in his Hard Rock Cafe T-shirt, had my dark suit slung over his shoulder.

"Nice touch, Delmas." Simpson looked up at the young cop. "Check it in. Make sure there's nothing in the pockets." Then he turned toward me. "He your lawyer or something?"

"He's my brother. He's a lawyer over in Mississippi, but he's got somebody else handling this."

"This other lawyer, he wear Hard Rock T-shirts, too?" Simpson chuckled, "Humphf!" He sat up, twisted his chair around, and beckoned for a guard standing beside the iron door. "You'll get your suit later."

I've seen a few fresh-faced cops. I've never seen a fresh-faced guard. New Orleans, Detroit, Omaha—they all look the same. Low forehead, jutting jaw, little black eyes set deep in dark cavities. This one didn't stoop; he was just squatty and compressed. His short hair was slicked down, and he had an indoor pallor and smelled of cigarettes and coffee.

We walked to the iron door and I stopped for the guard to open it. As I walked through, I turned and looked at Neal. He gave me a thumbs-up just before the door clapped shut behind me.

It's called the bull pen, an undivided holding tank in the center of the lockup where they keep prisoners who've just been booked and are waiting for their case to be called or for a cell to open up. They put me there by mistake; when you're booked for murder, you're supposed to be put into a single cell. After two or three minutes in the bull pen, I began to wonder why murderers get such special treatment.

My cotenants were generally a disagreeable lot. A couple of red-eyed winos, one with dried vomit down the front of his greasy shirt. Four snarling drag queens who had just been booked following the breakup of a table-busting fight at a gay bar on Esplanade—sequins, ostrich feather stoles, fishnet stockings, and miniskirts. The drag queens looked pretty good compared to the two hookers; the hookers didn't even try to hide their needle tracks. Several drunk bikers, mad at the world. Three bull dykes who had been run in for brawling; even the bikers weren't messing with them. And a black man, probably forty, could have passed for sixty, who had stabbed his girlfriend with an ice pick two hours earlier in the Desire Project. His eyes were yellowed and he smelled like an open bottle of Colt 45 Malt Liquor.

Outside the bars, a trusty swabbed the slick concrete floor with milky water from a tin bucket, the oblong kind with a mop wringer on one end. The place smelled like a backed-up urinal with a bottle of Pine Sol poured into it.

I walked over to the long bench set against the bars on the far side of the bull pen where a fifty-year-old man—a balding white guy—sat alone on one end. A borderline DUI, nabbed on his way home from the club, waiting for his wife to spring him. He still had the golf glove on his left hand, and his face and ears were red from sipping screwdrivers in the sun all day. He rested his face in his hands, his eyes covered, elbows propped on his knees. I plopped down hard beside him and he flinched. He looked at me, blew out a breath of relief, and tried to smile. The previous hour had not been one of his best. The guard who had brought me in came to the door and called his name, and he scrambled to the door like he was trying to catch the last ferry back to the mainland before the hurricane hit.

The shift must have changed right after that because a different guard—who could have passed for the first one's younger brother—walked through the iron door right after my golfing buddy left. This new guard was two inches taller and ten years younger, same bone structure, same hair, same grim mouth. He had so much hair on the back of his hands that it curled.

"Aw right, Delmas, Jack. Front and center, daulin'. It's show time." .

He opened the door, stood beside it, and gave a little bow as I walked by him, like a doorman at the Monteleone Hotel. No doubt the rest of the shift regarded him as funny. I took two steps toward the front.

"Whoa, Delmas. Follow her."

She was stubby with big forearms, fifty years old, and looked like she had been born right there in central lockup. She jerked her head to the side toward the hallway and plodded off ahead of me, a clipboard in one hand and a Marlboro in the other. She stopped by a door, twisted the handle, pushed it open, and pointed into the empty room with the clipboard.

"In there."

She walked on down the hall and never looked around.

It was a ten-by-ten room with a poured acrylic floor and concrete block walls painted pale green. An institutional odor of coffee cups and ashtrays filled the air. One of the fluorescent lights flickered and buzzed. A long steel table, with six metal chairs around it, and a clock set high on the wall behind a wire screen. It was five o'clock; not even four hours had passed since I'd heard those knocks on my front door.

I had been in the little room ten minutes when Josh Hallman breezed in. "So nice to meet you," he said. "I'm Josh Hallman."

"Uh . . . I-I'm . . ."

"You're Jack. Yes, I know."

"You?" I said. "You're . . ."

"Josh Hallman. Your lawyer."

A white powdered wig balanced on his head. A ruffled lace collar circled his neck. His face was covered with a base of tan makeup, and his eyebrows had been penciled black. White satin shirt, brocaded white knee pants, white stockings. He looked like he could break out into a minuet at any moment.

"I, uh, I'm . . ."

"Let me get comfortable," he said. "The heat has been simply unbearable."

He removed his lace collar and hung it on the coat rack, but he left the wig on. He stepped over to a chair across the table from me, swept his forefinger across the seat and examined it before sitting.

"In case you're wondering, it's dress rehearsal. Molière's *L'Avare*. We open at the Saenger Theater on Monday night."

I managed to close my mouth.

"I received a call from your brother," he said, "a dear, dear friend of mine. Said you were in a jam. A murder charge, I'm told." He glanced around at the floor and the table while he talked. "Do they ever clean this place?"

"Mr. Hallman . . ."

"Josh. Do call me Josh. Everyone else does."

"Josh, I've been set up."

"Yes, yes, Neal told me all about it. I read the file, and it looks bad. But, yes, it does appear to be a setup." He fidgeted around, tapping his fingers on the tabletop.

"I met this girl last week in a bar here in town. She was worried about a friend of hers . . ."

"Toulouse. Yes, Neal has told me."

"Well, let me back up. That morning I had driven up on what was obviously a murder scene. I was working . . ."

"I hate to interrupt you, but could we discuss this somewhere else?" He had crossed his legs and was inspecting the bottom of his shoe. "I mean, we would be a lot more comfortable discussing this in my office."

"Josh, that caveman who runs this place is not likely to let me run down to your office, even if I promise to come right back."

"Oh!" He laughed and put his hand up to his mouth. "I guess

that did sound silly. I mean after you make bail. That's an hour from now."

"You think I can get out on bail? On a murder charge?"

"Of course I do."

"I'm from out of state. They found the murder weapon in my truck . . ."

"Here are the facts. The deceased was a junkie who'd drifted into town recently and was mixing drinks in a dive with, shall we say, an unsavory reputation. She was known to hang out with a drug pusher, who himself had been murdered a few days earlier . . ."

When you write something down, see it in black and white, it can become stark and cold. Josh was verbally writing down the bare-bones outline of the life of Barb Novak—a junkie working in a dive and hanging out with dope pushers.

". . . she dropped out of college and couldn't hold a job . . ."

"You're being mighty rough on her," I said.

He stopped and his eyes hardened. "Don't go defending poor Miss Novak. I'm sure she had some good qualities, but my job is to get you out on bail and then to clear you of this murder charge. Agreed?"

I nodded and leaned forward, propping my forearms on the table.

"I'm not unfeeling. It's my job."

I nodded again.

"I don't know how much Neal has told you about me."

"He said you're the best."

"He's right," Josh said. "I'm the best criminal defense lawyer in New Orleans." He stared at me as if waiting for some reaction. I still wasn't sure he was in his right mind, so I stared back and kept quiet for a few seconds.

"Do you believe that?" he said.

"I believe Neal."

"In that case you can believe that the best criminal defense lawyer in the city is telling you that the only mission we have is to clear you of this charge. It's not to preserve the reputation of some unfortunate young woman you met in a bar."

"You're the lawyer," I said.

"And there's another matter we need to get straight. Neal tells me your involvement with Miss Novak grew from your desire to avenge the death of a friend of yours."

"That was part of it."

"Would you care to expand on that?"

"If she could have pinned this murder on André Mouton, it would have helped my feelings enormously. Six years ago he gunned down a good friend of mine. The guy was the investigator who brought me into the business. He was on a stakeout and witnessed Mouton execute a rival drug dealer on a street near the projects."

"Was your friend tailing Mouton?"

"No," I said, "he was looking for someone else and accidentally walked up on the murder. He tried to run away, but he was a big, easy target. One of Mouton's henchmen brought him down with a shot to the back. Hollow point .44. Mouton strolled over and popped another slug into his head to finish him off."

"I don't recall André Mouton ever being charged with murder," Josh said.

"There wasn't even a damned investigation, at least not by the police. I did my own. Found witnesses. Got statements. Turned it over to the cops. Nothing."

"That's not a happy story," he said, "but it's not something we'll be working on right now." He tugged at one of his lace cuffs, pulling it down over his wrist. "I guess that's all for now . . ."

"Not quite," I said. "Was there any evidence of a ritualistic killing at Barb's house?"

"Not that I know of."

"What would you say about that?"

"It's too early to say anything about it. It could be that the murders are unconnected and were committed by different persons."

"It could," I said.

"Or it could mean that the same person committed both murders but for different reasons."

"That's possible."

"Could mean a lot of things, or nothing," he said. "But I'm betting it was the same person."

"Well, it's not me."

Josh rose from his chair. "Night court begins at seven, that's in an hour and a half. The judge said she'll let us go first. She's such a dear."

"When do I get my suit?"

"They'll let you change ten minutes before we go in. I've learned the hard way not to let my client sit in that dreadful bull pen in a suit. God, that place is disgusting."

At a quarter to seven, the guard—the funny one—called me out, and we went through the iron door back to the booking room. Neal was standing on the other side of the front counter.

"Neal, have you lost your mind?"

"I know what you're thinking . . ."

"No, you don't, or you wouldn't be standing so close."

"It was a dress rehearsal for some play. Trust me, Jack. Josh Hallman is as good as you'll ever see."

"This is a nightmare."

"It'll be okay. Sergeant Simpson said you should change in that consulting room. Your suit's in there."

"Have you called Mama and Daddy yet?" I asked. "You can put a better spin on it than they're likely to get from the blue-hair network."

"I told them it was all a big mistake."

"For God's sake, don't let them come over here."

He nodded.

"I'll have to take your word for it on Hallman," I said. "Are you hanging around for court?"

"Of course. Oh, before I forget it, I gave Simpson the keys to your truck. I drove it over. I'm trying to get in touch with Billy McKay up in Tupelo to see if we can use his place for a while."

"His apartment on Dumaine?"

"You're going to be a resident of Louisiana for a while, son."

I hoped it wasn't twenty years to life.

Of course, Neal had forgotten my wing tips, but at least I was wearing Top-Siders and not white jogging shoes. I changed in the consulting room and followed the same guard—I found out his name was Clarence—through a series of hallways and into the courtroom.

Fifteen or twenty people sat in the spectators' gallery in the back of the courtroom. I sat inside the railing in a wooden arm-chair against the wall. In a few minutes the main doors of the courtroom flew open and a man walked down the aisle in brisk, deliberate steps. He pushed through the waist-high swinging doors of the railing and headed toward me.

"Is this better?" he asked.

It was Josh. He was a slender five-eight, with sharp and hand-some features. Strong jawline, aquiline nose, clear hazel eyes. His dark blond hair was cut short. It was flecked with gray and nearly white around his temples.

"You'll have to excuse me for a few minutes," he said. He stepped across the room and started talking to the court reporter. She nodded toward the visitor's gallery, and Josh looked out at the spectators. Then he walked through a door on the back wall beside the judge's bench and disappeared into the back room.

The guards brought in two prisoners—orange jail jumpsuits, chained at wrists and ankles—and sat them beside me. I looked out past the rail. A young woman with short hair, brown-blonde, walking toward the rear doors. A middle-aged couple, chunky blue-collar types. A swarthy, redheaded woman, late thirties, who kept glancing at her watch. A white-haired black lady in a flowered Sunday dress, with the impassive gaze and patient bearing of one who has spent a lifetime having to wait for something. Several wives and mothers waiting to once again bail some man out.

The bailiff crooked his finger, signaling for me to follow. We walked through the same door Josh had used, down a short and poorly lighted hallway, into a carpeted conference room with a table in the center and wooden armchairs all around. I had just sat down when Josh walked in.

He turned and held the door and a woman stepped in behind him. She was a tall, stern-looking woman about my age. Hard mouth, mean eyes. Could have been pretty if she'd tried. No makeup and dark brunette hair cut short. Her skin was pale; didn't spend much time outdoors. She said nothing and, other than a first glance, didn't look at me.

"Miss Cole, this is my client, Jack Delmas." Josh gave me a little smile. "Jack, this is Assistant District Attorney Karen Cole."

She looked up at me from her file and frowned. I nodded to her, and she glanced back down at her papers. She put her left elbow on the table, propped her forehead on her hand, closed her eyes, and sighed.

"There's not much I can agree to here. We've got a strong case. Your client is from out of state, likely to run. I can't recommend bond in any amount."

Josh sat three feet from her at her side. "Your strong case is a setup. You've got an anonymous tip, a shaky search warrant, and an eyewitness who can barely see. Mr. Delmas has no criminal record. There's no reason to deny bail."

"The nature of the crime is reason enough." She snapped the folder shut and glared at me.

"It's a serious crime; I don't deny that. But my client didn't do it. He has absolutely no motive."

"Dammit, Josh, there never are any motives! Some woman gets killed by a different creep every week in this city! Why? Who the hell knows? Maybe they hate their mothers or some crap like that. I really and truly don't care why they do it."

"He didn't do it."

"Tell it to the jury."

"No priors, no motive . . ."

"A million dollars, Josh. I'll take a million-dollar bond."

"That's ridiculous. You know the judge won't set any million-dollar bond."

"She's done it before."

Josh leaned back in his chair. He closed his eyes and ran his finger up and down the bridge of his nose. When he spoke, it was in soft, measured tones. "I know that violence against women is of particular concern to you. But don't let that cloud your outlook on this case."

"Don't patronize me, Mr. Hallman."

"I'm just saying that this particular female victim was involved with some very disreputable characters. Her best friend was that drug pusher the police found carved up in that vacant lot on Chef

Menteur. She was tending bar in a veritable drug supermarket . . ."

"Blaming the victim, are we?"

"I'm doing nothing of the kind. I'm merely pointing out that the deceased was on a first-name basis with a dozen people who could be suspects."

"The victim's lifestyle has nothing to do with this. The worst prostitute in the French Quarter deserves better than to be stabbed to death."

"I quite agree. You seem to forget the nature of my usual clientele. But there are circumstances in this case that are relevant to a bond hearing—the circumstances of her 'lifestyle,' as they say—and I intend to bring all of them out unless you agree to a reasonable bond. Do you wish for her family to . . ."

"Mr. Hallman, you're free to do whatever you . . ."

"Wait!" I held my hands straight out. "This little Ping-Pong match is fascinating, but it doesn't seem to be going anywhere."

Josh gave me a stern look—he can glare with just his right eye. "Jack, believe me, it's better for us to work this out now than it will be in court."

Miss Cole studied me like I was a bad oil painting somebody was trying to sell to her. "Your client is right. We don't seem to be getting anywhere."

"Make us an offer," he said.

"Very well. I'll make no recommendation to the judge as to any amount. I'll argue high, you argue low, and the judge decides."

"That will be fine," Josh said.

She stood, tapped the edge of the file on the table, gave me a cold glance, and stalked out.

Josh turned to me, his lips pressed together in a tight line. "Don't do that again. You broke the momentum. If I had made her angry enough, she would have laid out her whole case. I know these people, and I know what I'm doing."

"I'm sorry."

"As you can see, Miss Cole is particularly sensitive about violent crimes against women."

"So am I."

"We all are. But it's a blind spot with her. She's angry and she's going to charge ahead—but she's headed in the wrong direction."

"What do you mean?"

"She's going to try to paint this as a crime of violence against a woman. Didn't you hear what she said? 'Maybe they hate their mothers?' She hasn't thought this one through. Barb Novak wasn't raped. She was stabbed one time. This wasn't a murder by some lunatic with a sexual hang-up."

The door opened and the bailiff stuck his head in. "Josh, the judge is ready to start."

"Thanks, Dave," he said. "Well, Mr. Delmas, it's time for us to go to court. Your silence in there will be greatly appreciated."

"Do you think the bond will be anywhere close to a million dollars?"

He shook his head. "Not for the murder of any Barb Novak."

"All rise! Hear ye, hear ye. The Magistrate Court for the City of New Orleans is now in session, the Honorable Patricia Moret presiding. All who have business . . ."

Josh leaned in close and whispered, "Don't look around. Barb Novak's family is out there: her mother, father, and sister."

I felt their eyes on the back of my head. My ears and cheeks grew hot, and a trickle of sweat ran down the side of my face.

"Are you all right?" Josh asked.

"God, this is tough. I wish they weren't here."

"Wouldn't you be?"

"But I thought since they had kicked her out . . ."

"She was their little girl."

I nodded and looked down at my shoes. The hair on my neck seemed to rise.

"You're not guilty," Josh said.

"They don't know that, dammit. I've got to say something to them."

"Like what? They're hurting. They're angry—at you, at me, at themselves—they're mad at the bailiff for Christ's sake. And from what I hear, they're feeling a lot of guilt. There's nothing you could do or say . . ."

"Mr. Hallman, may we proceed?" Our case had been called, but we had not heard it. Josh sprang to his feet, light as a dancer. "Ready, Your Honor." He smiled at the Judge.

"Case number 426843. *State versus Andrew Jackson Delmas* on a charge of murder in the first degree," said the bailiff.

"Madam District Attorney, what says the state?" asked the judge.

"Thank you, Your Honor." Miss Cole rose and stood at the table, reading from an open manilla folder. "Mr. Delmas is before the court on a charge of murder in the first degree pursuant to a complaint filed by the New Orleans Police Department, Homicide Division. He is charged with the murder of Barbara Denise Novak in the City of New Orleans on or about June the fifth of this year. This case will be presented to the Orleans Parish Grand Jury next term. The purpose of this hearing is to determine whether the defendant is to be released on bond pending the action of the grand jury."

"Mr. Hallman," the judge said, "I take it you represent Mr. Delmas."

"Yes, Your Honor."

"You may proceed, Miss Cole."

"Thank you, Your Honor." She looked down at the folder and continued reading. "Mr. Delmas is a resident of the State of Mississippi. He has no property and no family in Louisiana. Your Honor, the record shows that the state has an eyewitness who will place the defendant at the crime scene near the time the murder occurred . . ."

"Your Honor, that has yet to be determined," Josh said. "The witness is eighty-eight years old and has given only a vague description of a person she allegedly saw on that day."

"I understand, Mr. Hallman," the judge said.

"The murder weapon was found in Mr. Delmas's vehicle on the day of his arrest," Miss Cole said.

"Defense contends that this search was pursuant to an invalid search warrant . . ."

"Mr. Hallman—" the judge tilted her head down and looked over her bifocals at Josh—"you will be given an opportunity to respond. Please allow Miss Cole to present her statement."

"Yes, Your Honor."

When the district attorney finished, Josh stood and buttoned his coat. He took six or seven slow steps around the table. "May it please the court. I am J. A. Hallman, counsel for the citizen accused, Jack Delmas." He spoke in a clear, loud voice. "Your Honor, defense contends that the state's case is built on circumstantial and suspect evidence alone. No motive has been established."

Josh stepped toward the judge and stood halfway between the defense table and the bench. He looked up at the judge and swept his arm back in my direction.

"I would submit that my client has no criminal record. On the contrary, he has an exemplary record of public service. While it is true that Jack Delmas does not share in our good fortune by residing in the State of Louisiana, he is a lifelong resident and a property owner in Bay Saint Louis. I would further submit that Jack Delmas is highly unlikely to attempt to leave or to evade the process of this honorable court . . ."

Josh had known about the case, and about me, for three hours, and he presented a case most lawyers could not have prepared in three weeks. I would love to see him in action at a trial—somebody else's trial.

He continued telling the judge what a great guy I am. His delivery was as good as I had ever seen. I saw why Neal had insisted on using him. Three or four minutes later, she interrupted him.

"Mr. Hallman, the court has heard enough. The setting of bond, is, as we all know, to ensure the presence of the defendant at subsequent court appearances. It is not meant as a punishment. It is a constitutionally guaranteed right to all citizens accused, but not convicted, of crime."

I suspected the judge was speaking to the audience, but I couldn't read what she was about to do.

"Bond is set in the amount of eighty thousand dollars, but is granted subject to certain limitations." The judge turned toward me, and Josh signaled me to rise. "Mr. Delmas, upon the posting of a surety bond in the amount of eighty thousand dollars, you will be released from custody to await the action of the grand jury.

If at that time you are indicted, a new bond will be set.

"If and when you post bond, you shall remain in the State of Louisiana. You shall obey all the laws of the state. You shall refrain from carrying or having in your possession firearms or weapons of any type.

"You shall not frequent disreputable establishments, nor any establishment that sells alcoholic beverages. Nor shall you be found in the company of persons of bad reputation."

The judge listed some more restrictions from memory in the flat cadence of one who gives the same speech several times each day. She finished, the gavel fell, and I turned to Josh.

"I forgot," Josh whispered, "don't shake hands. We don't want it to look like we got by with something."

"Eighty grand seems low for murder one," I said.

"It's exceptionally low, but I didn't have much to do with it. Judge Moret saw your last name and asked if you were related to Neal. She worked with him on a case some years ago and thinks highly of him."

"I guess respectability does come in handy every once in a while," I said, "even if it's only borrowed."

Across the room, Karen Cole glowered at me as she slapped papers into a manilla folder.

"Karen takes these things personally," Josh said. "I suggest you follow the conditions the judge laid out, at least until after the grand jury meets. That's two weeks from Monday. Don't give Miss Cole a second shot at you."

We walked to the docket clerk to sign some papers as the bailiff called the next case. As I waited for the clerk to fill out a form, I looked around the courtroom. The blue-collar couple I had seen earlier glared at me with red and teary eyes. I spun around and turned my back to them. I had a sick sensation in my stomach and prayed for the clerk to hurry.

TWELVE

Billy McKay, this rich friend up in Tupelo I went to school with at Ole Miss, keeps an apartment in the Quarter for Mardi Gras and a few Saints' games. It's a townhouse built around a courtyard, 150 years old. Billy—make that Billy's wife—is dividing it into four apartments. She's completed renovation on one apartment so far; the other three are empty. The one finished apartment is the front, upstairs quarter of the townhouse. It has a balcony on the street and one overlooking the inside courtyard: French doors open to both balconies. Billy said I could use it as long as I needed, but the Forty-Niners would be in town on September the tenth.

The morning after I moved into Billy's townhouse, I called Cotton Broussard. He was bringing his family downtown for Sunday mass at Saint Louis Cathedral and then a visit to the shark exhibit at the Aquarium of the Americas. He'd drop off his family at church, skip the nine o'clock mass, and meet me across the square at Café du Monde.

I was wiping the powdered sugar from my first beignet off my lips when I saw Cotton. He was getting out of a truly ugly dark green Caprice he had parked—in true NOPD tradition—in front of a fire hydrant across Decatur Street. He wore a shiny brown suit with tan stitching and a yellow shirt, open collar.

"How's the family, Cotton?"

"I dropped the kids off at the cathedral. Janelle was having a bad morning; she decided to stay home."

"I'm sorry to hear that."

"It's tough, Jack. The doctors at Ochsner's say she's got a good shot at recovery. Maybe seventy-five percent."

"Good odds."

"Yeah, but we gotta keep up the treatments. Looks like we might have to sell the house to do that. You know, the bad thing is I'm not that far away from being able to pay for it. I could swing it if I could make captain. The promotions list comes out next month."

"You think you've got a good shot at it?"

"I ain't had much luck before. And this time I've missed so much work because of Janelle's illness."

"Sounds like you're in a box."

"Yeah. But at least I don't have no more car payments." He pointed across the street.

"Unmarked car?"

"How'd you know?"

"Somehow a dark green sedan with black-wall tires and a radio antenna on the trunk doesn't look like what you'd choose."

"Looks beautiful to me, Cap. The department said I can use it as long as I need it, unless things change."

"They can do that?"

"Ain't nothing been put in writing, if you follow me."

"Dark green was the best they had?"

"They was fresh out of red," he said. "Anyway, enough of this. What's the deal with you getting arrested?"

"I've been set up. I met this girl at the Comus Bar . . ."

"The Comus? Man, that place is like a 7-Eleven for drug dealers. You sure know how to pick 'em, Cap."

"Hey, cut me some slack. It was a dockworkers' bar when I used to go in there. Besides, it only took me ten minutes to figure out what it's turned into. If I could make the place in ten minutes, where the hell is NOPD?"

"I'm a detective," he said, "I ain't in Vice. You prob'ly never thought you'd hear me say this, no, but it ain't my department."

"You're right. I never thought I would."

"It's like this, my friend. You remember back when we was in the MPs, everybody always fighting over whose turf was where? Like that time we needed some stun guns, us, and we went over Sergeant Koscovich's head. Whooo-eee, we paid for that one, didn't we, Cap?"

"Thought we never would get off latrine duty."

"I tell you, NOPD is worse. Drugs, they come under Vice. Yeah, I know about the Comus, just like every freshman at Tulane. I don't like to say it, but it ain't my department."

"But, Cotton, that place . . ."

"You know I never played office politics. You and me, we don't do shit like that, right? Well, it's really paying off. You, you got Sandy and your little girl living in Memphis. Me, I got fifteen years on the force and done been passed over twice for captain. Got hospital bills up to my ass, and I'm driving a borrowed car. This ain't the right time for me to start tellin' Vice how to do *their* job."

A tourist carriage rolled by, the horse's steel shoes clopping a steady 2/2 time. He sighed and stared toward the dark green sedan. Cotton always had a bulldog face, broad and big-jawed, but he had started to jowl a little since the last time I'd seen him. The morning sun accented the puffiness, the dark circles under his eyes. Not angry. Not irritated. Just worn down.

As I walked him through the details of what had happened, our tiny Vietnamese waitress brought Cotton's order and poured me what was at long last a decent cup of coffee. It was deep brown and fresh and had a strong chicory smell. I sniffed it and sipped it and swirled it around my mouth like it was a fifty-dollar wine. Cotton bit one of the beignets in half and chewed in silence, while he looked at the tourists walking along the sidewalk.

"The way I got it figured," I said, "Mouton sent somebody, and they saw I was in the house. They waited until I left, and then went in and killed her before her ride got there. They called it in to the cops and planted the knife in my truck later. They knew my tag number. It wouldn't take five minutes to get my name and address."

"Computers are wonderful things, Cap."

"I need some background on these people." I handed him a list—Barb, Toulouse, Rickey Dee, and Mouton.

"See if there's some connection between the Novak girl and Toulouse," I said. "I'm thinking that Mouton killed both of them."

"Well, Cap, that might be, but it seems like he's been slowing down some lately."

"You think so?"

"He's getting older. Plus, I hear he's almost out of the cocaine business. I think it's that new federal prosecutor. She'd love to bust Mouton, and he knows it."

"You mean LaShondra Batiste?"

"LaShondra, she grew up two blocks from Rampart Street. Lafitte Project, close to Louie Armstrong Park. You know the area?"

"I know the Lafitte," I said. "It's a war zone."

"Her mama, she was sixteen when LaShondra was born. Three years later, her mama was dead from heroin. Not an overdose, just bad stuff. It came from Mouton."

"I've heard a thousand versions of that story. Nothing changes but the names."

"She was raised by her grandmother," he said, "studied with the sisters at Saint Teresa's, and got real religious, almost became a nun. When she was growing up she saw lots of friends from the neighborhood die. Some became hookers. A lot of 'em got on drugs."

"So she wants to do something for the 'hood?"

"It's more personal than that. Them voodoo murders ten years ago, one of them bodies was her cousin. They was real close, them. She was in Tulane Law School when it happened. Got out and worked her way up in the U.S. Attorney's Office, but they never would go after Mouton. New president gets elected, and now she's the U.S. attorney. It'll be tough nailing Mouton hisself, 'cause he's been sockin' his money into real estate and turning the drug business over to the younger guys. He ain't interested in mixing it up with LaShondra. He's lookin' to retire, Cap, and he'll make it 'cause she'd need a federal charge, which he ain't gonna give her, no. But believe me, she'd love to nail that old bastard."

I finished my coffee. "I need the police report and crime lab stuff. I've got two weeks before Karen Cole indicts me."

"Cole's got your case?" He blew out a short breath and shook his head. "I never believed in reincarnation until I met her."

"What do you mean?"

"She was around for the Spanish Inquisition, Cap. I'm sure of that."

I had parked on Decatur Street down from the French Market near Esplanade. After Cotton left, I walked past the market and looked back over my shoulder before crossing the street. A yellow Chevy Lumina with tinted windows headed my way, and I paused to let it pass. I crossed the street and walked to my truck. The Lumina pulled over by the curb ahead of me.

My truck was pointed uptown, back toward Jackson Square. As I pulled away from the curb, I adjusted my rearview mirror and noticed the Chevy make a U-turn in front of an oncoming station wagon. It amazes me the risks people will take to claim an open parking space in the French Quarter.

I planned to go to Barb's house on Jasmine Street and see if I could find anything the cops might have missed. Traffic was heavy for a Sunday and I caught every red light. On Saint Charles, I got behind a streetcar that stopped twice to take on passengers. I got cut off by a cab on Lee Circle, had to slam on my brakes, and a shuttle bus that had been riding my bumper almost ran up my tailpipe. Then he blasted his horn at me like it was my fault he was tailgating. I hate to drive in New Orleans.

Once I got out of downtown, the traffic thinned out and I got in step with the synchronized lights along Saint Charles and moved at a steady pace, maybe thirty miles an hour. Up ahead two kids on bicycles were in my lane, sticking out into the road enough to cause me to edge to the left. I checked my side mirror. That yellow Chevy Lumina was behind me, maybe half a block. Big Jim always said that paranoia is your friend. But if somebody was tailing me would they be in a Lumina?

I took my foot off the gas and hugged the right shoulder. The Lumina slowed down. My pulse quickened. My eyes danced between the rearview mirror and the road ahead. Come on, fella, pass me. He hung back three car lengths.

Jackson Avenue was ahead, a wide cross street with a traffic light. The light was yellow so I gunned it. It flipped to red a split second before I went under it. The Chevy ran through the red light and a van coming into the intersection from the left hit its brakes, slid to the right, nearly slammed into the side of the Lumina.

I opened the glove compartment and reached for the Smith & Wesson out of habit before it hit me that it wasn't there. I cursed myself for being enough of a wuss to worry about whether some judge thought I ought to be carrying one. She wasn't the one whose ass was getting chased.

I floored it. The big V-8 roared, and the mud grip tires squealed. The truck rose like it was taking off from a runway. A cloud of blue exhaust and the black smoke of burning rubber covered the Chevy like a ground fog. I was a block down the street before it whipped out of the gray haze and came at me fast.

I raced around the next right on two wheels. I gripped the wheel so tight my nails cut into my palms. The Chevy nearly spun out when it took the corner. I whipped around the next two left turns, which circled me back to Saint Charles. The yellow car was losing ground; whoever it was couldn't take a corner worth a damn.

When somebody tails you, his purpose is to find out where you're going. If he knows you've spotted him and he keeps it up anyway, he's not tailing—he's chasing. He's either out to kill you, hurt you, or scare the hell out of you.

I waited at the Saint Charles stop sign. He pulled by the curb four car lengths back and stopped. He didn't know if I had a gun or not, so I let him think about that while I waited for the right moment.

A knot of eight cars came toward me on Saint Charles. When the first two got close enough for me to count their bug specks, I stomped it. My tires screamed as I jumped in front of the lead cars. Horns blared, tires skidded, and both of them flipped me off. I streaked ahead and jerked into the left lane. A streetcar in the neutral ground lumbered toward me. I raced it to the crossing and whipped in front of it. I could read the driver's lips and made out the vile name he was calling me. I scooted across the neutral ground and the opposite two lanes of Saint Charles into the residential area. Two or three more moves and I lost the Chevy for good.

I pulled over to the curb and turned off the engine. I rolled down the windows to let the cross breeze dry the sweat on my face and neck. My pulse raced through my ears as I ran through the list.

NOPD would have no reason to chase me.

None of Rickey Dee's men would be caught dead in a Lumina.

Mouton didn't even know I was alive.

Of course, when you've tracked down cheating husbands for eight years, the list of people who'd like to see you dead grows a lot longer than you care to think about.

But I had to think about it.

A dime store FOR RENT sign with a hand-painted phone number was taped to one of the grillwork columns on the front porch. Somebody had already stolen the Boston fern. A shred of yellow police-line tape fluttered in the front yard. The place looked deader than a burned-out headlight.

I parked in front, across the street, in the same place as before. When I got out, I looked toward the nosy neighbor's house and thought I saw a curtain move, but I wasn't sure. No matter. By the time she called the police, found the right department, and got a squad car sent out, I'd have had at least thirty minutes to look around. I thought about walking over to her house and asking her a few questions. But I've seen enough courtrooms to know how that could blow up in my face.

I put my handkerchief across my palm and tried the front door. It was locked so I followed the alley beside the house to the back. The back door was also locked, but not dead bolted. I jimmied the handle lock with a credit card, popped the burglar chain with a sharp push, and walked in.

The bloodstain had seeped into the scruffy planks of the kitchen floor. It was gut-wrenching to think that it had come from Barb. There were a few utensils—a black iron skillet that hadn't been used in so long it had some rust, a banged-up aluminum coffeepot, a few speckled Melmac dishes. It was the kind of stuff you see in a cabin at a state park. A double bed in the rear bedroom, no sheets, nothing in the closets. The other bedroom, up at the front of the house, was empty except for a painted bureau

Across the hall, the living room was just as I had seen it a few days earlier.

The cops had left a few things: advertising flyers and bills on the coffee table, a full trash bag in the kitchen with the twist tie still in place, some winter clothes hanging in the closet.

I slipped on a pair of latex gloves and went through the bureau from the top drawer down. The top three drawers were empty, but the bottom one looked like the treasure chest of any new college graduate. A lot of maize-and-blue junk from the University of Michigan, some stadium cups, a pom-pom, a Wolverine plaque.

I closed the drawer and stepped toward the closet. A board on the front porch creaked. I slid against the wall to the side of the front window, but the angle was too narrow and I couldn't see if anybody was at the front door. I looked across the street. The yellow Chevy Lumina that had chased me around earlier was parked behind my truck.

I tiptoed into the hall. I heard a metallic jangle from outside, then the thump of a key slipping into the front lock. I scurried down the hall, still on tiptoe. As I closed the back door behind me, I heard a clunk from up front as the deadbolt slid unlocked.

I slipped along the wall down the alley toward the front of the house. I stooped low, staying below the windows, out of sight of anyone inside. I reached the corner of the house and got down on one knee. I put my head at the level of the front porch and peeked around. The porch was empty and the door was open. I bolted down the driveway to my truck and drove off.

I checked the rearview mirror. No one came out of the house. I circled the block and parked around the corner out of sight. I scampered across two front yards and knelt behind a thick hedge of oleander six lots down from the house.

Minutes later, someone walked down the steps. I was looking through thick leaves and tall stalks, so I couldn't see him too well. He was small: baggy jeans, denim shirt, baseball cap, and sunshades. He got into the car, drove down Jasmine to the corner, and turned back north in the direction of Saint Charles. I got in my truck and went after him. I spotted him on Saint Charles and tailed him to Prytania, a parallel street one block riverside.

He pulled into the parking lot across the street from the Prytania Inn, a bed and breakfast. I whipped in behind a van parked on the street half a block away. I got out and ducked behind it. Through the van's rear window, I had a good view of the Lumina.

The driver got out, removed the sunshades and baseball cap, reached up, unsnapped a big clip, and her hair fell to her shoulders. She tossed the cap and the shades into the car and walked to the curb. She turned in my direction to check for cars.

I got a good look at her. The hair was dark blonde, a shade or two darker, and it was shorter. But there was no doubt about it . . .

I was looking at Barb Novak.

THIRTEEN

After Barb crossed the street, I dashed toward the little hotel and followed her through the passageway to the rear courtyard. I stopped short of the courtyard, heard a door shut to my left, and peered around the corner. The curtains were being closed in one of the ground-floor rooms.

I tapped on the door.

"Maintenance," I said.

It opened just a crack. I slammed against it and plowed into the room. The door knocked her back two steps. I pushed my hand over her mouth before she could scream. I kicked the door shut, threw her onto the bed, and jumped on top of her.

She clawed at my face, yelled into my hand, and tried to knee me in the groin. I fell on one of her arms, grabbed the other with my free hand, and sat across her thighs. She strained and jerked. She screamed against my palm and tried to bite it. She screamed muffled screams and strained against my weight until her strength was spent. She made one last push and fell limp beneath me.

"I want some answers, Barb—now!"

She growled into the palm of my hand.

"If I let you up, are you going to behave?"

She nodded.

"No screaming—right?"

She nodded.

I moved my hand from her mouth and she panted, catching her breath.

"Get off of me, you son of a bitch!"

The voice was harsher, huskier.

"Barb, what's going on?"

"I'm not Barb, you dumbass!"

I pushed up and stood beside the bed.

"Who are you?" I said.

"I'm gonna kill you, you son of a bitch!"

I hopped back and put out my arms in case she still felt like kicking. Her eyes were hot with anger. If it wasn't Barb, it had to be . . .

"You're Barb's sister."

"That's right, you bastard. You gonna try to kill me, too?"

I raised my hands up to my shoulders, palms toward her. "I didn't kill your sister. I know you don't believe that. But it's the honest-to-God truth."

"You lying bastard!"

"I didn't do it."

She pushed herself up, sat on the side of the bed, and rubbed both temples with the tips of her fingers as she watched me out of the corners of her eyes. She lunged for her purse at the foot of the bed. I snatched at it, ripped it out of her hand, and shoved her back down. I reached in and pulled out a blue steel .32 revolver. I jammed it in my pocket.

"Stand up," I said.

"For what?"

"Stand up and put your hands against the wall."

"Are you going to frisk me?"

"You pull another stunt like that and I'm gonna to whip your ass but good. Get up!"

She stood, gave me a look that was absolutely poisonous, and assumed the position. She was clean. She plopped back on the bed and pressed her palms on the mattress.

"What's your name?" I asked.

"Angie."

"Angie, I know it looks like I did it . . ."

"You're damn right."

"But I'm telling you, I was set up."

"Then why were you at her house today?"

"Looking for clues. I've got to get this thing solved. I'm charged with killing some girl I barely knew, and I was only trying to help her."

"Oh, sure! Help her do what?"

"Help her get out of the mess she was in. Help her get home, back to her family. When I left her at her house that day, she was alive."

"You were trying to help her get home?"

"I offered to take her to the airport right then and pay for the ticket."

She straightened up. "What did she say about going home?"

"She said she couldn't go."

"What else?"

"She said they had kicked her out."

"Damn!"

She nibbled on her lower lip and studied her fingers as she tented them against each other. She spoke in a low voice. "Mom and Dad didn't want to kick her out." She drew in a deep breath and blew it out. "They didn't know what else to do. It was those drugs."

"She never told me what the problem was," I said.

She stared at me for a while in an unblinking examination of my face. This woman was tough. Here she was, unarmed, facing the guy she thought had knifed her sister, and she was sizing me up as cooly as if I were across the desk from her applying for some job.

"Why should I believe a word you're saying?" she asked.

"I had no reason to kill Barb."

"Not that I know of. But maybe she had something you wanted. Maybe that's why you were at her house today . . ."

"Angie, I'm sick of this interrogation. I've had enough of them lately to last me awhile. I work out on a punching bag everyday, and I learned hand-to-hand combat in the military police. I know every inch of the coastline from here to Appalachicola. I've got access to any kind of boat I need. I could have killed your sister with my bare hands and put her body in a section of the marsh even the alligators couldn't find. Why the hell would I have used a knife, left my blood in her house, spread my prints all around, and then put the knife in my own damn truck?"

She held her stare a long time, didn't look like she was eve[n] breathing. And somehow I was the one who felt nervous. Aft[er] what seemed an hour, she nodded, stood, and straightened h[er] clothes.

"Well, Mr. Delmas, if you didn't do it, I guess we'd better fin[d] out who did."

It was a flat, clinical statement. Hypothesis A disproved, pr[o]ceed to Hypothesis B.

"The name is Jack," I said. "Why don't we go somewhere el[se] and talk about it?"

She followed me to the Camellia Grill, all the way out Sai[nt] Charles then a few blocks up Carrollton. We sat at the count[er] breathing in the smell of the frying burgers and onion rings.

"Barb was my younger sister, but we were just thirteen month[s] apart. Sometimes people thought we were twins."

"Tell me about her."

She dipped an onion ring in some ketchup on her plate. "Bar[b] was fine in high school, real popular. She was a cheerleader. B[ut] then she started dating the quarterback. He was gorgeous, b[ut] sorry as hell. Wasn't much of a quarterback either. Mom and Da[d] hated him and let her know it."

"Which made him completely irresistible," I said.

"He wasn't really such a bad guy, he was just kind of a pothea[d]. Nothing heavy, just a lot of grass."

"When did Barb graduate to cocaine?"

"At college. University of Michigan. Mom and Dad were [so] glad she was getting away from lover boy that Dad worked a[n] extra shift to pay for it. Neither of them ever went to college a[nd] they thought it would cure everything."

"Were you at the university at that time?"

"I was going to Wayne State part-time and working in Detroit[.]"

"Did that bother you?"

"What do you mean?"

"Sounds like Barb got a free ride and you paid your own way[.]"

"It was my choice. We all knew that if we left it up to Bar[b] she'd hang around Grand Rapids and wind up in a dead-e[nd] marriage. She never was much for responsibility."

I studied Angie's face as she talked. Except for hair a shade darker, she and Barb had identical features. Same height, same build, small nose turned up, smooth skin with a touch of natural tan. The eyes were the same emerald green, yet they constituted the difference. Barb's had been the eyes of a girl, not a woman. Even in fear they had shown a childlike belief that someone would make the trouble go away. Not so with Angie. Hers showed she had already learned some hard lessons somewhere.

"Barb was fine for two years until her grades started slipping. Dropping is more like it. She dropped out of Michigan in her junior year, moved to Chicago, and got a job as a waitress. She lived in what she called an 'urban commune.' Three other girls and God knows how many guys on any given night."

"How long ago was this?"

"Seven or eight years ago. She had turned twenty-one; I remember that. That was when she started snorting coke pretty regularly. I think she wanted to grow up some and be on her own, but she didn't know how. Like she wanted to rebel but not to hurt anybody's feelings doing it."

"When did your parents kick her out?"

Angie sighed. "She had really kicked herself out by that time. When Mom and Dad went down there and saw how she was living, it was really too late. They told her not to come home until she straightened up."

"Did they stay in touch with her?"

"They couldn't handle it. I served as the go-between. I'd talk to her by phone about once a month. You've got to understand; we loved Barb. We thought if she had to make it on her own, she'd come around. She never really seemed that far gone." Angie looked out the window, to a far-off place and a far-off time. A few seconds later she blinked hard and came back. "You want a beer?"

"I'd love one, but I've got to keep a clear head until I find out what happened. They don't serve beer in Angola."

"You going to Africa?"

"Angola is the Louisiana State Pen, darlin'. And I'm way too pretty to be going there."

I caught the waitress's eye, pointed to the beer tap, and held up one finger. "What do you know about Toulouse Caron?" I asked.

"Barb mentioned him some. I figured he was her supplier. I've learned more about him in the newspaper since he got killed than she ever told me."

"How about Rickey Dee McCoy?"

"Oh, yeah. Mr. Wonderful. I've heard all about Rickey Dee. She seemed to think they were in love."

"Have you ever seen him?"

"No, not even a picture. I just heard he's rich. Owns some icehouses."

"He's rich, all right. Those icehouses are a front for a drug operation."

"Rickey Dee sells drugs?" Her face said she was hearing that for the first time. Her eyes turned inward for a few seconds. "Was Barb selling drugs? Is that why she was killed?"

"I don't think she was selling. But some people may have thought that. Toulouse and Rickey Dee had been moving in on the territory of a psychopathic drug lord named André Mouton."

"You think this André Mouton killed her?"

"I think he killed both Barb and Toulouse, but I don't have any proof."

"You didn't find anything back at her apartment?"

"I was interrupted before I could finish."

"Don't you think we need to go back there?"

"I don't think *we* need to," I said, "but I plan to."

"I'm going with you."

"I really don't need you getting into this."

She cocked her head back slightly and looked down at me. "You don't think I can handle it?"

"What do you do for a living?" I asked.

"I work for the Department of Public Welfare in Detroit. AFDC eligibility."

"Is that where you learned to tail somebody in a car?"

She pouted and sipped her beer.

"I'm not being unkind, but the people I'm looking for don't play games. If I had been the killer, you'd be dead now."

She turned her stool until she was facing me head on. "I'm

staying down here until I find out who killed Barb. I can work with or without you. I admit you know more about this than I do. But you might just need me."

"I don't think . . ."

"After they convict you, do you think the New Orleans police are going to spend even one more minute on this case?"

She had a point.

"This is dangerous," I said. "You'd have to do what I tell you." She started to speak, but I cut her off. "First of all, I'll need some legwork done in Bay Saint Louis."

"Where?"

"It's forty miles from here on the Mississippi Gulf Coast. I live there. Also, Coastliner Ice Company is there, Rickey Dee's company. I need to check on Coastliner."

"What do you need?"

"I need to find out who owns it. I believe it's the Dixie Mafia."

"The *Mafia*?"

"*Dixie* Mafia. There's a difference," I said. "How long are you going to stay down here?"

"Until thirty minutes ago, I wasn't planning to stay but one day. Just long enough to kill you." Her lips formed a smile, but her eyes showed she meant what she was saying.

"You can stay at my place in Bay Saint Louis tonight. Let me call my brother and tell him you're coming." I stood to go to the pay phone. "Oh, by the way. How did you know where I was today?"

"I got your address from the bail bondsman, Jimbo, Jumbo, something like that. Told him I was your sister. I've watched you since you left home this morning. After I lost you in traffic, I guessed you were going to Barb's place." She sipped her beer. "I might be better at this detective business than you think I am."

FOURTEEN

"Here's the report from the scene on Toulouse. Nothing much from your buddy at the TimeSaver."

Cotton pushed the Tabasco sauce and horseradish to one side of the little marble-topped table. The smell of frying batter filled the room. He laid three manilla folders on the table and handed me the top one.

"He said there was a dark sedan that pulled around to the side of the store and stayed awhile. But there're no windows on that side so he didn't see nothing."

"How about the cause of death?"

"Five stab wounds and a slit throat. Musta been somewhere else; not much blood at the scene." He slid the next folder across the table.

"Here's the jacket on your boy, Rickey Dee McCoy. He ran a strip joint in Memphis 'til the feds busted his boss for racketeering. Then he teamed up with the Dixie Mafia. They sent him to Miami to run call girls for the convention trade. Rickey Dee's quite a ladies' man."

"How'd he end up in Bay Saint Louis?" I asked.

"It was sort of a promotion. More profit in a thousand bucks' worth of coke than a thousand bucks' worth of working girl, and it's a hell of a lot easier to handle. Rickey Dee's on what you'd call the fast track. If he can move in on Mouton, he'll move up in the organization. In other words, it might prove unhealthy to mess up his plans right about now."

"Is he violent, Cotton? Any record of assault, murder, anything like that?"

"One arrest, aggravated assault. Beat the shit outta some guy with a tire jack."

"You mean a tire tool?"

"Naw, Cap. He used the whole jack."

I picked up the folder to take a closer look at that one. "Says here those charges were dropped."

"The victim and two witnesses hadda charge of heart. Decided Rickey Dee deserved a second chance."

"What's that story?"

"One of the witnesses went to pick up his four-year-old daughter at day care. She wasn't there, no. They told him somebody who said he was her uncle had picked her up earlier. That night, about eight hours later, they got a call and somebody told them where they could find their little girl."

"Was she . . . ?"

"Didn't harm a hair on her head. They had left her at a McDonald's with one of them playgrounds, and she was having the time of her little life. But as the lawyers would say, it had a chilling effect on her daddy's testimony against Rickey Dee. Scared off everybody else, too."

Cotton took a big drink of tea and gave me a somber look. "I called a buddy in Miami. He said Rickey Dee ordered two hits he knows of. Says he started out as a bone breaker for a loan shark in Memphis. He's bad, Cap. He just ain't got caught gettin' his own hands dirty. All in all, just your basic white trash sociopath, who does most of his thinking below his belt."

Cotton took a bite of his oyster po'boy as I looked through Rickey Dee's folder. Fairly predictable stuff, starting with a stretch in a reform school in Arkansas at age thirteen. I closed that file and reached for the one on Toulouse Caron.

"This is pretty thin," I said.

"Toulouse was clean, Cap. At least in this country. Green cards, they try to avoid the law. Not much in that folder. But I found something on the Novak girl that might help."

Cotton reached into his coat pocket and put on his glasses. He opened the next folder and picked up the top page.

"Barbara Denise Novak. Twenty-nine years old. From Grand Rapids, Michigan. Her record's almost clean except for a misdemeanor marijuana bust in Chicago seven years ago. Came to New Orleans six months ago and waited tables at Julio's for a while. Only been at the Comus about five weeks, maybe six. Not much here you don't already know, Cap, except for this one item. You said her phone had been disconnected, so I checked to see if she had gotten a new one, and guess what? She had. Got one three weeks ago, unlisted. I traced it to an apartment on Conti Street, 236 Conti, Apartment B, one of those remodeled French Quarter townhouses. Pretty rich digs for a bartender. More like where a doctor would live."

"She got some help with her living expenses," I said. "Has Homicide checked out this second apartment?"

"Negative, Cap. Their report shows her residence as Jasmine Street."

"Damn, they're sloppy."

"They get ten new cases a week. A case like this—where they got fingerprints, blood samples, an eyewitness, and the murder weapon in the suspect's truck—hey, they call it solved and move to the next case."

"Have you told them about the second apartment?"

"It's my sworn duty." He looked over his glasses and grinned at me. " 'Course I sent it an hour ago by hand mail so they won't get it 'til about four o'clock this afternoon."

I put on my RayBans, adjusted my tie, took one step out of my front door, and nearly crashed into her.

"You going to court or something?" she asked.

"Angie, I thought you were in Bay Saint Louis."

"I had a few things to take care of. What are you working on?"

"Neal's expecting you. He's all set to help you get your stuff unloaded."

"You said it's less than an hour's drive over there. I might as well help you with whatever you're working on. So what are you working on?"

"Nothing."

"I see. You've got two weeks before a grand jury indicts you for murder. The cops have stopped looking for any other suspects. Your only way out is to find the killer. So you decide it's a good time to dress up and kill a few hours playing tourist. Take one of those carriage tours around the French Quarter or something."

"You're supposed to get some background on Coastliner."

"Which will take maybe two hours," she said. "You do have computers in Mississippi, don't you?"

"Yeah, but they're old and slow. You'd better get on over there and get started."

"Where are you going, Jack?"

I looked down at my watch. A quarter of two. If I could get in through the manager, I could be in Barb's townhouse in twenty minutes. If not, a break-in could take an hour or more, depending on the alarm system. Couldn't risk being in there past three-thirty.

"Okay, you win. I'm going to Barb's apartment."

"We can take my car," she said. "It's parked down the street."

"It'll be quicker for us to walk."

"But it's a couple of miles . . ."

"My, God, I can't believe this was Barb's place," she said. "Those leaded-glass doors alone cost a fortune."

"This is the manager's office." I pulled out my wallet, flipped it open, and set the fake badge into place. "You wait here in the car. I'll be right out."

"I'm going in with you and there's no time to argue about it."

"Just let me do the talking, Angie." I swear, sometimes they can make you so mad.

A group of bells mounted to the upper, inside corner of the door announced our presence. The place smelled of scented candles and potpourri. Slow footsteps came from the next room. I reached for the badge and had my right hand on my wallet when a stooped, gray-haired little dandy in a blue seersucker suit shuffled through the door.

"May I help . . . Oh, hello, Miss Novak. What can I do for you today, dear?"

"I'm afraid I left my key at work," Angie said. "I hate to bother you, but . . ."

I moved my hand away from my wallet.

"Oh, no trouble at all." He waved away the notion with his bony hand. "I'll be right back."

He plodded back through the doorway.

"Well?" she said.

"Well, what?"

"I got us in and you didn't even have to commit a felony."

"He's probably almost blind. Just don't say much when he comes back."

"Would it kill you to give me some credit?"

"Okay. That was quick thinking."

As we waited, Angie stepped over to the door. "I just realized that he doesn't know Barb was murdered." She looked out through the leaded glass and her voice grew quiet. "I can't understand why not. After all, it was such *big* news around here. Right there with the new car ads at the bottom of page twenty-three . . ."

"That's a good example of why I live in Bay Saint Louis," I said, "but it'd be the same thing in Detroit."

"Here you are, Miss Novak." He held the key out as he stepped back into the room and padded toward us. "I haven't seen you around lately."

"I've been pretty busy," she said, "and I went out of town for a few days."

"Well, just drop off that key when you find your other one. And if I can help you, give me a call."

Cotton was right, it was a lot better place than any bartender could afford. I walked in but Angie stood a step inside the doorway, gawking like a tourist at the Natchez Pilgrimage standing behind some velvet rope.

"Here." I tossed her a pair of surgical gloves. "We don't need to be trying to explain any fingerprints."

I did a quick walk-through to make sure we were alone. Two bedrooms, a living area, big kitchen, and two bathrooms. A balcony over Conti Street. The furniture hadn't been there long; it smelled new. There were new clothes in the closets, an answering machine by the phone, a VCR, and a television. Rickey Dee had been generous.

Angie was still gazing at the couch and love seat when I walked back into the living room. I stepped over to the fireplace. On the mantle above the fireplace sat a wedding picture, a large group shot. The bride looked familiar.

"Some wedding, huh?" Angie had slipped in behind me.

"Is that you, or Barb?"

"Me, unfortunately."

"I take it you're no longer married."

"It lasted fourteen months, which was about thirteen months too long."

"And he looks like such a nice guy."

"He is. He's the nicest carpet installer who ever wore a UAW cap."

"Is there something wrong with that?"

"GM offered to pay full tuition for him for night classes at the local college. But Donald Trump there decided tossing darts with the boys down at the Pink Cadillac was a better use of his time than going to Accounting 101."

"You can have a good career in the automobile industry."

"With some ambition. He peaked at age twenty-five. He'll have the exact same locker when it comes time to retire, if they don't move the whole plant to Mexico first."

At the other end of the mantle was a photograph of two girls, five or six years old, laughing round faces, golden hair bright with sunlight. They were on a beach; waves were breaking in the background. One child stood an inch or two taller, her brown arm draped around the other one's shoulders. Both wore yellow Donald Duck sunglasses, propped on their heads like hairbands. Even back then they looked like twins.

Except for one more faded ancestral picture, there were no other traces of Barb in the living room. Everything else came from some interior decorator, some pricey one. Heavy, light green sofa and love seat in a velour material, drapes of emerald chintz, mahogany coffee table.

"Look at this," she said. "This piece alone costs as much as that dump she was living in over on Jasmine Street." Angie stood beside a mahogany armoire, a nine-foot-tall antique that had been fitted with shelves for a television, a VCR, a CD player, and four Peavey speakers. "She had to be selling drugs."

"More likely this whole setup belongs to Rickey Dee McCoy."

"I hope you're right." Angie walked across the room and into the kitchen.

The bottom drawer of the armoire held at least thirty videotapes. *When Harry Met Sally, Pretty Woman,* Barbara Streisand movies, two aerobics tapes, and five or six blanks. One of the blanks was a little Hi-8 cassette with a stick-on label that read "Toulouse." I stuck it in my pocket and followed Angie to the kitchen.

It was too large for the kitchen of a mid-nineteenth-century home in the Vieux Carré. Probably a converted bedroom. White tile floors, a big island with a wooden chopping block, new oven with a separate range, and a side-by-side refrigerator. A shiny set of copper-bottomed saucepans that hung on the wall looked like they had never been used.

"Doesn't look like Barb was into cooking," I said.

Angie shook her head. "Mom tried, but I was the only one who learned how to cook. Barb would have starved if it hadn't been for microwaves and pizza delivery."

"So you cook," I said. "That's good."

"A woman ought to be good in the kitchen, right?"

"It helps."

"You're sounding like my ex."

"I'm sorry if I offended any of your northern sensibilities, but I didn't say anything wrong. I cook a lot myself."

She sighed. "I'm pretty edgy. I apologize."

"Apology accepted."

Angie turned toward the refrigerator. "Did you ever see Toulouse?" She pointed to a collage of photographs next to the wall phone, an eight-picture, do-it-yourself frame with built-in matting. It held a couple of family shots, one or two photos from college days, and a posed studio portrait of Angie.

In the biggest square was a shot of Barb and Toulouse, had to be Toulouse. They were leaning against the stern rail of some yacht. A big boat, probably Rickey Dee's. The water behind them was crystal green, which means the shot was taken out in the Gulf, past the muddy waters inside the barrier islands.

Toulouse had both palms flat on the railing behind him. He wore a white tank top, a muscle shirt, and a faded, baggy swimsuit pulled tight at the waist with a draw string. The white shirt made him look pretty dark, but he was lighter than I had expected. New Orleans calls it *café au lait,* coffee and milk. Wavy hair, black and thick, close-cropped on the sides of his narrow face and swept straight back. He wasn't big, but solid, with hard-edged muscles. He didn't smile so much as sneer.

Toulouse wore a necklace chain that suspended a gold dollar with a pea-sized emerald set in its center, and around the emerald was a ring of diamonds. A crude design, like something he'd thought of himself. Custom-made but still gaudy, what would pass for elegance to a street punk. He also wore the Rolex that Roger Partridge had told me about.

Barb stood beside him. She wore a bikini, mirrored shades, and a green plastic visor. She held a beer can in a foam rubber cooler, up and forward in salute. God, what a smile she had.

"Look at her," Angie whispered. "She was so happy." Her eyes went deep into the picture for a long time.

"Angie?"

"We've got to hurry." She wheeled toward the bedroom, leaving me standing in the middle of the kitchen.

Not much in the refrigerator. A quart of milk, some diet margarine, a few eggs, some sliced ham, some leftover macaroni and cheese, and two Diet Cokes. Nothing in the pantry; nothing in the cabinets.

Barb's bedroom was frilly and soft and smelled like a candle shop in the Quarter. She had a four-poster canopy bed with a three-layered dust ruffle and a mattress so high it took a two-step platform to get on it. A white eyelet bedspread with a cream-colored Afghan folded at the foot gave the bed the appearance of a big wedding cake. On the nightstand sat a French phone, ivory with gold trim. It was hooked to an answering machine, and the tiny red light was glowing. Angie stood beside it, pushing the rewind button.

"(Click) *This is Barb. I'm not able to come to the phone right now, but if you'll leave your name and number, I'll return your call. Thank you.*"

(Beep)

"Hey, baby, I got your message. Don't be scared. I'm sendi[ng] somebody to pick you up at your old place. Got it? They'll be the[re] around noon. They'll knock five times and shout 'Coastliner [?] Company.' Got it? I'm sorry about Toulouse. Don't worry. Lo[ve] you."

(Beep)

"Hey, where were you? My man said you didn't show. Call m[e] babe, okay? Love you."

"Rickey Dee?" she asked.

I shrugged. Could he have been smart enough to plant tho[se] messages?

"Pop it out and take it with you," I said. "We've got to get o[ut] of here."

A two-tone chime rang through the room.

"Oh, my God!" we both said.

"What are we going to do?" she said.

Several hard knocks sounded through the door. "Police! Op[en] up!"

"I'm going out that window," I said. "You stay here and [let] them in."

"Thanks a lot!"

"You've got every right to be here. You're Barb's sister. Gi[ve] me those gloves and that phone tape."

She peeled off her gloves. "What if a cop's outside looking f[or] you to climb out?"

DING-DONG!

"They don't know I'm here. Cotton just misjudged the time[.]"

"You sure about that?"

"I'd bet my life on it."

"That's exactly what you're doing, Jack."

I had been back at Billy's townhouse a little less than an ho[ur] when the phone rang.

"I'm on my way out of town," she said.

"What did the police say?"

"They were very polite. They asked me for permission to sear[ch] the place, and I said okay. I told them I had been looking for an insurance policy that Barb had."

"Good work, Angie."

By the time we got off the phone, it was after four o'clock. I wanted to view the tape, but it was an Hi-8 and Billy only had a VHS player in his townhouse, so I hustled to Canal Street and caught Paul before he closed. Orleans Photography is owned by my friend Paul Simms, the best in the business. He said he'd make the transfer to VHS and have it ready the next day, but it would be late in the afternoon.

Forensic photography is Paul's specialty and tight lips are his trademark. Any photo lab could transfer the cassette to VHS, but Paul would keep his mouth shut about anything he saw on it. That had been important to me many times before.

But never as important as it would turn out to be this time.

FIFTEEN

It began with a daytime scene, bright sunshine, at a sidewalk in the Projects. It was shot from inside a vehicle, and occasionally I saw the blur of a car driving by and heard the swish of tires rolling along the asphalt. The camera swept up and down the sidewalk across the street and zeroed in on a stocky black man as he stepped through the kicked-out screen door of one of the apartments and walked toward the person filming the scene. The picture zoomed to his face when he reached the street.

"*Toulouse!*" he said. "*Hey, man, check it out.*" He rolled up the sleeve of his T-shirt, crooked his arm, and flexed his muscle. The picture focused on the grapefruit-size bicep, then faded to black. When it faded back in, that same man was standing six feet away looking into the lens.

"*Today we be interviewing Little Boy Perryman . . .*" Little Boy waved at the camera. "*Little Boy gonna show us today's special. What's the special today, Little Boy . . . ?*"

Little Boy showed a lot of teeth and held up a sandwich bag containing eight or ten white rocks, each the size of a butter bean. He reached in for one and held it up between his thumb and forefinger. "*Dis today's special. Top-quality rock. Guar-on-teed, please.*" He held it in his palm and the picture zeroed in on what appeared to be a dingy piece of broken chalk. "*Little Boy be making a limited time offer. Just a dime a rock. First-time customer get a free sample.*"

"*Hey, Little Boy, you take food stamps?*"

Little Boy laughed and the picture went back to his face. His eyes were red, pupils wide. "*Hell, I'll take anything, specially poor tang!*" They giggled like a pair of thirteen year olds.

Little Boy looked over his shoulder and turned back around. *"Hey, turn that thing off. Here come the man."*

The camera faded to black then into the next scene. Little Boy stood across the street beside a gold Lincoln Town Car, talking to the driver while handing him some money. A kid in shorts and a Georgetown T-shirt walked up to them. It was someone they knew; they hardly looked up. The driver, a broad black man with short hair and a trimmed mustache, leaned his head out of the car, his left arm resting on the window. The kid in the Georgetown T-shirt said something, and Little Boy reached in his pocket for a sandwich bag of white powder. The kid took it and gave Little Boy a wad of bills. Little Boy handed them to the driver with his right hand and pinched off two or three of them with his left. Little Boy and the driver laughed. The kid walked away.

The rear window slid down and from inside the car, a gray-headed black man leaned forward. My heart jumped into my throat. I only caught a glimpse of him but it was enough.

Mouton hadn't changed in the past six years. The hair was still salt-and-pepper. The eyebrows were still snowy white, so white they glowed in the sunlight. The eyes were still as depthless and as cold as a shark's.

He said something and Little Boy stepped back two steps. Two young men approached the car. They were older than the first kid, probably in their twenties. They made a buy, one bag each, and that time one of them gave some money directly to the driver. Mouton put his window down all the way. The sun shone bright and it looked like a hot day. Another kid, maybe sixteen or seventeen, walked up to the car before that sale was over.

"Whooo-man! Look like a ice-cream truck." Toulouse talked to himself as he filmed. *"They be needin' one of them music boxes."*

When the last kid had walked away, Mouton stuck his head out the window.

"There you go," I said aloud, "stick that ugly face out a little farther and smile for the camera."

He said something to Little Boy and stared at him as the car's window rose, sweeping across his face until it closed. It was a shot good enough for any post office. I got that same rising feeling that had hooked me on this business eight years earlier.

The driver held out his hand, Little Boy slapped his palm, and the car drove away. The camera held on Little Boy and then zoomed to the car as it stopped at the corner stop sign. It had a Louisiana tag with a border around it fashioned out of heavy links of golden chain. The picture faded and electronic snow on the screen signaled the end of the tape.

Through the open French doors a breeze blew in, whipping the curtains around, the clean smell of coming rain filling the room. I walked out to the balcony and sat on a wrought-iron chair. The sky darkened and claps of thunder grew louder and closer and soon the first fat drops of the storm splatted on the street. The leading edge of the blue-black front slid across the sky until it was straight overhead, and the wind rose and the air chilled. The rain moved through the city in gray waves, and the stinging drops sizzled against the balcony floor around my feet.

I tilted back and closed my eyes and felt my lips rising into a smile.

SIXTEEN

A street washer showered the pavement and sloshed last night's half-eaten hot dogs, broken Hurricane glasses, and empty beer cans against the gray stone curb. A sour smell rose from the sewer grates. The sun had not yet risen high enough to clear the buildings along the Quarter's eastern edge.

I headed to a Bourbon Street joint named the Gator's Den. The Gator is trashy even by Bourbon Street standards, at least it was when I first knew it. But I hadn't been in there since Candy bought it.

Two years earlier, when it was being used to fence hot CD players out of the back rooms, I had worked undercover as a bartender and bouncer for three weeks before I figured out the pattern and when the loot would come in. One morning, around two-thirty, I gave the cops a call, told them when the buy was going down, and delivered buyer, sellers, and thirty CD players still in their crates. Came from a department store in Metairie insured by my good friends at Bayou Casualty.

Candy was a stripper when I worked there. She had been in the business a rough sixteen years, mostly on Bourbon Street. She was ready to get out, at least from stripping and hooking, tired of drunk Kiwanians down for a convention grabbing her ass and fraternity boys on road trips throwing up at her feet.

I took her to lunch two or three times while I was on that job. Once we went to a movie out in Metairie. We got to be friends, mainly because I didn't try to get in her pants. Candy didn't tell me much about her history. She said she was from around Knoxville, but that was about it. I figured it was not a happy story.

Candy always told me she was saving her money. I guess she had, because when Gator's went up for auction after the stolen property bust, she bought it. Mostly for cash.

At the icehouse, Roger told me that Rickey Dee's foreman, Bruno Hebert, was seeing some Bourbon Street stripper. That meant Candy would know more about him than he could remember about himself. The girls do get together and talk.

The door stood open to let the fresh air in as the maid mopped and swept. I stepped around the chair propping open the Gator's front door. Candy was sitting on a stool behind the register with her back to me, her auburn hair pulled up in a bun. She was counting money and making entries in a ledger. She wore glasses and a New Orleans Zephyrs T-shirt and looked for all the world like some PTA mother ready to help with the junior class homecoming float.

Even with the door open the room was dark except for the spot lamp on the bar shining down on her ledger. It was as cool as a cave. Candy punched the buttons on a handheld calculator and didn't see me until I was only three or four steps away.

"Buster!" That alias must have fit me somehow; it has stuck. "Come here, darlin'." She leaned over the bar and kissed me.

"How's it going, Candy?"

"Just great. A few months ago I had the best Mardi Gras business I can remember."

"You're not retired yet?"

"If that piece of shit air conditioner holds out for one more summer, and I can keep the cops in line, I'll make it in probably three years."

"Cops giving you a rough time?"

"Same old shit. A new one transferred in a few months ago and the son of a bitch got greedy. I had to get the precinct captain to straighten him out."

"What did you tell the captain?"

"I told him I'd pay what was fair and that I knew enough dirt to make things hot for everybody if he didn't put a leash on the new guy. I didn't have to tell him that last part; he already knew it."

"Candy, you be careful . . ."

"You don't last in this business without making friends on the force. I've made lots of friends, lots of different ways. Any cop comes after me, he's got twenty cops coming after him."

I nodded. "So what else has been going on with you? You married yet?"

"You know, I'm pretty close. Can you believe it? Hey, maybe fourth time's a charm. I think my odds are a lot better on this one."

"What makes you say that?"

"I didn't meet him in here," she said. "So what brings you in, honey?"

"Trouble. I've been booked on a murder charge."

Her eyebrows lifted, showing a bit more of the white around her blue eyes.

"Damn, Buster, you don't screw around when you talk about trouble. What's the deal?"

"You probably heard about it. It was that girl who tended bar at the Comus. She hung around with some bad folks. One of them started selling dope on André Mouton's turf, and he showed up dead."

"That was Toulouse. God, what a dipshit! So that girl at the Comus was tied in with Toulouse."

"You knew him?"

"In this business, pretty soon you get to know every lowlife in a hundred-mile circle. That punk Toulouse came in here once a week. I'll give him this much; he naturally spent the hell out of some money. I knew he was a dealer when he first walked in."

"How'd you know?"

"Twenty years of lookin' at 'em." She propped her glasses up on her head, pushed back her stool, and lit a cigarette.

"What about a guy named Bruno? Worked for the same company as Toulouse. I hear he came over here a lot."

"Yeah, I know him, too. He's worse than Toulouse. That son of a bitch is just plain mean." She swung down from her stool. "You want some coffee?" She walked to the bar and poured us two cups. "So, how do you fit in to all of this?"

"I met the girl at the Comus. She said she was a friend of

Toulouse's. Turned out he worked for Coastliner Ice Company in Bay Saint Louis, where I live. Coastliner's a front for drug operations."

"An icehouse. Sounds like a good cover."

"It is. But Toulouse tried to move in on André Mouton's turf and ended up as the sacrifice in a voodoo church service. I tried to help the girl after they found Toulouse because she was scared that Mouton was coming after her, too. I was the last person anybody saw her with, so I got pegged with the murder."

She drilled me with her eyes, her lips in a tight line. "Shit, Buster! How old are you now?"

"Forty-two in September."

"When you gonna learn you can't help anybody over the age of twelve?"

She took a short drag from her cigarette and blasted a puff of smoke straight out.

"Are you going to help me?" I said.

She stubbed out her cigarette, mashing it hard into the ashtray. "Oh, hell, of *course*. But I swear I don't know why."

"What do you know about Toulouse?"

"Dammit, Buster, I can't believe you."

"Please, Candy."

She shook her head. "I don't know much about him. He was a real wiseass, but he didn't really seem all that tough. He came in with that Bruno every week. It started to look like Little Miami when they'd come in. I mean open collars with these gold chains, rings on every finger. They'd wear sunglasses, like it's too bright in here or something. Looked like the friggin' Cuban Mafia."

"Was it just Toulouse and Bruno?"

"Oh, hell no. It was a whole bunch of them."

"Was Rickey Dee McCoy ever with them? About my height, blond hair, pumped up . . ."

"A white guy?"

"Yeah."

"Never were any white guys in that crowd. Strictly Caribbean. Like I said, I called 'em the Cuban Mafia. They'd sit there and wouldn't say a word, at least not to anybody who wasn't with them. Acted like they were in some gangster movie. But that's what it was—an act. All except for Bruno. Now he's the real thing, a genuine badass."

"Did they have a kinda short guy with them, about as big around as a barrel?" I held my arms out before me in a big circle.

"Yeah. His name's Roberto, but they call him Bobby. One of my girls tied up with him one night. Said he's built like a bull, and she didn't mean muscles."

"That's the icehouse crew, all right. Bruno's the number-two guy behind Rickey Dee."

"Well, he's bad news, Buster."

"Why do you keep saying that?"

Candy lit another cigarette. "He's S and M. Took one of my girls out and hurt her bad. Two black eyes, fractured jaw. She looked awful. Who knows what set him off. He's into bondage, handcuffs, all that shit."

"I take it you don't approve."

Candy shook her head. "Getting the shit beat out of me ain't my idea of fun and games. Some sicko gets outta control and kills one of my girls, I'll have to blow the son of a bitch away." She carries a 9-mm rubber-grip Glock and practices at a shooting range in Westwego at least twice a month. "It'd be a real pain to have to go to court."

"Have you seen Bruno lately?" I asked.

"See his sorry ass every week, but not in here. After he beat up Gina, I stuck my nine in his face and told him to stay the hell outta here. So now he goes to the Roman Orgy across the street. Goes with a girl named Lola, and they fit together real good. She's into whips and chains and stuff. They go out to one of those hot-sheet joints out on Old Highway 90—you know, mirrors on the ceilings, skin flicks, the whole bit."

"You say this place is on Old 90? You mean Chef Menteur?"

"Yeah, the Crescent City Courts. He'll be there with Lola this Saturday night; you can bank on it."

I set my mug on the table. "Have you heard anything about André Mouton being involved in these murders?"

"Only what everybody else has heard."

"Which is?"

"That Mouton did it because he's the Undertaker. It's like

everything else; people talkin' and don't know shit. There's a rumor they found a voodoo coffin near Toulouse's body."

"That's true. I've got a friend who saw it."

"Mouton's not the only one around here who knows anything about voodoo. That only trims it down to two- or three-hundred-thousand suspects."

I couldn't argue with that.

"Suppose Mouton did kill him," I said. "You think he'd kill the girl, too?"

"Maybe."

"Would he kill her just because she hung around with Toulouse?"

"He don't kill just for no reason, honey. But if he thought she was selling with Toulouse, or she saw something, or knew something . . ." She took a deep drag on her cigarette. "Let me tell you a story about Mouton. Years ago, before he slowed down, he used to come to the joints all the time. Used to come in here a lot. He had this one stripper running smack for him out of Big Daddy's on Decatur. I knew her. She stripped under the name Sweet Charlotte. This was about the time I was getting started in the business. Anyway, she got busted and was lookin' at twenty or thirty years of hard time. So word got out that she was going to the grand jury and turn Mouton for them. She disappeared; nobody knew where she was. Hell, the cops even asked me what I knew about it."

"What did you know?"

"As far as they were concerned, not a damn thing. I really didn't. I had heard some stuff, that's all. Anyway, a few days later, they go into the old Kit Kat Klub—that's what they used to call Big Daddy's—they walk in to open up one day and there on the stage, there's this girl's head. No body. Just her head."

"God . . ."

"That was not too long after that *Godfather* movie. I guess Mouton liked that horse scene." She took a sip of coffee.

"Damn. You mean just her head . . ."

"To this day, every stripper in the Quarter is scared shitless of André Mouton. A lot of them weren't even born when that happened. But believe me, they all know the story." She put out her cigarette. "He's mean, Buster. He'd have killed her as fast as you'd swat a fly if he had some reason."

"The dead girl told me she used to ride around with Toulouse a lot. She could have been selling."

She laid her elbow on the arm of the chair, rested her chin on her hand, and thought for a few seconds. "Maybe I know somebody who knows something. Come back tomorrow night around ten. You'll need some cash; two hundred ought to cover it."

I reached out and squeezed her hand. It was warm; Candy sends out heat. She smiled and took my hand in both of hers and laced her fingers with mine. She moved it to her lips and started kissing my wrist. She moved up my palm with soft little kisses, then lightly ran the tip of her tongue across my knuckles while making a low, moaning, feline sound. She slowly raised her eyes to meet mine as she pressed my hand against her cheek and leaned toward me.

"Buster, honey, the next time you really get the urge to help some girl out, you come back here and see sweet Candy," she said softly, "and I'll personally kick your ass from here to Canal Street."

SEVENTEEN

ack, somebody broke into your house." The tremor in Angie's
voice came through over the phone. "Neal followed me there
and was two minutes behind me. Stuff from your cabinet drawers
was scattered on the floor, and there was this guy standing in the
den."

"Please tell me you ran away," I said.

"He asked, 'Where's that damn tape?' Then he lunged at me
and I ran out the door. About that time, Neal was pulling into
your driveway so the guy took off through those pine trees."

She paused. She was breathing hard, like she had been running.

"What was he talking about, Jack?"

"I . . . don't know," I said. "Where are you?"

"At Neal's."

"Have you called the sheriff?"

"Deputy Partridge came out." She pulled in a deep breath and
let it out with a puff.

"Let me talk to Neal."

"One more thing. This guy who broke in; I've seen him before.
Something about him was familiar—his voice, clothes, something."

"You think he's from Michigan?"

"No, it was down here somewhere."

"Down here? You've only been here for three or four days."

"I've seen this guy before, and it wasn't in Michigan. It'll come
to me. Here's your brother."

Neal got on the phone. "What's this tape business?"

"Did you see who it was?"

"No. He had on a stocking mask and he was running away. Kinda tall. Must have been young, judging from the way he ran."

"Was he white, black, what?"

"Couldn't tell. What tape was he after?"

"I took a videotape from Barb's apartment."

"And?"

"You keep Angie over at your place tonight."

"I'll take care of things on this end. Now let's get back to that tape."

"Yeah. But before I forget it, what do you know about a federal law named RICO?"

"The Racketeer Influenced and Corrupt Organization Act. I know it well."

"Would the sale of crack cocaine in three separate incidents come under it?"

"Yes. Drug cases are covered and three offenses is a pattern. Now, what were you going to tell me about that . . ."

"Even if they're state offenses? Can that get you into federal court?"

"They're drug offenses! It doesn't matter! Three will get you in! Two can get you in! You want to know more, go back to law school! Now, dammit, what's the deal with that tape?"

They knew who I was. They had broken into my house. And they'd keep on coming if I didn't throw one hell of a counter-punch.

I took the tape back to Orleans photography and caught Paul a few minutes before he left for lunch. He said he could do what I wanted, no problem, and it would be ready the next morning. "A piece of cake," he said.

But I knew that when I served up that piece of cake, I wouldn't be in for any party.

EIGHTEEN

Having the goods on Mouton was something I had dreamed of for six years, but, dammit all, now I was going to have to lay the stuff in his hands in exchange for him turning the killer over to NOPD. As far as being amusing, this irony shit is badly overrated.

ARM, Inc., and company president André Richard Mouton, businessman, were headquartered on the twentieth floor of the World Trade Center. The center is at the foot of Canal, right on the river.

I wore my good suit, clean socks. A fresh, stiff white shirt, a burgundy paisley tie, and a pair of polished black wing tips. I carried my briefcase and bought a pair of eight-dollar reading glasses at the corner K & B drugstore. I also had a few of the phony business cards I usually carry, which show me to be an associate of Taylor, Brock, and Johnson, P. A.

After announcing me over the phone, the receptionist directed me to the end of the hall. Her radio was up so loud that even when she switched it to the headphones I could hear it across the room.

Three offices lined the hallway. Two appeared to be empty, but coming from the closest one I heard the electronic voices of some radio or television. I recognized the driver from the video sitting in there by himself, leaning back in an armchair with his heels resting on a coffee table. He was watching *Oprah* and tossing popcorn into the air, catching the puffed kernels in his mouth.

Before entering Mouton's office, I paused for a last glance at the photographs. Paul had taken the videotape and produced a series of eight-by-tens that showed three drug sales, in broad daylight, on a street in the Desire Project. Ten shots. A time spectrum from the sale to the kid, through the other sales, to the exchange of money, to the last glimpse of the eyebrows of André Mouton as the rear window rose. I adjusted my tie, pushed my glasses up the bridge of my nose, knocked on the door, and stepped into the room.

Behind Mouton's desk was a floor-to-ceiling plate-glass window, a moving picture of ships, tugs, barges, paddle wheelers, and ferries on the broad, brown river. The desk sat on a foot-high dais as wide as the room and extending ten feet in from the window. The dais had dark green carpet, new from the smell. The floor in front of the dais was white marble.

In the dreams I had let him take the first punch, had grabbed his wrist and slammed him to the ground, had stood above him, taunting, had kicked the breath out of him when he lunged at me again. I had heard the crack of his ribs, seen the blood at the corner of his mouth, felt his weight as I leveraged him over my hip to bounce on the ground again, and again, and again . . .

"Yes?" he said.

"Mr. Mouton, I'm John Doggett of Taylor, Brock, and Johnson. We represent an investment company and have been authorized to make an offer for the purchase of certain properties owned by ARM."

"I have no properties on the market at this time." Mouton's voice was deep, a full voice accustomed to command. But he spoke too slowly, too precisely, like he was reading from an unfamiliar text.

I nodded. "We are aware, Mr. Mouton, that these properties are not listed for sale. However, my clients are prepared to make an offer you may find attractive."

Mouton circled his chair around and looked in silence out the plate-glass window. I glanced down at the framed photograph on his desk. Her black eyes bore into mine, and I saw why they feared her. An ancient evil ran through that family and showed itself in the eyes of *Mère* Marie.

He spun back around, propped his elbows on the arms of his chair, and rested his chin on his knuckles. "Who sent you?"

"I'm not at liberty to say at this time."

"Then we have nothing further to discuss, Mr."—he looked down at my card—"Doggett."

"Perhaps you would have more interest in discussing these." I laid the photos flat on his desk and fanned them out.

Mouton's chin remained on the back of his hands, but his eyes grew wider. He bit his lower lip and reached for the photograph that showed him looking out over the window of the car.

"We still have nothing to discuss," he said quietly.

His right hand dropped below the desk. I planted my palms, pushed with my legs, and jumped over it. My heel hit his ribs and knocked him and the chair against the plate glass. I grabbed his shoulder and flipped him over on his stomach. I twisted his arm behind him, jerked him up, and pushed him across the room.

We barely got behind the door before the guy from down the hall burst in waving a .38. Before he could turn, I shoved Mouton into his back. The gunman stumbled forward and put his foot forward to regain balance. When he turned, I swung my foot and kicked the gun. It slid across the floor. A kick to the sternum staggered him to his knees. An outside leg spin held Mouton in check. I bolted to the gun. I spun around and held it on them.

"Hands behind your head," I said.

The hall was empty; the receptionist nowhere to be seen. I shut the door and gestured them down to the floor with the pistol. The guard sat, catching his breath, and laced his fingers behind his head. Mouton gave me an indignant glare and held his ground.

"I don't have a lot to lose here," I said. "Get those hands behind your head while you still got a head to get 'em behind."

He did, then he started to speak.

"Shut up!" I said. "I don't have time to listen to any of your crap. I've got enough here to bust your ass wide open. Those pictures are just the start."

"Where'd they come from?" Mouton said.

"I want the goons you sent to kill Toulouse Caron and Barb Novak."

"I didn't . . ."

"You got three days. The cops get the killers; you get all the pictures. Cops don't get the killers; the eight-by-tens go to La-Shondra Batiste."

"You crazy, man. I don't know nothin' about none of this. I'm out of the drug scene. I don't know where you got those pictures, but they don't prove shit. All I was doin' was sittin' in a car."

"LaShondra would love to nail your ass, André."

"I'm a businessman," he said. "You want to sell me the negatives, we'll talk. But I don't know nothing about no murders."

"Two men, André. The one who killed Barb Novak and the one who killed Toulouse."

"Whoever you are, you make a serious mistake. You in deep shit, man."

"Hey, three days from now—Saturday noon—the cops don't have the killers, we'll see who's in deep shit."

"Those pictures," he asked, "where they come from?"

"You sent your man to break into my house. You know where they came from."

"I didn't send nobody after nothing. This the first I know about any of this."

"Mouton, I'm tired of fooling around with you."

I pulled a switchblade from my pocket. Mouton's glare didn't change. But the guard started squirming, and when the blade flicked open he flinched. I walked behind them and cut the wire leading from the alarm button. Then I cut the phone cord. I pushed open the door to the walk-in closet. It was solid wood and heavy with small gaps at the top and the bottom between the door and door frame. I grabbed a handful of pencils from a jar on Mouton's desk.

I shut the closet door behind them. I jammed six pencils into the space above the closet door and nailed them in snug with the butt of the pistol. I did the same at the bottom. That jammed the door shut tighter than deadbolts could.

"Saturday noon, Mouton, or the pictures go to LaShondra." I slid the photos under the door between two pencils. "Run these by your lawyer and ask him if he's ever heard of RICO. And I don't mean one of his Hispanic clients."

———

Up and down the narrow streets of the French Quarter I rode, keeping one eye on my rearview mirror. My truck's air conditioner roared at full speed and blew out a white fog as it started freezing over. I loosened my cuffs and my collar, and rolled down the windows, but I was moving too slowly for any breeze.

After twenty minutes of crawling around the Quarter, I knew I had gotten away clean. Nobody could follow me in those cramped, closed-in passageways and not be seen. But there was no percentage in hanging around within five miles of the Trade Center, so I got on Rampart, headed uptown to Canal, and hung a right to the I-10.

The wind racing through the cab cooled me down and dried the sweat from my face and back. As I sped down the interstate I replayed in my mind the scene in Mouton's office. I was on the crest of the Industrial Canal Bridge when it hit me what Mouton had said.

"Negatives!"

He never said videotape.

Next off-ramp. Pay phone outside a Chevron station. Neal answered.

"Did you get the tape?" I asked.

"Got it this morning. It's in the safe deposit box. I didn't even keep it long enough to look at it."

"I think you need to send Kathy and the kids up to her folks in Yazoo City for a few days."

"What's up?"

"That tape shows Mouton himself knee-deep in a drug sale. I had some still shots made and went to see him."

"You went to *see* him? Are you nuts?"

"I told him I'd give him the pictures when he turned over the guys who'd killed Barb and Toulouse."

"Are you calling me from some padded cell?"

"You know a better way to get some names out of Mouton?"

"He'll kill you, Jack. He's a mobster. You know mobsters. They're those people who recycle bodies along with their oil drums."

"It's the only bargaining chip I had," I said, "but there's one problem."

"Oh, Lord."

"The problem is that Mouton didn't know about the pictures until I showed him."

Neal paused. "How do you know that?"

"When I showed the pictures to him, he said that was the first time he knew anything about them . . ."

"Well, that's sure as hell good enough for me," Neal said, "long as he said 'cross my heart.'"

"Neal, he said he'd buy the negatives.'"

"You're not thinking about selling them to him. Tell me you're not."

"You're not listening," I said. "Mouton said 'negatives.' He thought the shots came from a camera. If he had known it was a tape, he would have said tape."

A few seconds went by. "I don't follow you," Neal said. "If Mouton didn't send somebody after the tape, who broke into your house?"

"No idea. But you can count on one thing—whoever did is still looking for that tape. And as soon as Mouton figures out who I am, he'll come for it, too."

"I'm sending Kathy and the kids off as soon as they can pack," he said. "What about Angie?"

"Any chance of sending her to Yazoo City with Kathy?"

"I doubt she'll go. She appears to be kinda stubborn."

"Give me until day after tomorrow," I said. "You can bring her here on Friday. We'll meet where the old White Kitchen used to be."

"Does Mouton know where you are?"

"Since I'm still alive, I don't think he does. Like I said, he doesn't even know who I am—but that's just a matter of time. I've got a place where Angie and I can hide out, so bring her Friday at noon. Oh, and one more thing, okay?"

"What?"

"If I turn up missing, give the tape to LaShondra Batiste."

NINETEEN

It was deep enough into the night for the French Quarter to have become brassy and wicked. The front door of the Gator's Den stood open, and from the street I saw a long-legged nude dancer under a blue spotlight grasping one of the chrome poles at the front of the raised stage, suspending herself above a stage-side table, and lowering her bare bottom toward the two howling drunks seated below. I stepped through the wreath of clear lights that rimmed the door and flashed in running sequence, creating the illusion that a little dark spot was continuously circling the door frame.

A big-busted blonde wearing only a white, tassled G-string and white, sequined high heels stepped in front of me before I was three feet inside the door. The G-string and shoes glowed under a black light mounted over the door.

"Table for one?" she asked.

"I'm here to see Candy."

Candy was already coming my way. She slipped her arm through mine and leaned in close to my ear.

"Let's go back to the office," she shouted over the blare of the music.

We crossed in front of the stage to the door under the green-lighted exit sign on the far wall. She shut it behind us and the sudden quiet made me dizzy. The hallway led thirty feet to a steel door with an emergency push bar, the rear passage to the alley. A light scent of hair spray and baby powder drifted from the dancers' makeup rooms to the left. Along the right wall were Candy's office and a storeroom. I followed her into her office.

"You remember to bring some cash?" she said. "If not, I'll lend you some. It's gonna take two hundred dollars."

I pulled the two bills from my shirt pocket and held them up.

"There's somebody back there you need to talk to. He's behind the rack in the storage room. No names, okay? And he wants you to leave the lights off."

"What's he got?"

"A name."

"Does he know who killed Barb?"

Candy shrugged. "I told him what you're looking for, and he said he'll give you a name. I don't want to know the name."

"Is he back there now?"

She nodded. "Stand right inside the door and tell him you're here. Remember, no lights. Hold the money over the top of the rack, and he'll take it from there."

We walked out of the office and Candy went back up front without another word and without a look back.

I stepped through the door of the storage room and shut it behind me. The only light came through the ventilation transoms up near the ceiling, gray shafts of second-hand light from the alley, which struck the opposite wall and made pale rectangles above my head. A free-standing metal rack stood in the middle of the roomful of paper towels, toilet tissue, cocktail napkins, and plastic cups. Looking through a gap where the rack was empty, I guessed his height to be five-eight, five-nine, and the weight maybe one-eighty. I couldn't see his face.

"I'm here," I said.

He tapped on the top shelf. "Lemme see the cash."

I had heard the voice before, but couldn't remember where or when. I pinched the bills between my thumb and forefinger, and I held them up above the rack. He plucked them like a trained seal snatching a fish.

"Ain't sayin' this but once. You aksin' about Toulouse. Toulouse had a big mouth; he lucky to last long as he did. He always braggin' and shit. Said he had some juice on Mouton."

"Juice?"

"Had some shit on him, shit he could take to the cops."

"What was it?"

"Don't know, man. Toulouse just say he got it."

"What else did he say?"

"Toulouse was a fool, man. They was ripping off their own people, and the fool would talk about it. They was stealin' from Rickey Dee; then they was movin' it in Mouton's turf. They dissed both of them, man. I guar-on-tee you."

It was a voice from the tape, the guy who was selling for Toulouse on the street, Little Boy.

"Dissed?" I asked.

"Dis-re-*spec*-ted, man. They dissed Rickey Dee. They dissed Mouton. Hey, they dissed 'em both. They even used Rickey Dee's truck, man. Had the name on the side."

"What name?"

"Coastliner Ice. This Rickey Dee, he own it. They haul the rock over here in his truck."

"You keep saying 'they.' Did Toulouse have some help?"

"Toulouse be workin' with one of Mouton's guys. This guy tol' Toulouse when it be safe to come over and sell."

"Isn't that what Rickey Dee wanted?"

"They were skimming from Rickey Dee, man."

"Did he know that?"

"What do you think, man?"

"I think I paid to find out who killed Toulouse and Barb Novak."

"Don't know that."

"Hey, you mess with me and I'll jump over this flimsy-assed rack so fast . . ."

"Whoa, Ram-*bo!* I gonna tell you the dude who know. His name be Nate. He run the Comus Bar. He know who did it."

"Nate? What the hell did this Nate have to do with Toulouse?"

"Hey, Nate be the one telling Rickey Dee when to bring a load over. But Nate and Toulouse, they be partners on the side. Check it out."

"What do you mean?"

"Hey, these c-notes done used up."

TWENTY

The offices downtown were still open, so the crowd and the coke dealers hadn't shown up at the Comus yet. Two junior executive types, shirts and ties, and some guy about my age in an LSU T-shirt sat down at the far end of the bar, arguing about some of the trades the Saints had made. A barmaid I had seen the last time I was there stood behind the bar across from them. Two guys from Zappit! Pest Control Company sat at a booth across the room. They both wore green jumpsuits with beetle logos sewn across their backs. Other than that, the place was empty.

I shuffled toward the bar and by the time I reached it, I had acclimated to the dark. Nate stood at the near end of the bar, slicing lemons and oranges and occasionally looking up at the television. I kept my eyes on his hands.

I sat on the stool in front of Nate. He looked up and wiped his hands on a wet dish towel.

"Can I get you something?" He hesitated just a bit and flicked his eyes up and down my face as he tried to remember where he had seen me.

"I'll take a cream soda."

He put the bottle in front of me. "Anything else?"

"Yeah, Nate, there's something else. I need a name."

"Do I know you, pal?"

"We have some mutual friends. Toulouse Caron for one. Shame about Toulouse, wasn't it?"

Nate chewed on the inside of his cheek, thinking hard. He snapped his fingers and pointed at me. "You're the guy who came in here looking for Barb the day she got killed. What the hell you want?"

"The guy who killed her. I believe you know who it is."

"Hey, man, I don't know nothing about that. I already talked to the cops."

"Did you tell them about Toulouse?"

"I don't know nothing about him neither. He used to come in here, that's all."

"You don't know anything about your own business partner?"

Nate glanced up the bar and stuck his face close to mine. "Hold it down, man. What the hell you talking about?"

"I'm talking about your partner." I got louder.

"Shh! Don't say that!" He looked around. "I wasn't his partner. I didn't hardly know him."

"You've got the name and you're going to give it to me."

"I don't know nothing about it!"

"If you won't tell me, I'll have to get it from Mouton."

"You're nuts, man."

"Of course, Mouton doesn't do anything for free. I'd have to give him something. Like maybe the name of the guy who told Toulouse when the coast would be clear. You know, his partner."

Nate ran his tongue across his bottom lip. "It wasn't me."

"You know, you might be telling the truth. You know why I think that? 'Cause you're still alive. If I go to Mouton, he'll probably laugh in my face, don't you think?"

"Look, Toulouse was on his own. He was selling on his own."

"Where did he get his drugs?"

"How should I know?"

"You know what I think? I think you were the one who was ripping off the cocaine from Mouton and giving it to Toulouse to sell."

"Hey, man! Toulouse was the one stealing the drugs. He was ripping off his own organization."

"What organization?"

"Coastliner, dammit! He was stealing them from Rickey Dee McCoy!"

"I never mentioned any Rickey Dee McCoy. You sure seem to

know an awful lot about this Toulouse and Coastliner. Things I'm sure you told Mouton."

Nate wiped his hand across his mouth. "What you want from me, man?"

"Like I said, a name. Somebody in Mouton's organization killed Toulouse, and then Barb. You give me his name and I forget I ever heard of you."

Nate looked around. He pinched his nose and blew out a hard breath. "You got it wrong, man."

"Nate, I've had enough of your bullsh . . .".

"I mean you're after the wrong guy. It wasn't Mouton."

"Who was it?"

"Hey, I ain't positive. I mean, I can't prove nothing . . ."

Light flooded the room. Nate glanced past me, over my shoulder toward the door. His eyes swelled and his mouth dropped open. He dived to the floor. I looked up at the mirror behind the bar. Three men, silhouetted by the sunlight, stood in the open doorway. All three carried sawed-off pump shotguns. The one in the middle raised his gun to his shoulder and pointed it our way.

I lunged sideways and hit the floor. I rolled toward the far end of the bar just before the first shot. The shots came fast; the explosions slammed against my ears. Bits of glass sprayed around the room. Shards from the shattered mugs hanging above the bar peppered my head and back.

The whole scene went into slow motion. The gunmen chewed up the room with buckshot. I saw the girl at the other end of the bar screaming, but I couldn't hear her over the roar of the shotguns. The guy in the LSU T-shirt dropped to the floor. The two young guys scrambled over their stools toward the rear of the room.

The blasts kept coming, hitting the bottles and mirrors behind the bar. The burning sulfur smell of gunpowder smoke filled the air. I rolled to a wooden post in the middle of the room and tried to make myself small behind it. One slug splintered a hole in the bar, sending chips of wood flying. A chair beside me exploded as it was hit. A boom from a shotgun, and the beer-wagon lamp over the pool table shattered.

Two gunmen stepped forward, aimed at where Nate had

ducked behind the bar, and ripped the front of it open with four blasts. One of them ran and jumped up on the bar. He aimed his shotgun down at the floor and fired.

And that was the last shot.

The room rang with the echoes of the blasts. Then it grew still and quiet, except for the ringing in my ears, and there was a flat, blue cloud of smoke, shoulder high, over the room. The odor from the shattered liquor bottles mixed with the pungent smell of cordite. I heard the barmaid whimpering behind the bar.

I peeked around the post and saw the three gunmen in the light near the door in a loose phalanx. One gunman stepped forward, and the broad shaft of sunlight from the open front door shone on his face.

Bruno.

"Hey, Mouton! A little calling card from Rickey Dee!" He shouted to the open room, as if he were addressing the bar itself. "You'll pay for Toulouse, you dried-up old bastard!"

Bruno took a quarter turn toward the door, lifted his shotgun, and fired at the ceiling. Bruno's face was half in the light, half in shadow. A glint of sunlight danced on the gold chains around his neck and flashed from the jeweled pendant suspended at his breastbone. He shouted a laugh and ran out between the other two men, who kept their guns trained on us as they backed out the door.

I pushed up, dashed to the bar, and leaned over it. The eye on the side of Nate's face that had not been blown away was wide open. Tiny bits of skull, like pieces of eggshell, were strewn across the cushioned mat behind the bar along with bright red chunks of his brain. Blood had splattered along the angle of that last shot and crimson spots ran a foot or two up the back wall. A red liquid circle grew as it oozed across the mat and dripped onto the floor.

I rushed to the front door and stood beside it, flat against the concrete block wall. I shoved it with my foot and jerked my leg back behind the wall. Nothing, no shots, so I crouched low and looked outside. The gunmen were gone.

Faraway sirens were rising. I didn't need to be talking with any cops, so I walked out the door and toward my truck one block over, moving slower than I wanted to so I wouldn't attract attention. Over my shoulder I saw two guys from a warehouse up the street pointing toward the Comus. They watched, didn't follow. A dozen shotgun blasts can make you cautious. I turned the corner, started trotting to my truck, and ended up running. When I drove off, I kept it under fourth gear to force myself to stay under the thirty-miles-per-hour limit and not give anybody anything to notice, much less remember.

As I reached Canal Street, two police cars raced by me headed back to the Comus, wigwag headlights flashing and sirens blaring. When I stopped at the red light on Canal, chest pounding and hands shaking, I realized that the man, maybe the only man, who could tell me who had killed Barb and Toulouse had just died.

TWENTY-ONE

I had witnessed a murder and I knew the killer's name. Trouble was, it had happened in the Comus. And the Comus, by any standard, was one of the disreputable places the judge had told me to avoid if I didn't want my bond revoked. It was time to see Josh.

Josh's office is on Tulane Avenue near the Orleans Parish Courthouse, a converted two-story warehouse that used to belong to Purity Sugar Company. I parked in a CLIENTS ONLY space beside the building in front of a yard-wide strip of white periwinkles and red caladiums, which ran the length of the wall. A mist from the underground sprinklers glowed white in the sunlight and deepened the green of their foilage. The sidewalks were washed gravel, and there was a grassy island in the parking lot where crepe myrtles shaded a concrete bench. A miniature park without the graffiti.

The two front doors were of clear, leaded glass, and beside them was Josh's brass nameplate: JOSHUA A. HALLMAN, ATTORNEY-AT-LAW. Josh has associates but he has never had a partner.

A pebble stuck in the tread of my Top-Siders tapped on the shining marble of the foyer. The air was perfumed with cappucino. I was greeted at the receptionist's desk by a handsome and pleasant young man with a diamond ear bob. I asked to see Mr. Hallman and gave him my name.

Josh's office is up a narrow staircase with a runner of deep red carpet held fast to the stairs by a series of brass rods laid over the carpet against the inside of each step. The largest portion of the second floor, toward the rear of the building, is the library. But

Josh's office is almost as big and takes up the front section over-looking the street. It's a yellow room trimmed in white with two small crystal chandeliers and French doors on each wall opening to a balcony that encircles the building.

The young receptionist and I had been upstairs no more than thirty seconds when Josh walked in from a side door like he was late for something.

"Oh, Jack, I'm so glad to see you away from that dreadful lockup. Kurt, I'm sure Jack would like something to drink." Josh held up his wrist, tilted his head back, and looked down at this wristwatch. "It's a little early, but I'm sure it's five o'clock some place. Tanqueray and tonic with a slice for me. Jack, you must try Kurt. He's the best. I have to constantly give him outrageous bonuses to keep him from going to Brennan's as head bartender."

Kurt blushed.

"Coca-Cola would be fine," I said. "I've sworn off for a while."

"Oh, I really should." Josh patted his flat tummy. "But I simply can't forego all vices." He walked around the desk to his chair, fished out a long, thin cigarette from his top drawer, and lit it. "I'm down to five a day."

Kurt frowned at him and walked out of the room.

"Josh, I have a problem."

"You mean another one?"

"I've witnessed a murder."

"Oh, my God! When did this happen?"

"An hour ago. I saw three of Rickey Dee's men walk into the Comus Bar and shoot the manager."

"The *Comus?* Don't you remember our friend Miss Cole, the assistant DA? Would you really want to give her a second shot at revoking your bond?"

"That's why I'm here. I want to know if I should take this to the police."

He took a long drag from his cigarette and let the smoke escape slowly. "Tell me what happened."

"I'd heard that the manager, a guy named Nate, could tell me who killed Toulouse and Barb. I went to the Comus and while I was there three guys walked in with sawed-off shotguns and started shooting up the place. They killed Nate . . ."

"You said they were Rickey Dee's men. How do you know that?"

"I recognized one of them. Plus, he said that it was a calling card from Rickey Dee. Said Mouton would pay for killing Toulouse."

"Why would they shoot up the Comus?"

"Mouton owns the place. The manager was on Mouton's team. That's what my source had told me."

"Your source?"

"You know Candy Dixon?"

He nodded.

"Candy lined me up with a snitch who told me that Nate worked for Mouton but also had some action of his own on the side with Rickey Dee. Nate acted as lookout so Toulouse could sell in Mouton's territory. Toulouse stole drugs from Rickey Dee and sold them over here. Then he and Nate split the profits."

Josh put his cigarette in an ashtray and stood looking out the window, his hands behind his back, rising up and down on the balls of his feet. "If Rickey Dee found out about it, that would account for going after Nate."

"That's right."

Josh turned to me. "Would he have killed Toulouse and Miss Novak?"

"I still think Mouton killed them," I said. "But, then, just before the three shooters came in to the Comus, Nate told me Mouton didn't kill Toulouse."

"Who did he say did it?"

"He didn't. I think he was about to tell me when he got blasted."

"Do you believe him? Do you think it was somebody other than Mouton?"

"Hard to say. Nate had plenty of reasons not to snitch on Mouton."

Kurt brought the drinks back in on a silver tray, which he sat on Josh's desk, close enough for me to smell the juniper scent of the gin. "Will that be all?" he asked.

"Yes, thank you," Josh said.

Kurt reached over to the ashtray, put out the smoldering cigarette, and dumped it in the trash can. He shot a disapproving glance at Josh and walked out.

Josh took a sip of his drink. "Mmmm—the best," he said and sat down. "Well, I'm afraid the picture is as cloudy as ever when it comes to the killer of Miss Novak. But as entertaining as your story is, it makes little difference to me. As I told you earlier, that is not my primary concern. Nor is it your concern at this time." He held up his hand to stop me from talking. "My job is to keep you out of jail. And if you go directly to the police with the story you told me, that is where you will go—very soon."

"Why? What have I done?"

"You consorted with a woman who's on a first-name basis with the entire Vice Squad. I dearly love Candy Dixon, but she's been busted for prostitution so many times that they've stopped counting. You also approached Nate, a witness, or potential witness, in your own case. I've been on top of your case and I know that the police interviewed Nate."

"He told me that."

"You also frequented at least two establishments that sell alcohol and God knows what else."

"What should I do?"

"This is not the right time for you to play good citizen." He sipped his drink, set the glass on the desk, and rubbed his palms together briskly. "Now, before I tell you what I've done on your case, are there any other adventures you'd like to tell me about?"

"Well, yes, there is one."

"Only one?" Josh's lips were in a tight line, and I could tell he was irritated.

"I discovered that Barb Novak had a second apartment. It's in the Quarter. Very upscale, very expensive. Rickey Dee apparently set her up. I guess Neal told you that Barb was Rickey Dee McCoy's girlfriend."

"Neal told me most of what you told him. My question is, if she were his kept woman—indulge me, Jack, I don't get to use that term much these days—if she were, why on earth did she work at that god-awful Comus?"

"The only thing I can figure is that's where her friends were."

"I suppose," he said. "What do you know about this second apartment?"

"I found out about it before the police did and I went in for a look."

"You were careful. Weren't you?"

"Very. I didn't find much. Or I should say we didn't find much."

"We?"

"Barb's sister, Angie, was with me."

"Do you call taking an amateur with you being careful?"

"It's a long story," I said. "I didn't have much choice."

"I've talked with Neal and he told me about Miss Angie. It sounds as though she is in what the psychologists refer to as denial in regard to her sister's death."

"That may be true."

"It has been my observation that when such denial occurs, the emotion of grief often catches up with a person quite suddenly."

"I don't doubt it."

"What I'm saying is that these dangerous little games you play are made even more dangerous when you include someone who may be on the edge."

"Point well taken, Counselor."

"End of sermon. For now at least. Please proceed with your story about Miss Novak's second apartment."

"I found a videotape Barb was holding for Toulouse. It showed André Mouton in three drug sales. I mean he was right there when the money changed hands. That's a conspiracy, isn't it? Isn't that a federal crime under RICO?"

"Very likely. There are certain specified offenses that come under RICO. Drug sales are in the group. You say three *different* sales?"

I nodded yes.

"That establishes a pattern of criminal activity. The RICO law is an abomination that allows federal prosecutors to do as they please. Stalin would have loved it. I'd have to see the tape, but, if it's as you say, it's probably a RICO violation."

"It's there, and the shots are daytime clear," I said. "Toulouse was planning to use the tape somehow. To blackmail Mouton, probably. But I know Mouton wasn't aware of the tape's existence until after Toulouse and Barb were both dead."

Josh raised his right eyebrow and glared at me with only that one eye. "How do you know that?"

"I had some still photos made of some of the juicier parts. I went to his office and told him he had forty-eight hours to deliver Barb's killer or the tapes go to LaShondra Batiste."

Josh dropped his feet to the floor, pushed up from the chair, and glowered at me, breathing through his nose hard enough for me to hear it. "Dammit, Jack! You're not making this easy!"

He wheeled around and looked out the French doors, saying nothing, pushing up and down on the balls of his feet, his hands clasped behind him. After a long ten count, he turned back around and gave me that one-eyed glare. "I'm curious. One, what did he say? Two, what did you possibly hope to gain? And three, have you lost your frigging mind?"

"He denied knowing anything about the murders, of course. But he wants the tape, no mistake about that. And it was a surprise to him, Josh. He didn't know about the pictures until I showed him."

"Congratulations! Now you've got Mouton after you, too."

"I had to try something. Who knows? Maybe he'll turn over the killer to save his own hide."

"Or, more likely, he'll just kill you."

"I told him if he does, LaShondra gets the tape, and he goes to the federal pen for a RICO violation. I couldn't let him sit idly by and watch me take a fall for him."

"You don't even know if he did it."

"Even if he didn't, he can find out who did."

Josh took a deep breath, held it, then blew it out in a puff. He walked around his desk and put his hand on the back of my chair. "You realize that you have an excellent chance of beating this charge entirely. From what I know so far, the eyewitness won't hold up. We're sending our man out there this afternoon; but from talking with her on the phone, she sounds like she would be very weak on the witness stand. She's eighty-five years old, almost blind, and she picked you out of a photo lineup in which you were the only white guy above the age of twenty-two. They've broken the chain of evidence on the blood samples, left them out on a desk unmarked for two days. They're already talking plea bargain."

"Beating this rap is only half the battle," I said. "It's your half. I'm looking for a killer."

"For the killer of Barb Novak, dammit! You don't have the time to go after the killer of Big Jim Brannan. You keep screwing around with André Mouton and you're going to end up dead. Or back in jail, which, thanks to these latest shenanigans, is now the same thing."

"The same thing as what?"

"It's the same thing as being dead," he said. "Bear in mind, Jack, the tentacles of André Mouton are long and they reach far."

"I never was good at poetry," I said.

"Mouton has a number of New Orleans police officers on his payroll. They take orders from him. Since your confrontation at the World Trade Center, I would not advise you to do anything to place yourself in the custody of the police department. You've turned any stay in the New Orleans jail—however short—into a death sentence. You hear me, Jack? A death sentence. You wouldn't be in there fifteen minutes before somebody jammed a shank into your ribs." He sat on the front edge of his desk. "Your sense of justice is admirable, but you're going to get yourself killed. You're also running the risk of facing other charges by withholding evidence."

"You mean the tape? I'm not withholding it, I'm just borrowing it."

Josh stalked back around to his chair, plopped into it, and threw his feet up on top of his desk. He snatched a file, opened it, and started reading. "I'll stop by your apartment tonight," he said. "I'll drop off some copies of the police reports."

"Thanks, Josh."

He didn't look up as I walked out.

TWENTY-TWO

T he sunset's pink reflection on the high clouds to the west was growing dim and night was coming quickly. I walked through the damp, brick corridor to the courtyard, then up the outdoor staircase to my front door. The lock is contrary and it took some jiggling around to get the key to fit. Cool air from the apartment rushed out with a sweet, smoky smell, not uncommon in the French Quarter, like a candle or incense.

I had to walk around the door to get to the light switch, one of the eccentricities of Billy's apartment. I was feeling for the switch when a blast of pain shot down the back side of my head. My knees folded and I fell backward. As the world faded, two dark forms stood over me, looking down.

The icy water slammed against my face and shot up my nose, sending me into a coughing spasm. It clouded my sight as I pushed my eyes open. I couldn't move my arms or legs; they were lashed to the chair. I tried to blink the water out of my eyes; then I tried to shake it out, and a sharp pain shot through my skull with each move. When my eyes cleared, I saw a big black man standing in front of me in a wide stance, arms crossed. A second man, same size, stood at my side. The one in front slapped my head right at the ear, and I thought my brain would explode.

"You can make this as hard or as easy as you want to, homeboy. We want that tape NOW!"

He punched me in the stomach. It knocked me and the chair over. My gut heaved and an acid burn shot up into my throat. My heart pounded, each beat shooting pain. The guy on the side jerked the chair back up. The one in front grabbed my shoulders and leaned down in my face.

"It ain't gonna get no easier, sucka. Where's the damn tape?"

His face was a blur. His breath was hot. He smelled of cheap wine and cheaper cologne. He shoved the chair over backward and I strained against the ropes. A kick to my ribs knocked the air out of me, and I gasped until I could suck down a breath. They both hoisted the chair, one on each side, and slammed it down upright in the middle of the floor, jolting my spine up to my skull.

"I don't have it . . ." My voice had been burned by stomach acid. "It's not here . . ."

"Wrong answer!" He kicked my shin and my eyes watered. A knifepoint pricked me below my chin. "You miss another one and you ain't gonna be around for the big prize. I'm gonna give you one more chance to . . ."

Five sharp raps at the door.

"Are you in there, Jack? What's all that noise?" It was Josh.

"SHOOT 'EM!" I screamed. "BLOW 'EM, JOSH!"

One of them nodded toward the French doors, and they calmly stepped over to them. "We be back. Them tapes get out and yo' country ass is dead."

"THEY'RE GETTING AWAY, JOSH!"

"Jack? Are you all right?" Josh yelled.

Against the lights of the street, they slid unhurried over the balcony railing. The front door eased opened, Josh eased his head in, and his eyes nearly popped out.

"Oh, good Lord."

"Lock the doors." I pointed my head toward balcony. "My gun's in the bedroom, nightstand drawer. Go get it, quick."

He turned the front door deadbolt, dashed across the room, and flipped the handle locks on the French doors. He ran to the back of the apartment. I heard water running and a few seconds later he returned, a wet cloth and a butcher's knife in one hand and my .45 in the other. He pinched the handle of the gun between his thumb and forefinger like it had germs. He set it on the coffee table.

"Who *was* that?" he asked.

"A pair of Mouton's enforcers. They wanted the tape."

"Oh, good Lord . . ." Josh cut the ropes from my arms and legs. He wiped the cloth across my forehead. "How bad is it?" He touched the cloth to the blood behind my ear and I jerked away.

"It was about to get a whole lot worse."

"I can't believe they ran away so easy."

"They can't kill me until they find out where the tape is. We were making so much noise that we were about to draw a crowd. They were sending me a message. They'll be back."

Josh handed me the damp cloth to let me wipe my own face since I knew where it hurt, at least where it hurt the most. I rubbed it on my eyes. They stung with tears and the salt of sweat, and white flashes came and went. The smell and taste of acid in my throat set off a spasm of nausea, and I staggered to the bathroom and got on my knees in front of the toilet.

When I walked back into the living room, Josh was sitting on the edge of the couch, puffing on a long, thin cigarette, his hands shaking so hard the ashes kept flaking off.

"Where is it?" he said. "I'll not have you killed over the damn thing and some macho code of chivalry or vengeance or whatever the hell it is." He stood up and held his hand out, palm up.

"You want something?"

"I want that tape—right now!" He tapped his foot.

"It's in a safe deposit box in Bay Saint Louis. Neal has instructions to give it to LaShondra Batiste if something happens to me."

"Shit!" He took another angry puff of his cigarette and plopped on the arm of the couch.

"Josh, you're upset and angry. You're a smart lawyer . . ."

"Some people think so. Some people actually follow my advice."

"But think this one through. First of all, that tape is keeping me alive. And if I take it to the cops or LaShondra Batiste or the FBI before Saturday, where am I going to say I found it?"

"You seem to think this tape is providing you with some sort of security," he said. "All the tape does is make kidnapping Mouton's first option. If that's not convenient, he'll kill you without hesitation. And if you *are* kidnapped, I suggest you surrender the tape immediately. You'll still be killed, but you may spare yourself the torture session. What you just went through is a warm-up. Mouton's goons can be quite creative with a pair of pliers."

I eased down into the chair, tilted my head back, and laid the cloth across my forehead. "I'll do better," I said. "I'll worry about finding Barb's killer later. I promise. I'll help your guys with their investigations or just lay low. I'll do whatever you want me to do."

I closed my eyes. The coolness of the facecloth drew the ache from my head, and Josh remained mercifully quiet. The soft breeze from the ceiling fan lapped at my face, and I drifted into a light sleep. Some minutes later, when I opened my eyes, Josh was down on one knee at the table beside the French doors, his head tilted, looking at a foot-long box set on the tabletop.

"I thought I smelled incense," he said. "I didn't notice these candles earlier."

The candles were black. Squatty votive lights like they burned on the altar at Saint Louis Cathedral. They had burned down to the sockets, and the black wax had flowed to the table and hardened into flat pools at each end of the box. The box was ten or twelve inches long, maybe four inches wide and three inches deep, homemade from scrap lumber, slats, rough-sawed and unhanded, tacked together with one-inch brads. It was light-colored wood, cheap white pine with a few knot holes. It wasn't fitted together very well and the angles were off enough so there were some gaps where the boards met.

A dark stain covered the top of the box, the remains of some liquid that had been sprinkled or poured on it. It was slippery and some of it stuck to my fingertips. It had a sweet smell a lot like licorice. Behind the box, stuck into a glob of paraffin, were the burned stems of what had been, or at least looked like, three sticks of incense.

Josh pulled an ink pen from his shirt pocket and pushed against the box, turning it around so that the rear side was visible. Someone had drawn three designs on that side with a felt-tip pen.

"What is it?" I asked.

"It's an *ouanga* of some sort. A magical charm."

"A charm?" I said. "Well, good. I need all the help I can get."

"I have the distinct feeling that this is no good luck charm. I think this is a warning to let you know you've been hexed."

"Voodoo?"

"Right this minute they're probably sticking pins in some doll that looks a lot like you."

"Well, that's a hell of a lot better than sticking a switchblade into my ribs."

"I don't think we should make light of this. Do you have a camera?"

"I'm an investigator. I sleep with a camera. What do you need one for?"

"I need a few shots of this. We'd better not disturb it any more." He was bent over very close to the box, looking over every inch of it.

"You don't believe in this, too—do you?"

"I was raised down here as a Catholic. I have gone through periods in my life when I rejected all religion—embraced atheism, if you will—until I realized that atheism is itself a form of religion. I then became an adherent of eastern religions and their emphasis on reincarnation, then a deist, then I came full circle and am now a Catholic—a bad one, but still a Catholic. I believe in the power of God and of spirits, and I cannot reject anyone's spiritual beliefs if they are strongly held."

"You think somebody can hex me?"

"I have seen people who have been hexed."

"Are you serious?"

"It works. Now I will admit that the ones I have seen under a hex really believed in the power of such things, and that may have been the reason they were effective . . ."

"Exactly."

". . . but whether they work or not, whether you believe in it or not, we ought to find out what this means. We need to find out what Mouton, or Mouton's mother, has in mind."

Josh remained on his knees, sniffing the burned-out candles, staring at the symbols painted on the side of the box. He had not looked up the whole time he was talking to me.

"I'm going to clean up. I don't think anything is broken, but I probably need to get checked out for a concussion. I still have white flashes in my eyes . . ."

He kept staring at the little box.

"Where's your camera?" he asked.

After I showered, I put on baggy jeans and a Jazz Fest T-shirt and went back into the living room. Josh sat on the couch studying one of several manilla folders he had brought from his office.

"Feeling better?"

"My head's still sore right here." I pointed to the area behind my right ear.

"I took some extra shots for you." He held up four Polaroid shots of the voodoo display on the table. In one shot the designs on the side of the box were clear.

"What's in the folders?"

"Police reports, mainly the crime scene investigation. They don't have the final results from the lab, but I'll get them as soon as they review them. I've got a friend in the lab who says Miss Novak had some fragments of what appeared to be skin under her fingernails. She didn't scratch you, did she?"

"If it's skin fragments, they aren't mine."

"Well, it wouldn't clear you, but it would help. Their case is falling apart. If you'll be patient and let me . . ."

"You've convinced me, okay?"

He flipped through the papers in the folder. "Oh, here's the photo lineup. Here's what they showed the eyewitness." He handed me five black-and-white photographs, glossy mug shots, front and side views on each print. The first one was me. One was a black guy who had a huge Afro like I used to see in the late sixties and early seventies. There was one kid who couldn't have been over eighteen or nineteen years old—Josh said he was twenty-two—and he had a hood-ornament earring. The other two suspects were shown in mug shots straight from the files. Glum, impassive men with the mean eyes that spoke of years behind bars. One of them was a white guy, nearly bald, with a neck so fat it bulged out past his chin. The other was ebony black.

"I'm the only guy in here who even remotely looks like me."

"It obviously wasn't a fair lineup," he said. "And I told you about your blood samples from Barb's house, didn't I?"

"You said they left them unattended on a desk."

"Right. They're now inadmissible."

"Sounds good. Anything else?"

"I sent my investigator out to see the eyewitness today. She's an eighty-eight-year-old lady named Julia Desporte. My man showed her six photographs. None of them you, not one of them. Yet she picked out the man she had seen—two times. And it was two different men. Unless you continue to go to that neighborhood so she can really get a good look at you, you'll be home free as far as her testimony is concerned."

"She won't see me again."

"Mrs. Desporte has a niece who was visiting her the day of Miss Novak's murder. This niece didn't see you. But she told my investigator that a police car drove up to Miss Novak's house after you left."

"Of course."

"This car only had one officer in it. He went in, stayed maybe five minutes, and left. He left before the other squad cars arrived."

"He left her body unattended?"

"I'm looking into that possibility. We're going to follow up on it. We're also looking for the niece to see if she'll tell us anything else."

"I could check with this friend I've got on the force."

"Don't you even *think* of talking to anybody with NOPD," he said.

"You think the cops had anything to do with this?"

"What I suspect is that the first car arrived after the tip came in, and there were actually two officers but the niece only saw one of them. One must have stayed inside to secure the crime scene while the other one went out for doughnuts."

"I get the feeling that NOPD may not be real strong on procedure."

"How do you think I got to be such a rich man?" He broke into a grin. He closed the file and stood. "Put your clothes and personal effects on the bed. I'll send somebody for them."

"Am I planning to move?"

"Be sure to mind your manners and send a thank-you note to that nice man in Tupelo who allowed you to stay here."

"Where am I going?"

"Since you seem to relish flopping around with the lowlifes, I'm taking you to a place where you'll feel right at home. We're off to the emergency ward of Charity Hospital. You may have a concussion, remember?"

"And after that?"

"You'll stay in my guest house as long as necessary. They've found this place. You're now officially in hiding, my friend."

I was not the only one who needed to go into hiding. Somebody outside Mouton's organization had already confronted Angie about the tape. And my visit to the World Trade Center had raised the stakes since then.

TWENTY-THREE

The student doctor on call said there was no lingering evidence of a concussion. I didn't have time to hang around for a second opinion. Besides, my head didn't hurt as bad as my gut, and he said the tests showed nothing there—so we left.

I woke the next morning to a room so glaringly white it sent a stabbing pain into my already hurting eyes. Everything gleamed like polished alabaster; the walls, the carpet, the bedcovers, the phone. The morning sunlight bounced around the walls like the room was a handball court. The air was chilly. The air conditioner must have run all night. The windows were fogged around their edges, but they were clearing quickly as the eastern sun rose above the shield of a live oak some two hundred feet away.

I sat cross-legged on the bed, working out the kinks and finding sore spots I had forgotten about. My ribs and the left side of my head were way past what I'd call tender, but it was not as bad as I had expected.

I pulled back the curtain and looked out across the lawn. Josh wore a pale blue linen suit and sat by the pool in a dark green wicker chair beside a glass-topped table. He saw me looking out the window and beckoned for me.

"How would you like an omelet?" Josh asked. "Irma makes the best."

"I'm afraid I'll have to pass. I swear when that guy hit me in the stomach, he must have broken something."

"I wouldn't be surprised . . . oh, before I forget, I called Neal last night and told him about your run in with Mouton's goons."

"What did he say?"

"Something most strange. I really didn't understand. He asked me if I could pull a few strings and get you admitted to Tulane Law School."

"I'll never hear the end of this one."

"Do you know what he meant?" Josh asked.

"I'll tell you some day when we have plenty of time. Did he say he was bringing Angie over?"

"He said you were meeting somewhere around noon."

The morning was warm and pleasant as I walked to the pool; it was too early to be too hot. The omelets looked so good I tried one, but it hurt so I settled for a glass of milk.

"I've got to move out this morning," I said. "If I stay here, you'd be in danger. I'm going back to the Alamo Plaza, where I stayed when I was working that undercover job."

"That fleabag! You're welcome to stay here as long as you wish."

"Those guys who beat me up last night surely know you're my lawyer. They'll find out if I'm staying here. You don't want them around. They tend to be pretty messy."

"I can hire a guard."

"I think you should do that anyway." I finished my milk. "I can't tell you how much I appreciate all you're doing for me, but you know I don't have that much money and I . . ."

Josh held his hand up, palm toward me. "Your brother Neal—my dear friend—got me out of a serious situation involving some redneck cops in Poplarville when I was handling a case there some years ago. For some reason, they had taken a dislike to me and had planted some LSD in my car while I was in the courthouse. I have no doubt that had not Neal interceded, I would now be incarcerated in your state's Parchman Prison. I have already been paid for whatever bill you may run up."

"But I'm afraid I've put you in a dangerous situation."

"It comes with the territory. But I will put on a guard this evening. I've done it before, believe me."

Old U.S. Highway 90 comes in from the Mississippi Gulf Coast along the edge of the Gulf and cuts through the broad swamp along the inlet from the gulf to Lake Ponchatrain, the area known as the Riggolets. The old trail was the gateway to New Orleans until thirty years ago, when it lost out to the Interstate a few miles to the north. Now it's a back road. I take back roads every chance I get.

Old 90 meets Highway 11, which runs south from Slidell, at a point just inside the state line. At the intersection, there's a road-house turned truck stop, a low, blond-brick building with tinted picture windows. That's where we met.

"Oh, man, that's bad," Angie said. She looked at the side of my face like it was a wad of gum in her glass of tea.

"They were waiting for me when I walked into the apartment last night. If Josh Hallman hadn't walked in on them, I'd be dead now."

"This is getting scary," she said.

"It was real scary last night," I said. "I've moved out of Billy's apartment. I'll be checking into the Alamo Plaza the same time you do."

"Are you all right?" Neal asked.

"To be framed on a murder rap, running from the mob, and nursing a sore head and sore stomach, I'm doing great."

I told the details of my encounter with the two henchmen from Mouton. For some reason, they both thought it was hilarious that one of them had called me homeboy. After I told the whole story, they sat staring at me, or at least at the swollen right side of my face. I decided to change the subject and asked them what they had found out about Coastliner.

"I heard Rickey Dee sent a goon squad to the Comus and shot it up. Killed some guy," Neal said. "I'm sure Sheriff Wade will be right on top of that."

"It was Bruno Hebert and two other guys. I was in there and saw the whole thing."

"*In* there!" he nearly shouted. "What in the hell were you doing *in* there?"

"Shhh . . . hold it down." I glanced around. "The manager, the guy who got killed, was named Nate. He was Toulouse's silent partner in the drug-skimming operation. Your source was right, Neal. Toulouse had been skimming. Nate was one of Mouton's men, and he told Toulouse when and where it was safe to sell."

"How do you know this?"

"I've got some sources of my own. I heard Nate would know if Mouton had killed Toulouse and who the triggerman was. I swear, he was about to tell me when they walked in and shot him."

"You saw him get shot?" he asked.

"I got a good look at the whole thing. Hell, I was close enough to count the links in Bruno's gold chain."

"But why did they kill this Nate guy?" Angie asked.

"They said it was payback for Mouton killing Toulouse. Neal, you be careful around those guys. They're bad, real bad. And one more thing. Don't trust the sheriff . . ."

"That guy gives me the creeps," Angie said. "When we walked out the front door of your house, he was parked at the curb. Just sitting and watching. I felt like he was staring a hole through me. Never got out of the car."

"He didn't go into my house?"

"When we drove off, he fell in behind my car and followed us all the way to Neal's place. When I turned into Neal's drive, he drove on past us without stopping. I mean, the guy is weird."

"Neal," I said, "watch your step around him. If he tries to question you about the break-in, don't let it slip where Angie and I are."

"He can't bother you in Louisiana," Neal said.

"Barb told me she saw Rickey Dee give a big stack of hundreds to some guy with dark hair. If that guy was wade, that means anything he sees or hears is going straight back to Rickey Dee. I'm sure y'all talked about the videotape in the report Roger made . . ."

"Excuse me," Neal said, "but if you'll recall, at the time of the break-in you hadn't chosen to share with us any information about any videotape. Of course it's in the report. It's also in the report that Angie is Barb's sister."

"I'm not fussing at you. It's just that if Rickey Dee thinks I've got something Mouton wants, I don't want him knowing where I am. McCoy doesn't have much respect for a state line."

Along one stretch of Highway 90, called Chef Menteur Highway inside the New Orleans city limits, interspersed among the used-car lots and self-storage warehouses, is a series of relics from the heyday that was the 1950s. The Flamingo Courts, the Pelican Motel, the Alamo Plaza, the Andrew Jackson Inn, and the infamous Crescent City Courts. Their gaudy neon signs stand near the highway, sputtering and flickering in blues and pinks and greens, with messages such as AIR-CONDITIONED or TV. The offices are up front, little cubicles surrounded either by plate-glass or jalousie windows, each with a counter for check-in and a drive-up window at the side to accommodate late-night guests.

The Alamo is the nicest of the group. A family from India bought it, and they live there and they all work on it all day long. It's clean and freshly painted, and the family is saving to buy a Comfort Inn franchise in Hammond. The Alamo mostly rents by the week, but it has begun to attract some overnight business, mostly truckers in town for one night. The other motels in the group usually rent to transients and construction crews, except for Crescent City Courts. Their clientele usually rent by the hour and they feature in-room, triple-X movies.

Angie pulled into the space beside me, but after driving past the auto-body shops, adult bookstores, honky-tonks, and hubcap shops along that stretch of Chef Menteur, she stayed in the Lumina with her doors locked. I walked to her window and she let it down.

"I'm not going in there," she said.

"Don't judge it by the neighborhood. The rooms are cleaner than you'll find at most hotels in the Quarter."

"I'd be scared to death."

"I promise you, it's OK. Come in with me and I'll introduce you to the Srivastava family. If you don't like it, then we'll leave."

We went into the office and met the Srivastavas, and Angie fell in love with Suni, their four-year-old daughter who's got brown eyes as big and round as quarters. I had fallen in love with Suni several weeks earlier.

We were in our rooms fifteen minutes later.

We had adjoining rooms in a duplex unit in the rear of the motel. The nightstands and chests of drawers were knotty pine and showed the scratches, cigarette burns, and peeling varnish of the last forty years. But the beds were new and firm, the carpet likewise, and the pink tile of the bathrooms was clean and shiny. I helped Angie unpack, and I threw my stuff on my bed. I walked into her room while she folded her clothes and started putting them into the chest of drawers. When she finished, she walked to the dresser and began brushing her hair.

"I need to get out for a while," she said.

"I don't know that we should."

"For lunch. Somewhere for a sandwich. I'm too restless to sit here."

"I knew we should have eaten back at the truck stop."

"We'll keep our eyes open," she said.

Tujague's is near Café du Monde, off the corner of Jackson Square across from the French Market, close to the river. The main dining room is high-ceilinged and long—three tables wide and eight tables deep—with wood-paneled walls, darkened with age, black ceiling fans, and a white floor of ceramic tile. It smells faintly of roux and fried batter, and they keep the air conditioner set low. Tujague's is where my ex-wife Sandy and I went when we had some extra money, which is to say we went no more than three times during our marriage.

Back then, our usual table was in the right corner at the rear of the room. We'd set Peyton's carrier on a chair next to the wall. The waitresses brought her sweet wafers and orange juice, and if business was slow, they took turns holding her and trying to make her laugh. The last time I was in Tujague's, just before Sandy left me, Peyton had outgrown the carrier and was using a booster seat.

The image of Peyton when she was two, banging her heels against her Sesame Street booster seat, popped into my mind as the waitress led Angie and me toward that same corner. I stopped beside a station along the right wall, halfway between the front door and the back wall.

"We'll sit here if that's OK," I said, as I pointed to the table beside me. The waitress turned around and laid down two menus, one at each seat.

"I thought you wanted a table near the rear," Angie said.

"Not that one."

"Whatever." She shrugged as I pulled out her chair. "It doesn't matter to me."

I glanced over the crowd before I took the seat facing the front door. We ordered fried crawfish for an appetizer and a couple of Dixies. I deserved one. The saltwater smell of oysters on the half-shell from the table beside ours was too good to resist. I ordered a dozen (even though they aren't too good in the summer) and told Angie (who, being a Yankee, had never eaten a raw oyster) I was about to find out how brave she really was.

Twenty people stood around the walls waiting for an open table. Loud talk and laughter, the crash of silverware dropped into the busboy's trays, the hostess shouting out names as tables opened—all created a wall of noise sealing off our table.

"Why do you keep looking around? Are you concerned about being in here?" she said.

"We've got two groups of real bad people looking for us. And the French Quarter's not all that big. Coming in here is probably not the smartest thing I've done lately."

She huffed. "What I mean is are you worried about being in a place that serves alcohol?"

"Tujague's is not what the judge had in mind. The Comus is a different story."

"I'm sure you're right about that. At least I hope so. And maybe this isn't too damn smart. But I couldn't sit in your house, and I can't sit in any motel room."

"But, Angie, you've been going nonstop."

"And I'm going to keep it up until I get the son of a bitch who killed Barb."

She sounded like she was in a mood to bite somebody's head off, and I didn't want it to be mine, so I excused myself and weaved through the maze of round tables back to the men's room.

There was one stall and one urinal. While I was at the urinal, a man who had been in the stall came out, washed up, and left the hot-air drier running when he walked out. As soon as he left, someone else stepped into the room and I sensed him walking behind me.

"Remember me, homeboy? Don't turn around."

I recognized him in the wall mirror. He had a pistol pointed at my spine. A sport coat draped over his forearm covered all but the barrel.

"I'm not going anywhere," I said.

He poked me with the gun, right in the kidney. "I blow you away, you think one of these tourists 'round here gonna stop me? Get moving."

I walked out and he followed, the gun now fully covered by the coat. He stayed close, not quite touching, close enough for me to smell that syrupy cologne.

At our table, Angie watched me as I walked toward her. I pointed back over my shoulder with my eyes. Her eyebrows tightened down as she read trouble on my face.

I took two big strides—enough to make him uncomfortable with the distance, to make him scoot ahead to fill the gap. Maybe Angie would catch the signal. I glanced back and he scowled, a threat to me not to run. He quickened his pace to catch up. When I turned back around Angie was looking beyond me, right at him.

I walked him past our table and Angie kicked the natural hell out of his shin.

"*Yeow!*" he screamed. "Son of a *bitch!*"

I wheeled around as he reached down toward the pain. I popped him hard on the jaw. He flopped back on the table, crashing it against the wall. I grabbed Angie's hand. We scurried to the front door and pushed through the crowd to the street.

We ran along the curb toward Jackson Square. We bolted across the street through a moving gap between two cars. I glanced back. He was in front of Tujague's, scanning the sidewalk for us. He spotted me, threw his sport coat to the ground, jammed the gun in his waistband, and started running.

We sprinted down the packed sidewalk toward Jax Brewery. He was 150 feet behind and gaining. He ran like a sprinter, arms pumping, knees high, eyes straight ahead. A hundred feet behind. Eighty feet. Sixty.

He was flying past the crowd by Café du Monde. Some poor blimp in a tropical shirt stepped into his path. He slammed into the man's enormous side and knocked him sprawling. The gunman flipped high into the air, a full three-sixty, and came down on his back.

Angie and I burst through the doors of the Jax Brewery and scooted up the three steps to the expansive marble-and-glass mall of the first floor. We snaked through the crowd and jogged two flights of stairs to the third floor.

"Who *was* that?" she asked.

"One of the goons Mouton sent to beat me up."

"Oh, sweet Jesus!"

We ducked into a corner deli. No real cover, but it had an outdoor deck, quick escape. We sat low at a table by the rear door and looked out at the open mall, ready to run.

Each minute lasted an hour. I set a limit on how long we'd wait and checked my watch. Angie fidgeted with a paper napkin as we scanned the open area out the front entrance. When the five minutes were up, there were a pile of napkin pieces, each the size of a postage stamp, on our table.

"Let's go back to the motel," I said. I reached for her hand and felt moisture. "I think we lost him."

"But I don't feel safe on that sidewalk."

"The levee is right beside this building. We'll go to the other side of it and follow the streetcar tracks back to the French Market. You can't see those tracks from the street."

We walked toward the escalator, pushing along pretty hard. The echoes of our own footsteps on the marble floor sounded like somebody right behind us in close pursuit. On the ride down, I scanned the crowd below. Didn't see him. We reached the second floor and U-turned to the next down escalator.

Halfway down, Angie gripped my forearm. "Look up at the elevator!"

To our right the glass elevator was climbing at a slow, steady rate. Three short and gray ladies, their backs to us, green shopping bags in hand, stood inside it looking up at the lighted floor indicators above the door. Towering above them, also looking up and away from us, stood the tall black man who was chasing us.

Angie dug her nails into my arm, nearly drawing blood. We kept still, letting the escalator take us down, not wanting to make any movement to catch his eye. We had made it about halfway to the ground floor when he turned and spotted us.

We shoved past a teenaged boy and bolted three steps at a time down the escalator toward the exit. The man in the elevator reached over the little women, pounding on the buttons, trying to stop it.

We burst through the front door and raced up the ramp to the top of the levee. We ran down the steps on the back side. Fifty yards ahead, a streetcar slowed to pick up a bearded young man with a backpack. I shouted and held it, and we jumped aboard.

I spotted him at the base of the levee, running toward us. The streetcar gained speed, but he fell in behind and ran after us.

"What's he *doing?*" Angie asked.

"He thinks he can catch us."

We had put only a hundred yards between us when the streetcar slowed to a stop.

"Why the hell are we stopping?" Angie looked up front.

A new passenger was pumping quarters into the slot. The driver, a fat and sluggish kid, sat slumped in his seat. I startled him when I stepped past the fare box.

"You not s'posed to stand up here."

"Don't have time to say this but once. Now, listen . . ."

"What the hell you want?"

"Look in that mirror," I said. "That man running after us? He's got a gun and he plans to use it. He's one of André Mouton's hit men."

"Mouton?"

"Jack! Hurry, dammit!" Angie ran toward us. "He's about to catch us!"

The driver bolted up in his seat and shoved the brass throttle full ahead. His wide eyes stayed glued to the rearview mirror. The streetcar built to top speed. It swayed side to side as the electric motor whined and rose higher and higher in pitch. It blew past four shouting, waving, cursing people at the next stop.

"Won't it go faster?" she asked.

"No, ma'am. This's fast as she gets."

"Angie, go see if he's still back there."

"Y'all gotta get off. I don't want no trouble in here."

"Put some more distance between us and him," I said, "and we'll be on our way."

A few seconds later Angie walked back toward us, slower, no more tightness around her mouth.

"He stopped running," she said. "I guess he gave up."

TWENTY-FOUR

At the next streetcar stand, the driver put us out and gave us emphatic orders to stay out. We were at the Aquarium of the Americas across the tracks from the *Natchez*, a three-deck sternwheeler that cruises the river three times a day.

The steam calliope of the big boat played "Way Down Yonder in New Orleans" and shot white plumes of steam into the air with each note, shrill carnival tones audible all the way back to the Quarter. A thick and widespread crowd roiled around the waterfront as a Dixieland band on a stand near the boat's ticket booth played some tune that could be heard only when the calliope paused, the banjos and trombones no match for the power of the steam organ.

"Who are all those people?" Angie said.

"Some street party. Around here, it doesn't take much excuse. Probably Blanche Dubois's birthday or something."

We could walk along the promenade through the crowd down to the Riverwalk. We'd call a taxi from there; I'd pick up the truck later. The calliope stopped playing and the last piercing notes reverberated over the open space along the river. As we stepped across the narrow steel rails, Angie pulled at my sleeve.

"Look at that streetcar coming toward us." She pointed back toward Jax Brewery.

"What about it?"

"Standing beside the driver. Isn't that . . ."

"Yeah, hell, yeah. That's him."

"My, God!" Angie said. "He's got a gun on the driver."

We dashed toward the crowd and slipped into an opening at

the edge. We weaved our way to the middle of the revelers. I peeked back toward the tracks through a group of costumed men dressed like Las Vegas showgirls. Couldn't see him, but the street-car he commandeered had passed by when we were blending into the street party; he might have jumped off, might have ridden on by.

I looked for him in the crowd, but there were too many colors, too much movement. A prickling sensation ran up the base of my neck and spread out below my scalp, raising my hair. Was he near? Behind that clump of people? Ready to spring?

"It's too far to run to the Riverwalk," I said. "Too much open space if he's around."

She looked around and shuddered. "I can feel him."

A low blast rose from the steam whistle of the *Natchez*, that unmistakable riverboat song, climbing in pitch, the last call for boarding.

"Come on," I said.

We zigzagged through the crowd toward the ticket booth. Half-way there Angie sucked in a loud breath and jerked my hand. I spun around, my right hand in a hard fist, my left one pulling her around to my backside.

"What is it?" I said.

"Somebody grabbed my arm."

"Grabbed it like they were pulling you?"

"Just grabbed it, okay? Let's get out of here."

We ran through the maze six or eight steps at a time. At the ticket booth I handed Angie a twenty to buy our tickets. I stayed on my toes with my back to Angie, checking out the rear flank. I jumped when she tapped my shoulder with the tickets.

The celebration sheltered us from open view as we snaked through the dancing crowd. We hurried up the gangplank, trying to make ourselves small. We stepped inside to the main dining room, avoiding the outside deck in case he was still on the riverbank. The inside staircase toward the stern led up two flights to the very top, the Texas deck. While ascending the stairs, we felt steady engine vibrations through the steel floor as the boat pulled away from the dock.

Sunlight bounced off the white deck as we walked to the rail, swaying on uncertain landlubber legs, dizzy from the sensation of movement of the big boat. Behind us, the paddle wheel churned forward, as wide as the boat and rising a full twenty feet over the waterline. Each paddle was as big as a roadside billboard. The foaming water cascaded off the broad boards with a loud, sloshing noise, raising a thick mist that rainbowed in the sun and floated up to us, glazing the top deck, smelling faintly of mud and decayed river vegetation.

"You still want lunch?" I said.

"You were right. We shouldn't have left the motel."

"Look at it this way; we've worked up an appetite."

We stood side by side, leaning on the side rail and looking down at the dancing throng as we sailed away from them. I took a deep breath, held it, and let it out slowly. The soothing splashing of the paddle wheel slowed my pulse. The little red streetcars looked like toys as they rolled along the riverbank toward the Quarter, the faint clanging of their bells fading as we sailed away.

"I wonder if he's in that crowd," Angie said. She leaned forward and rested her elbows on the rail.

"Maybe he's looking at us right now," I said. "Why don't you wave to him?"

It was the first time I had ever seen Angie smile. It struck me the same way Barb's smile had.

She straightened to her full height and raised her arm high and moved it from side to side in a wide arc, a classic *bon voyage* wave.

"So long, homeboy!" she shouted.

"You be goin' somewhere, bitch?"

His gold tooth gleamed as pointed his .357 casually in our direction. The gun told me he was Mouton's muscle, nothing more. A pro carries a .22 with a silencer, not some cannon. I knew we had a chance.

"You've outsmarted yourself." I stepped in front of Angie.

"What you talkin' 'bout, man?"

"You're on a riverboat, fool. You pull that trigger and you got five armed security guards on your ass and a police squad waiting for you at the dock."

The corners of his mouth turned down and a flash of uncertainty swept across his eyes as he planned his next step.

"There's nowhere to go." I spoke with the soft tones I would use with a snarling dog.

He ran the tip of his tongue across his lips and swallowed. I took a step toward him and he stepped back.

"What do you want?" I said.

"The negatives, man. You stay where you are."

I stepped sideways, Angie close behind me, my eyes locked with his as we circled like two cautious boxers in a ring. Angie eased toward the storage bin at the corner of the deck, the only cover around. I sensed her stepping back, peeling away from us.

"You can't get us here," I said.

"Shut up, man."

I edged closer to him with each side step, keeping my eyes fixed on his, peering deep into his tiny black pupils, tightened by the sunlight to pinholes. He locked in on my stare, and we moved in a slow and heedful waltz, each footstep inching us closer together.

"You pull that trigger, you're dead meat. We're in the middle of the river, a boat filled with people. What are you planning to do when they start coming up here?"

"Shut up!"

"Any minute now somebody's going to come up those stairs over there. You plan to shoot them?"

We had rotated a quarter turn in our moving standoff. Angie had slipped over to the storeroom, a nearly forgotten onlooker as we squared off. Atop the storeroom sat the brass ship's whistle, big as a water heater, its pull chain running down into a hole in the deck that led to the pilothouse. In our stare down I caught a peripheral glance of Angie, over to our side, wrapping her hand around the chain.

She yanked it straight down with all her might.

The whistle's scream knifed through our ears. It startled him; he reflexively snapped his head toward it. I whipped my hand forward and popped the gun. It slid across across the slick deck and over the side. He spun with a roundhouse left. I blocked with my right and cracked a left jab square into his face, watering his eyes. He lashed out, a blind stab wide to the left. I snatched a handful of shirt and slammed my fist under his chin. He staggered back two steps and hit the stern rail. I rushed him and crouched for leverage. I smashed him in the jaw, aiming my punch all the way to the back of his skull. It flipped him over the rail.

I leaned over and looked into the churning paddle wheel and the cloudy white spray of water. He was gone, plunged into the swirling undertow of the swift, brown river. Angie came to me and peered down at the gigantic wooden blades.

"Is he dead?" she asked.

"Gotta be. Just hitting one of those paddles could have killed him. Then he got pushed below the surface sixty or eighty feet. This river runs so fast, if a deep current got him he won't surface for miles. He hits a snag down there and he may never come up."

We stood in silence, leaning forward against the steel stern rail, searching the foaming, white wake. He never came up. The boat rushed past a huge, bare tree branch from upriver, gliding on a rapid current toward the Gulf. We followed its downriver run for a few minutes.

Angie turned to me. "How many more are out there?"

TWENTY-FIVE

W e sat cross-legged on the bed in her room and ate carry-out pizza. The window unit roared and pumped out ice-cold air that condensed on the vent and fogged a plate-size circle on the window where one of the air streams caromed off it. The waxing orange moon cast a long, crisp line across the parking lot, the shadow of the roofline of the motel's office. We needed a few laughs, so we watched Andy Griffith. It was that one where Barney deputizes Otis and Gomer, but we couldn't get into it.

After eating, I started watching a debate on the crime bill of the month on C-SPAN, and Angie worked the *New York Times* crossword puzzle in the *Times Picayune*. She stared at it for three or four minutes and set it aside on the bed.

"I've been thinking about this tape," she said. "Are you sure it's Mouton who's looking for it?"

"No doubt about it."

"Who else could want it?"

"What are you thinking?"

She pulled an envelope out of her suitcase and tossed it on the bed in front of me. Printed across the top was the Coastliner Ice Company logo, the royal blue letters CIC shaped into an oval.

"Mom and Dad had the mail from Barb's box forwarded to them in Michigan. They sent this to me. It's a letter from Toulouse that came after Barb died."

It was a handwritten note on a plain white sheet of paper.

> Barb,
> Hide that tape and dont tell nobody you got it. To

many know about it. Im out of town a few days. Call
you when I get back.

                                        Toulouse

"Sounds like he had left the tape with Barb for safekeeping," I
said. "For some reason he got worried about it."

"I wonder how many people knew about it?" she said.

"Toulouse seemed to think it was too many. But I can tell you
that Barb never realized there was anything unusual about it."

"Why do you say that?"

"She didn't hide it; it was out in plain view. She didn't know
it was any big deal. This letter came after she died. She never knew
that the tape could put her in danger."

Angie read the note again.

"If Toulouse told anybody in Bay Saint Louis about that tape,
it wasn't Rickey Dee," I said. "If he had known she had any tape
and he wanted it, he would have gone to Barb's apartment. He
may have been the only person besides Barb who knew about her
new place."

"If Rickey Dee didn't know about it, who did Toulouse tell?"

"Toulouse was a cokehead," I said. "He could have told Mouton himself and not remembered doing it."

She held up a photograph and stared at it and sank to the edge
of her bed. "She wasn't just some worthless junkie," she whispered. "She had people who loved her."

Angie turned her face toward the wall, then covered her face
with her hands. Her shoulders quivered and I could hear the
small, stifled sound of tears. It pinched my heart and I sat,
wooden, awkward, until I couldn't stand it anymore. I stepped
around the bed and sat beside her. I rubbed my hand lightly across
her shoulders.

"It's OK to cry, Angie."

She turned, her eyes red and wet with tears. She reached her
arms around me and buried her face into my chest. "She was
alone, Jack," she whimpered. "Nobody to help her. God, she had
to be scared."

I held her tight against me and she started crying hard and

loud, and she cried until it was all out, all the hurt of the past two weeks, all the pain she hadn't shown, the pain I had sometimes wondered if she felt. I felt her soften in my arms.

When the sobbing was done, when the quivering stopped, she lay back on the bed, pulling me down beside her. She lay half on top of me and pressed the side of her face high on my chest.

"Just hold me . . . ," she said.

I felt each beat of her heart, each tiny shaking when she sobbed, each sniff, each little gulp, each warm exhalation against my throat. I smelled her hair as it brushed against my chin; I heard her whimper. A heated teardrop fell on my neck. My pulse raced through my head and my breathing quickened. I started to speak, but she put her finger to my lips to close them.

"Don't leave me alone," she whispered. "Not tonight . . ."

TWENTY-SIX

Maurice had set up by the iron gate of the park across the way from Saint Louis Cathedral and close enough to the Pontalba that I could smell the soft-shell crabs. The act lasted a well-planned ten minutes, short enough to hold the audience. For the finale, he placed a trick collar around the throat of some grandmother with a camera around her neck and ran a sword through it. Pretty good material.

I sat behind him and to his left, under the covered walkway of the Cabildo Museum. When the show ended, the crowd clapped and Maurice quickly passed his cigar box around for their quarters and dollars, cajoling some, shaming others, milking every cent out of the twenty tourists he had just entertained.

As the crowd scattered, I walked toward him across the expanse of dark gray slate. I flushed a covey of pigeons, which fluttered straight up, soared to the cathedral's steeple, dived in formation toward the lawn inside the fence, pulled up, and lighted on General Jackson. Maurice was separating the coins by denomination into the corners of the cigar box, keeping his eyes on the loot. I stopped beside him and dropped in a twenty.

"Ready to earn that?"

Maurice looked up at me, shielding the sun from his eyes with his hand.

"Don't stand here." There was urgency in his voice. "Go over to the Cabildo—inside. I'll be there in a minute."

I turned on my heels, walked back to the Cabildo, and went inside as he had said. Three or four minutes later, Maurice walked past me and jerked his head toward the rear of the building, a silent command to follow him. There were few other people in the old museum and we found a musty display room in the corner.

"Buster, what the hell you done, man?"

"What do you mean?"

"Mouton's after you."

"I'm aware of that."

"Word's out on the street; he wants you alive."

"That's good to know."

"He find you, you won't stay that way long. What's the deal, man?"

"Mouton sent two of his enforcers to work me over the other night."

"Why he do that?"

"I've got something he wants bad. They were trying to beat it out of me. Somebody spooked them and they ran away."

"You still got what he's after?"

"That's the only reason I'm still alive. They'll keep coming, Maurice. You got to tell me who they are."

Maurice reached for my chin and turned my head to the side. He winced at the blue-and-purple bruises. "You get a good look at these guys?"

"No. It was dark and they knocked me out. My vision was blurred, but I can describe at least one of them. He has a gold tooth." I pointed to my right front tooth.

"That's Truman Tyrone," Maurice said. "Tall? Little, thin mustache?"

"That's him. Or at least was him."

"Was?"

"Truman fell off a riverboat and drowned."

"I ain't heard nothin' about that."

"Nobody else knows it, Maurice. You need to keep it extra quiet."

He nodded. "Who was the second guy?"

"Not so tall. A good bit heavier. Had a high-pitched voice."

"That's what I figured," Maurice said. "Had big arms, big forearms, right? That's Popeye, like the sailor."

"What's his story?"

"He got his own territory. He work Armstrong Park. Truman be on the docks down to the river."

"Did he have the Comus Bar?"

"Yeah, you right. The Comus, that's Truman's," he said. "He sets up at a table way in the back."

"Another tradition down the tubes," I said. "How about this Popeye?"

"Stay outta Popeye's way, Buster. He real bad."

"I'm trying to, but I need to know where he hangs out."

"That don't sound like staying out of his way to me."

"I can't leave the city or they'll revoke my bond. Popeye'll be back, and somebody'll take Truman's place. I've got to dodge them for a while, but to do that I need to know where they stay."

"Go hide somewhere."

"I got things I need to do. I can't just stay holed up."

"You got to," he said. "This thing Mouton wants that you still got . . ."

"I can't tell you . . ."

". . . I don't want to know. What I be thinking, why don't you just give it to him?"

"He'd still be after me."

Maurice studied my face once more. "Man, whatever you done, you got Mouton out of retirement, that's for sure."

"Which reminds me," I said, "how much do you know about voodoo?"

"I grew up here in the Quarter. I know it all."

"The other night, while Truman and Popeye were waiting for me, they set this up in the room." I handed him the photographs that Josh had taken of the box, the candles, and the incense.

Maurice looked at the top photograph and his jaw went slack. He studied all four shots, shaking his head from side to side. When he got to the shot of the three inscriptions, he sucked in a quick breath.

"*Maître!*"

"What did you say?

"Look here, Buster." Maurice pointed to one of the inscriptions. "That's the sign of *Maître.*"

"Who's *Maître?*"

"He's a voodoo leader, a . . . what you call it?"

"I don't know, Maurice. You mean like a god?"

"No, man. *Maître* not a god. He like a guide. He helps the voodoo."

"Helps it do what?"

"Buster, it like this. The voodooine calls up *Maître*, and he help her power."

"You mean like some kind of patron saint?"

"Yeah, man. That's it. *Maître, Carrefour, Grand Bois*—these be they signs." Maurice pointed to each symbol on the side of the box as he called the name it represented. "This box is a coffin. It was concentrated. Look here." He pointed to a discoloration on the box. "That damnation oil—they anointed this coffin with damnation oil." He held the photo to the light. "These candles, Buster. Were they burning when you saw this mojo?"

"Mojo?"

"This coffin, man. It called a Mojo hand. It be like a magic charm. Those candles, were they burning?"

"No, they had burned down. But they were burning when I first walked in. I could smell them. I smelled candles and incense."

He kept looking at the photograph. "How 'bout this incense? Was it burning, too?"

"Yeah. Like I said; I smelled the smoke."

He handed the photo back to me. "That mean the coffin was concentrated on the spot. Truman and Popeye did it. It wasn't *Mère* Marie."

"She didn't do it?"

"She made it, but she didn't concentrate it."

"What does that mean?"

"She put a root on you, Buster."

"A root?"

"A hex. Hex, root, same thing. She wasn't there. That mean the spell maybe ain't too strong. Maybe it can be reversed."

"I'm just asking what the spell is. What does it mean?"

"It's the coffin spell. Turn the dead against the living. Worst kind, Buster. You got to reverse it or you'll die." Maurice narrowed his eyes. "You been feelin' awright lately?"

"No, I've been feeling awful. My face is sore and my gut aches . . ."

"Uh-huh." Maurice nodded.

"But it doesn't have anything to do with a curse. Mouton's men beat the crap out of me."

Maurice wiped his face with his palm, took a deep breath, and blew it out hard. "You got to reverse this spell, man."

"If it'll make you feel better, let's do it. How do I reverse this thing?"

Maurice frowned. I instantly felt bad about patronizing him. "This is serious; I ain't kiddin' around." He spoke slowly, "You use a pink candle and uncrossing oil. Get some uncrossing powder and sprinkle it into the flames. Gotta be done jus' right."

"I don't know anything about this uncrossing powder."

"I get it for you. This spell came from *Mère* Marie. You need to get the powder and the oil from a voodooine. You got to get somebody as strong as *Mère* Marie."

"Who's that?" I asked. "You?"

"Don't dis the voodoo. Not now. That new voodooine, I'll find her. She called Olivia. If she can reverse *Mère* Marie's coffin spell, she might get to be the new queen."

"Are you saying I may become the battleground to determine if the new voodoo queen's time has come? Is that what you're saying?"

"Yeah."

"And for Mouton's mother to win, I've got to die?"

"It look that way."

"No, thanks, Maurice. Don't you think he's got enough reason to kill me already?"

"You gonna die anyhow if you don't get that spell uncrossed."

"How will I die?"

"You'll get weak and sick. You'll jus' die."

"Somehow that sounds better than being carved up by Popeye or whoever else Mouton sends after me."

"You still don't believe me, do you? You already got pains, don't you? I'm tellin' you, man, this Olivia, she can beat *Mère* Marie."

"Tell her to mix up some powder."

"But she gotta go to where you stay, five straight days."

"I'm not telling anybody where I'm staying. Nobody."

He stared at me. "Don't wait too long. She gotta start *now*."

"I'll have to take the chance."

Six or eight tourists walked into the display room and we stopped talking. I didn't like the turn our conversation had taken, and when the tourists walked in it was a good time to break it off.

"I've got to go," I said. "Why don't you leave and I'll hang around long enough so nobody will put us together. Thanks for the line on Popeye."

"I'll find Olivia."

"Get some powder for me, okay?"

"You got to get help, Buster."

He started to walk off, but he turned and got close enough to whisper to me. "One more thing. It wasn't Mouton who killed Toulouse."

"How do you know that?"

"Them candles. I hear they was white. Mouton know better. The candles shoulda been black. Like the ones they used on you."

TWENTY-SEVEN

Her room had taken on that female atmosphere of hair sprays, perfumes, and powders. A hair dryer on the counter of the bathroom, a makeup mirror, and four pairs of shoes, neatly lined up on the closet floor. She had spread these things throughout her room and it looked as if she had lived there for years, as if a woman, by her mere presence, added a quality and air of home.

In my room, I was down to my last pair of clean underwear, yesterday's pizza carryout box was on the dresser, and my clothes were still in the suitcase.

"Did you see your friend?" she asked, as she plugged in her hair dryer. She was in a robe and had just showered.

"I did. I got the name of Mouton's goon who chased us around the Quarter."

"Did your friend say anything new about Mouton?"

"He said Mouton's mother has put a root on me and it's going to kill me."

"What's a root?"

"A hex. A voodoo curse. She's the reigning queen of voodoo in New Orleans."

"Like sticking pins in a voodoo doll or something? Do you feel any sharp pains?"

"Several."

"Well, it must be working. Did he know anymore about the murders?"

"He said Mouton didn't do it. The candles near Toulouse's body were white. The voodoo curse calls for a black candle."

"Toulouse and Barb were stabbed. They didn't die from any curse."

"Maurice may be right. Mouton takes this voodoo very seriously."

"Humph!" she sniffed. She flipped on the hair dryer.

I lay back, my head sinking in the softness of the pillow, and I watched Angie as she leaned forward to the hair dryer. It tossed her hair in the sunshine that slanted through the open window, wreathing her head in a halo of light. The electric drone of the dryer weighed down on my eyes as I slipped into the netherworld just before sleep. I didn't know if I had been there for minutes or hours when Angie laid her hand on my cheek and I flinched just enough to wake myself up.

"I didn't mean to startle you," she said.

"It's okay. I was drifting off."

"You've had a tough couple of days. We both have." She stroked the bruise on my face. "What do we do now?"

"There's nothing we can do today. I'm waiting for Mouton to make his move. If he doesn't give the cops a name by tomorrow, I go to the U.S. attorney. Until then we wait."

She put her head on my chest and we lay for a few minutes in silence and warm sanctuary from the exhaustion and fear of the days just past. Soon Angie rose and looked down at me. The corners of her eyes crinkled as her face lightened with a faint smile. She sighed and stretched and broke the spell.

She sat at the foot of the bed and opened the newspaper. I punched the remote control to the weather channel just in time to catch the temperatures and rainfall levels in southern Europe and northern Africa. After the weatherman showed the storms and heat waves around the rest of the world and got back to north Africa, I started thumbing through a folder that lay on Angie's bed.

It held a stack of papers, letters, photographs, and cancelled checks that had come from Barb's apartment. The phone bill showed a dozen calls to a Bay Saint Louis number, probably Rickey Dee's. I memorized it—it could come in handy and was probably unlisted. There were three letters from Angie, all with a

Detroit postmark. A couple of menus from carryout places. She favored Chinese. A dozen photographs, recent ones, from various places around New Orleans. Riverwalk, Mardi Gras, the Superdome. Barb and some friends, none of whom I recognized, smiling and laughing. There was the picture of Barb and Toulouse on the stern rail of that big boat, the same picture I had seen before. A few ticket stubs from Saints games.

When she finished reading the paper, Angie sat on the edge of the bed across from me. She picked up the various scraps of Barb's life that I was thumbing through and examined them one by one, smiling at some, sighing about others.

One of them caught her attention, some association was made, and her eyes disengaged and took on that unmistakable look of a daydreamer. After four or five seconds, she closed her eyes and swallowed hard.

"Angie, are you alright?"

"It was one of Barb's poems," she said. "She was really a good poet. She won a contest up at Ann Arbor." Angie rested her face in her hands.

"Angie . . ."

She looked up with moist eyes. "You know, yesterday was the first time I cried for Barb."

"There's no one right way to handle grief or loss."

"You must have thought I was the coldest person you ever saw."

"Maybe you need to get away from this for a while."

She picked up the photograph of Barb and Toulouse on the boat. She gazed at it for a few seconds. The gaze hardened into a stare. She sat up and held it out before her with both hands.

"I knew it! I knew I recognized something about that guy who broke in your house." She held the photo in front of me and pointed to Toulouse. "Look at this!"

"It was Toulouse?"

"No! You remember I said it seemed like I had seen him before? It wasn't the *man* I had seen. It was this."

She pointed to it, and it struck me, too.

And I knew who the killer was.

TWENTY-EIGHT

It wasn't the *man* I had seen before," Angie said. "It was that medallion. The man who broke into your house was wearing that damned, gaudy medallion."

The medallion now seemed to be the biggest thing in the picture. That garish gold coin with an emerald circled by diamonds.

"The greedy bastard stole it from a dead man," I said.

"Who did?"

"Bruno. He was wearing that medallion when he shot up the Comus," I said.

"Bruno?"

"Rickey Dee's foreman at the icehouse."

I sat on the edge of the bed and called the front desk to turn on the long-distance line. I made a credit card call and got Neal at his office.

"Neal, can you find out what kind of car our buddy Bruno drives?"

"I see him driving around all the time. It's a Cadillac, a fairly new Coupe deVille. Why?"

"What color is it?"

"Dark blue. He keeps it polished. I guess those icehouse boys wash it three or four times a week. You want to buy it or something?"

"The police reports when they interviewed my friend Tony, the night clerk at the TimeSaver? Didn't he say a car pulled around to the blind side of the store, but nobody ever came in?"

"He said people pull back there to take a leak. It happens all the time and he didn't pay much attention to it. Said it was a shiny, dark car. He couldn't remember what kind of tag it had. Couldn't remember anything unusual about it."

"You remember when I told you about seeing Bruno shoot up the Comus Bar?" I said. "I got a real good look. He was wearing a medallion. Angie and I were looking at a photograph of Toulouse and he was wearing the same medallion."

"Jack, they probably make those a thousand at a time in Hong Kong and sell 'em at the French Market for five bucks apiece."

"No, this is real gold. It's heavy and it's got a dull shine," I said. "Angie says the guy who broke into my place was wearing that same medallion. It's Bruno, Neal."

Angie laid the photo on the bed and stared at the medallion. "How would he know about the tape?"

"Toulouse probably told him," I said, "or let it slip. Maybe that's what he meant when he said too many people know about it."

"What was Bruno going to do with it?"

"Maybe give it to Rickey Dee and they could send the competition to jail. Maybe, but I doubt it. He probably thought he could blackmail Mouton."

"Why would he have killed Barb?"

"Maybe Bruno knew she had the tape, and he didn't want Rickey Dee to know about it. Didn't want to split any blackmail money. He might have thought he would kill her and then steal the tape. Of course, it could be that Rickey Dee really did order her killed. If that's what happened, he would have sent Bruno to do it. Either way, it was Bruno."

"Let's call the cops," she said.

"We can't. There's no way the New Orleans cops could get Artis Wade to arrest one of Rickey Dee's men, even if they buy our story. And I don't know that they'd buy it."

"Why not?"

"I'm the one with the murder weapon in my truck and my blood on the floor of Barb's apartment. So I go to the cops, what am I going to say? Hey, I didn't do it, that other guy did? Won't fly, darlin'."

"Well, what are we going to do?"

"We've got to get Bruno to come here and confess."

I figured I'd use a trap that had already been baited.

TWENTY-NINE

"W hy don't I wait for you out here?"

"They don't bite," I said. "It's not even noon. They're just in there getting everything set up."

"The strippers?"

"The bartenders and maids. Come on. I need you to listen to whatever Candy's got to say. I promise you, everybody's got their clothes on."

We had dropped in on the Quarter before it had a chance to clean up. Its walls, set only a sidewalk's breadth from the streets, resounded with the slams and bumps of garbage trucks lifting the Dumpsters and dropping them back onto the sidewalks. The stench of last night's decayed food and sewage wafted from the gutters and drew low clouds of fruit files. We stood in the middle of Bourbon Street in front of Gator's and Angie was being stubborn.

"How do you know this woman?" she asked.

"Candy was a stripper here until two years ago. I worked a case undercover as a bartender in there and got to know her then. We worked together, you might say."

"I thought you said she owns the place."

"She does. The owners were busted for receiving stolen property. When the bar was auctioned off, Candy bought it."

Angie looked the building over like she was afraid it would collapse on her if she walked in. I grabbed her hand.

"I need for you to hear this." I pulled her toward the door. "If you want to leave once you meet her, you can."

Gator's was getting a face-lift. Painters high on a scaffold scraped flaky paint on the eaves and wire brushed plaster off the bricks. They had already repainted the ornate cornice at the roof-line, and there was a sweet and heavy smell of paint.

The door was propped open and a box fan blew Lysol-scented air out into the street. When we walked in, a canister vacuum whined as a fat maid cleaned the floor near the door.

Candy stood beside the bar toward the front, her back to us, legal pad in one hand and pencil in the other. She wore a dark green, sequined cocktail dress, slit high up her left leg, and her auburn hair was in a French braid. But Candy's stance and movements were no longer those of a stripper. She had become a business owner. The Establishment in a push-up bra.

The vacuum shut off and whirred down to a stop, and the maid looked up at us. "You got customers, Miz Candy."

"Sorry, folks, we don't open today until . . ." She turned to us. "Buster! Come in, darlin'. " She smiled and walked to us. She kissed me on the cheek and held out her hand to Angie. "I'm Candide. Folks call me Candy."

"I'm Angie." Angie spoke in a small, shy voice and shook Candy's hand.

"Are you a friend of Buster's?"

Angie looked at me with a question on her face.

"Buster is the name I used when I was working here under-cover. Candy still calls me that."

"I like it," Candy said. "I've never met a bad Buster yet. Y'all come on over and have a seat. Maggie, would you bring us some coffee?"

"That would be nice. Thank you," Angie said, not quite as timid.

We sat around a small but sturdy round table near the stage. It had to be sturdy; Gator's is "Home of the Five-Dollar Table Dance." Angie's eyes roamed the cavernous room when she thought I wasn't looking.

"Place looks real good, Candy," I said. "Real good."

She smiled at the compliment. "Well, it might be sleazy, but it doesn't have to be dirty," she said. "Did you see what I'm doing to the outside? It's gonna look real good when I get it painted. Hell, this place had gotten so run-down even the drunks didn't want to come in. You keep a dirty place, you attract nothin' but scumbags, and I ain't just talking about customers. I'm so sick of these low-class coke whores nowadays. God, they'd get it on with a pig if they needed a fix..." She stopped in midsentence and looked at Angie. It was the first time I could remember seeing Candy embarrassed. "What I mean is, I want a decent place where boys can be boys. I'm not interested in sickos or perverts or druggies. I want my girls to feel safe and put on a good show."

"I noticed you kept the name," I said. "I thought you'd call it Candy's Gentlemen's Club or something like that."

"Buster, people can say a lot about me, but nobody can say I ain't honest. I see all these joints calling theirselves gentlemen's clubs. If they had a bunch of gentlemen going into them, why the hell you think they'd be hiring all those bouncers?"

Angie laughed and leaned close to me. "I like her," she whispered.

"Candy, I said, "you remember telling me that Bruno used to come in here?"

"Who?"

"The guy you said used to come in here with Toulouse Caron."

"Oh, yeah. Bruno. He used to come in here. Mean as hell. You know some of these girls used to hustle some on the side out of those booths over there."

Angie looked at the booths.

"Honey, for the right price a john could go to one of those booths and get an Oval Office special. I made them cut that out, at least in here. Don't need no more of that hassle. Anyway, Bruno comes in here one night and picks up this girl who's been here two or three weeks. She was from Alabama somewhere. I told her not to go off with him—I can spot that kinda trouble a mile off— but she said what she did after work was her business . . ." Candy tapped a cigarette on the table, lit it, and leaned back, blowing a long plume of gray smoke. "He took her to one of those hot-sheet joints on Highway 90, the Crescent City or something like that."

"Crescent City Courts?" Angie asked.

Candy stared at her, her eyebrows up a bit.

"Yeah, that's the name. *You* know that place?"

Angie glanced at me and blinked her eyes downward, her face reddening.

"I pointed it out to Angie when we drove in from Bay Saint Louis," I said. "I told her what you had said about the place."

"Does she know Bruno or something?" Candy asked.

"The girl who was murdered was Angie's sister," I said.

She turned to Angie. "I'm sorry, honey. That was just awful. Do y'all think Bruno was in on it?"

"I think there's a good chance he killed both Barb—that was her name—and Toulouse. That's why we're here. Go on and finish telling us what he did out at Crescent City Courts."

"What he did was cuff her to the bed and beat the shit out of her. He's a bondage freak. You know, handcuffs, ropes, all that. She must have struggled or resisted or something else that set him off. She's lucky he didn't kill her. I went to see her in the hospital. One eye was swollen shut, her face was purple; I mean her whole face. He'd knocked some teeth loose and cracked two ribs. Hell, her nose was broken. It was bad." Candy flicked some ashes from her cigarette and examined my face. She had not noticed the bruises earlier in the dim light. "You don't look so good yourself, Buster."

"An unfortunate misunderstanding. I'll tell you about it sometime."

"Uh-huh . . . well, I never saw that girl again. I guess she went back to Alabama. Then the next week here comes Bruno right back in here like nothing had happened. I got out my Glock and ran his ass off—permanently. Now he goes across the street to the Roman Orgy. Goes every Saturday, regular as clockwork."

"So he'll be there tonight?"

"Just after dark, around eight o'clock, he'll go in there and pick up Lola for their usual Saturday night date. Lola, she's not so smart, but she's real pretty. Got curly hair and dyes it red. They drive to Crescent City Courts for a bondage session. Handcuffs, leg irons . . ."

"How do you know this?" Angie asked.

"Honey, she tells me herself. Lola comes in here with Christi, who works for me. They're roommates. What Lola don't tell me, Christi does."

"I've got to know something," I said. "What do they do; and how long do they stay?"

"They play 'tie me up, tie me down' for two hours. She gets a buck-fifty."

"You mean she does that stuff for two hours for a dollar and fifty cents?" Angie's mouth was wide open. Candy looked at her like she had asked who was president of the United States.

"That means one hundred and fifty dollars," I said.

Candy laughed out loud. "Honey, I been around here so long I forget what real people talk like."

"Why do they go to the same place every week?" I asked.

"They got a reason." Candy crushed her cigarette into the ashtray. "It's specialized. You got some places that have plastic sheets so they can pour Mazola or whatever on each other. Some got waterbeds and mirrors on the ceilings. This place specializes in S and M."

"What?" Angie was lost in an unfamiliar world.

"Sadism and masochism," I said. "It's where a person . . ."

"I know what it is," Angie snapped.

Candy chuckled and sipped her coffee. "Actually, it's not the whole motel. It's just this one room. The last one on the second floor all the way at the back end of the building. I guess they put it way down there because of all the noise."

Angie winced. "Oh, God . . ."

"Yeah. I don't get into that stuff either," Candy said.

"Christi and Lola say the place has whips, cuffs, chains—anything to warm a bondage freak's heart. And the bed, it's solid iron and bolted to the floor."

"Candy, this is real important. Has Lola ever told you exactly what they do? I mean step by step."

"Yeah. She says it's the same thing every Saturday. They get high on whatever's handy and strip down. He slaps her around, sometimes with a whip. Then he cuffs her wrists to the headboard. She says he really gets into the movies while this is going on. When he gets worked up, he gets in back of her . . ."

"And she's in cuffs all this time?" Angie broke in.

"She's cuffed to the headboard."

"Any of this stuff on him?" I asked. "Cuffs? Chains?"

"No, just on her."

"You know who runs the place?" I said.

"Old pervert named Charlie Petro. You probably remember him, they call him Dirty Charlie. Used to run that adult book store a couple of blocks down. Cops got on his case pretty bad about something, and he sold out."

"Old guy?" I asked. "Wrinkled, kinda bad teeth?"

"That's him."

"Does he have security?"

"At the motel? Are you kidding? He sits up there drunk behind that bullet-proof glass and watches TV all night. He's got one of those slide-out cash drawers where cars drive up after hours. Hell, World War III could break out and he'd never know it. Wouldn't care."

"Sounds good," I said.

"What in the hell you planning to do, Buster?"

"I need to ask Bruno a few questions, and I need to ask them here in Louisiana. I've had trouble lining up a regular appointment with him," I said. "And I'd like for it to be a surprise, okay?" I put my forefinger to my lips.

"You might like to know one more thing in that case. Bruno doesn't carry a gun. Guns mean hard time. He carries a knife—and he knows how to use it."

Angie pushed her chair back from the table and looked to the side, her eyes focused on some place far beyond the walls of the Gator. She tilted her head forward and stared without focus at the floor.

THIRTY

We waited at a table off the sidewalk in the courtyard of Houlihan's, half a block down and across the street from the Roman Orgy. We ordered Perriers just often enough to keep the waiter from asking us to leave and scanned the sidewalks for Bruno. The sky darkened as the last sliver of sunset slipped below an unseen swampy horizon somewhere over Cajun country to the west. The neon glow of Bourbon Street rose in reciprocation so that darkness never came and never would.

The revelers came one or two at a time at first. Then they came in groups, and soon a constant flow paraded by, sipping beer and daiquiris from plastic cups. Some of them paused at the open doors of the strip joints, a few working up the nerve to go in, most content with the naughty thrill of a peek.

"Jack, that tall guy down there." Angie pointed toward Canal Street to a light-skinned black man in sunshades. "Is that him?"

He wore a blue, open-collar shirt with pirate sleeves, yellow-tinted sunshades, and gold chains around his neck. When he walked closer I saw it, even from across the street—the golden coin medallion from the dead Toulouse.

"Go to the truck and wait for me," I said.

"I want to go in." Her eyes locked on Bruno as he nodded to the doorside barker and walked in.

"Go to the truck."

"Why?"

"When you walked into Gator's this morning, you were positively addled and they weren't even opened. There's no way you could keep it in focus in there right now."

"And you can, I suppose? Naked women walking around and you won't be distracted."

"I'm damn near immune to anything I'll see in there. I've seen too much of it before. Besides, if you walk into the Roman Orgy, you'll draw more attention than the girls on the stage. Bruno would spot both of us in a second."

"What makes you think he won't spot you?"

"I'll lay low."

"I could lay low, too."

"You're not going in. Go to the truck and wait for me."

Angie stood and snatched her purse from the ground. She gave me a stormy look. "I'll be in the damn truck." She stomped off, not looking back.

I stepped to the sidewalk and watched her until she'd turned the corner, just to make sure. I crossed the street and skirted around a small crowd of college boys in front of the door.

"Best show in town! . . . Right this way! . . . No cover charge!" The barker ignored me as I walked past him. He was aiming at the college boys, five of them in Arkansas Razorbacks T-shirts, huddled around counting their money, sipping beer from plastic cups, and trying to decide whether to go inside.

"Seat near the front?" The hostess wore a red dress cut to her navel, her huge breasts squeezing out.

"I'll sit in the back."

She walked ahead of me, weaving through the tables and the crowd. I got the last booth in the far corner. It was the darkest and the one farthest from the stage, the best seat to survey the room. The air smelled stagnant, and the booth felt like it needed a good wiping. The red-and-green stage lights diffused through the smoke and dust motes and created the aura of a misty night in a boat channel. I ordered a four-dollar 7UP and rested against the corner where the booth met the wall.

The lights rose on the runway and a baby-faced girl, visibly stoned, in a green satin cocktail dress and uncertain high heels, slipped from behind the stage curtain and began twirling and stripping to some Rod Stewart song, strong on lyrics, weak on rhythm, and a beat or two ahead of her moves. The crowd didn't seem to mind.

Bruno's table was corner stage side, beside the door to the dressing rooms. He drank from a tall glass, gazing at the listless dancer from behind his sunshades. During the dance a girl almost my height, in spike heels and a short white dress, came through that rear door. She had high cheekbones and a narrow face, red hair in long, curling strands down to her shoulders, just as Candy had said.

A waitress set another drink before Bruno and a Long Island Tea on Lola's side of the table. It was automatic; no one had ordered anything. Bruno flipped a bill on the table and the waitress stuffed it in her G-string.

They drank in silence, both watching the jaded dancer above them, and downed their drinks before I could finish my second 7UP. Lola stood and led Bruno in front of the stage and through the crowd toward the front door. I dropped a ten on my table and followed them.

They walked down the sidewalk without talking. Halfway down the block, it was Lola who reached for his hand. I followed a hundred feet back, behind three drunk and laughing convention-eers.

Bruno had parked on the street two blocks toward the river, near the lot where Angie waited. The dark blue Cadillac shone like a tinted mirror under the weak French Quarter streetlights. As he unlocked the passenger-side door, I walked past them un-noticed. Before getting in on the driver's side, Bruno snatched a parking ticket from under his wiper blade, crumpled it into a ball, and threw it across the street.

I jogged across the street to my pickup. Angie was tapping her fingers on the steering wheel. I stopped at the driver's side, keep-ing my eyes on the Cadillac. Bruno's headlights came on and then his brake lights.

"Move over and let me drive," I said.

"I can drive."

"You don't know your way around the city like I do. Move over . . . please."

She huffed and slid across the seat.

"Keep your eye on that dark blue car," I said, as I started the engine.

The Cadillac eased away from the curb, creeping toward Decatur Street. I headed out of the lot and into the street and left my window down. The strong bass tones from the stereo in Bruno's car vibrated all the way back to our truck, and our car seats shimmied in rhythm to the music.

A yellow flicker from a lighter shone through the window of the big car. I didn't figure they were lighting up cigarettes.

Bruno was mean enough when his head was clear . . . I wondered what he would be like on crack.

THIRTY-ONE

W hat exactly are we going to do when we get there?" Angie asked.

"Here's the plan. First, we follow them until we see for sure that they're going to Crescent City Courts. Second, we park at the Alamo Plaza. Third, I walk over to where they are."

She nodded her head, keeping Bruno in sight. "And while you do that, what am I going to do?"

"You're going to wait for me back at the room."

She huffed. "Dammit, Jack! I want to do *something*."

"You want to break down their door and rush them?"

"No."

"You want to take Bruno down while I handle Lola?"

"Don't make fun of me, Jack. You know I can't do stuff like that. Why don't you let me drive the car or something?"

"I won't need a car."

She looked at me for the first time since we'd started tailing Bruno. Her eyebrows were bunched down in a tight knot.

"I'm counting on a couple of things to go right," I said. "Lola's got to be handcuffed to the bed, Bruno can't have a gun, I've got to surprise them . . ."

"What am *I* going to do?"

"I've got to ambush Bruno in that hotel room and make him talk. Ambush means moving fast and hoping things fall into place. Your being in the room is one more thing for me to worry about. I can't risk it."

She glared at me, breathing through her teeth.

"Watch the car, please," I said. I looked straight ahead but felt her scowl.

"You still haven't told me your great plan," she said.

"All right, here it is. I dress in dark clothes, sneak to their room, wait 'til just the right time, and break the door down. I get the jump on Bruno and tell him he's got a choice: he can either tell the cops he killed Barb and Toulouse, or I can tell Mouton who did it and who tried to blame it on him . . ."

She waited for the punch line.

"I'm leaving out some of the details," I said.

"Hmph!" She crossed her arms and looked straight ahead. "Some plan!"

It wasn't much; I'll admit it. Saying it out loud seemed to make it sound even weaker, and that's always a bad sign. But a custom-made gold medallion and a hunch weren't enough to take to the police; they were only enough to make a case against Bruno in my mind. He'd have to talk, and I was hoping that the threat of turning him over to André Mouton would loosen him up.

Not the best plan I've ever made, but it was all I could come up with.

On Interstate 10 we picked up speed and soon we reached the Chef Menteur exit. After a glacial drive past the auto parts stores and discount tobacco shops, we came to the area that had been my temporary, month-long home a couple of weeks earlier.

A long highway block before we reached the Crescent City Courts, Angie and I were caught by a traffic light that Bruno had ignored. His long, dark car drifted into the motel's parking lot. The light changed and we drove by. Bruno was leaning out the window, putting some money into the slide-out drawer.

"The parking lot looked pretty empty," Angie said. Her voice had softened some.

We reached the Alamo Plaza thirty seconds later. I went to my room and slipped on a pair of jeans. They were new and still dark blue. I put on a denim work shirt, black socks, and a pair of black Reeboks. I was lacing up the shoes when Angie walked to the door between our rooms and leaned on the door frame.

"You're not taking a gun?"

"I never use one unless I absolutely have to. If a private investigator shoots at anybody, he ends up doing paperwork for the next six months and is damn lucky if he keeps his license. Besides, Bruno doesn't have one."

"That's what Candy thinks at least."

"She told us which games Lola and Bruno are going to play and which toys they'll use. If she knows that, she knows whether he carries a gun."

"I still don't see how you plan to get the jump on him. Are you planning to knock, or are you just going to ask old Dirty Charlie for a key?"

"I'm going to use this." I held up the glob of soft plastic.

"Silly Putty?"

"Plastic explosive. I keep some in the toolbox. It'll blow the door open like this." I snapped my fingers.

"Won't that attract an awful lot of attention?"

"I'll use just enough to take out the dead bolt. There'll be more noise from the highway than I'll make with this."

"Are you sure?"

"It's one of those job skills I picked up in the army."

I stood up. "Wish me luck."

Angie stepped to me, reached around my chest, and kissed me. I wrapped my arms around her.

"Be careful," she said, then squeezed hard. She turned and walked to the bed. She sat on the edge, biting her lower lip and rubbing her hands.

"I'll be okay." I said.

She tried a smile, but didn't quite make it.

In the toolbox of my pickup I carry glass cutters, crow bars, an extra pistol, and various other handy instruments that would require some tall explaining if the cops ever pull me over. Among these devices is a set of police-issue Peerless handcuffs I picked up at last year's Delta Gun and Knife Expo.

I stuck the cuffs under my belt and started a fast walk up the road to Crescent City Courts. The worn-out neon signs of the ramshackle motels sputtered and glowed and lit my way. Disrespectful cars and trucks roared by me in a constant stream, and a city bus shot a cloud of hot diesel exhaust in my face. An inbound jet rumbled overhead, its turbines winding down as it descended toward Lakefront.

The guest rooms were behind the office in a rectangular building that resembled a shoe box. It was bisected the entire length, and across the middle, by open breezeways, so that there were four blocks of rooms, one in each corner, two stories high. Along the length of each block of rooms were three units, three upstairs and three downstairs. They opened to wide concrete sidewalks which looked out over the parking lot. From what Candy had said, their playroom would be at the rear, upstairs and on the other side of the building.

The only car I saw on the near side was a new black Lexus. In the lower, left-hand corner of the front windshield was the red circle decal of Fox Run, a gated subdivision north of the lake. Some one-night refugee from the brie-and-chablis crowd, out with a hooker for an hour-long waterbed party. Two hours if she'd take American Express.

I ran across the lot to the breezeway in the middle of the building and then through it to the far side. The only vehicle there was parked near the highway, a high-wheeled pickup with rooster tails of dried mud along both sides. To the rear of the building was Bruno's Cadillac. I stepped into the parking lot to get a better angle. The lights were on in the last room on the upstairs floor.

At the rear end of the building, a stairway led ten steps up to a landing, then ten more steps up to the second floor. When I reached the concrete walkway of the second floor, I hugged the wall and stepped lightly to the corner around from Bruno's room.

I heard and felt the vibration of a bass guitar slowly running a reggae scale. It came from their room, either from a TV or a boom box, I couldn't tell. I stepped around the corner and searched the edges of the plate-glass window, hunting a crack where the curtain didn't cover. But they were shut tight, even at the corners.

The music died. Then there were TV voices. Movietime. I heard a girl-squeal, sharp and short, and louder than the television. Had to be Lola. The squeals got louder and came more often. The whip must have come out.

The door was metal but worn at the hinges, the frame near the dead bolt bent a little and scratched, it had been pried open before. Thin shafts of light peeped through where the door and frame weren't quite flush.

I jammed the tiny blasting cap into the walnut-sized glob of plastic explosive, leaving three inches of fuse exposed. I stuck it into the crack near the exposed dead-bolt shaft. I flicked the butane lighter and moved it toward the stiff, green fuse.

Their light went out.

I jumped back around the corner, backed against the wall, and crouched low to get the leverage to slam Bruno good if he came out. My heart pounded. I coiled, ready to spring. I listened for the turning of the door handle.

Instead, I heard Lola. Long, slow, sexy moans. The whip had been set aside. I looked around the edge of the building. The plastic explosive was undisturbed. A blue lambency seeped through the curtains, a soft, flickering glow from the television. Lola kept getting louder, her voice higher, the moans quickening in a mounting rhythm.

I touched the lighter to the fuse. It sputtered as I ducked behind the wall. A flash, then a pop.

I kicked the door open and charged in. Bruno, stoned and stripped, stood beside the bed with both hands still around Lola's waist. The air was thick with the smell of burning cocaine; a clay pipe smoldered in the ashtray by the bed. She was naked and on her knees, her wrists cuffed to the headboard.

I charged and popped my shoulder into Bruno's gut. He doubled over and I hit him with an uppercut on the hinge of his jaw. His head snapped back and he dropped to his knees.

I pushed him to the ground, pulled his arm behind him, and slapped on the handcuffs. I put him in a choke hold and dragged him to the foot of the bed. I pushed his cuffed wrist through the iron bars of the footboard, pulled his other arm in, and cuffed it, too.

I ran to the door, which was still smoking from the blast, and propped it shut with a chair. Bruno lay on the floor at the foot of the bed, dazed and gulping air. Lola screamed and pulled against the headboard. She twisted on to her back and kicked at me, while trying to jerk the iron bar out of the headboard.

"Shut up, Lola!" It surprised her that I knew her name and she shut up.

"Hey, you the mon from the pool." Bruno had pushed up against the end of the bed but still had not caught his breath.

"Bruno, it's decision time," I said. "I know you killed Toulouse Caron . . ."

"You full of shit, mon!"

On the counter of the chest of drawers along the wall was Toulouse's medallion. I grabbed it and held it up, swinging it from the gold chain.

"I'm full of it? Where'd you get this?"

Bruno's eyes flickered. "That don't prove nuttin'. Toulouse give that to me."

"Cut the crap, Bruno. He didn't give you anything. I got a witness who saw you drive up to the place where they found Toulouse's body. It's decision time. I can call the New Orleans police and tell them . . ."

"You outta you mind."

". . . or I can call Mouton and tell him I've got the guy who tried to set him up. Then I let him come pick you up. Both of you."

"NO!" Lola screamed, "DON'T call Mouton! HE did it! He killed that guy! He told me he did!"

"Shut up, bitch!" Bruno tried to stand. I kicked his heels from behind and he plopped back down.

"He told me about it. Call the cops; I'll tell them." She was shaking. "God, don't call Mouton . . ."

"SHUT UP, LOLA!" Bruno shouted.

"Bruno and this other guy—uh, Bobby," she was crying, "yeah, Bobby! They did it! They killed him and dumped the body."

"I'll KILL you! I swear to God!" Bruno shouted over his shoulder.

"Lola," I said, "he means it. He'll kill you. You'd better make sure the cops put him away. Bruno here is going to do the same thing to you that he did to Toulouse if he gets out of this."

"I'll talk! For God's sake, mister, don't call Mouton!"

I stepped to the nightstand and got the key to her handcuffs. I unlocked them and slipped the key into my pocket. Lola jumped to her pile of clothes and raced to get them on.

"Lola, you'd better not run," I said. "If you don't cooperate with the cops and this scumbag gets off, he's going to put you through some real pain. No more of this fun and games. He'll slice you into little pieces and set the pieces out on trotlines."

"I know. I'll talk. Don't worry . . ." She had her dress and shoes on in seconds; didn't bother with the panties or bra. She threw the door open and ran out.

"BITCH!" Bruno yelled after her.

The tapping of her spike heels faded as she ran down the concrete walkway outside. He breathed hard through his mouth and glared at me. "You some kinda cop?" he asked.

"You'd be lucky if I was. I'm the guy they're trying to hang with the other murder you did."

"What other murder?"

"Barb Novak. Toulouse's friend. What's the matter, Bruno? Can't keep up with all the people you've killed?"

I pushed the door shut and sat on the low chest of drawers against the wall. "Oh, that reminds me, Mouton will also be delighted to learn that you're the guy who shot up his place and killed his man Nate."

Bruno bent his head forward and chuckled. "You are so full of shit."

"I was in the bar and I saw it. Me and about six other people."

"I ain't talking about Nate. Screw Nate. I mean the girl. I didn't touch no girl." He took on a sullen tone. "That's what thiz all about. You try to get me to take your fall for killing the girl."

"I know all about the tape. Toulouse screwed up and told you, didn't he. And you went looking for it at Barb's place and then killed her so Rickey Dee wouldn't know about it and you wouldn't have to share any blackmail money."

"You crazy."

"You couldn't find the tape after you killed Barb. You knew I had been there. So you broke into my place looking for it."

"I don' know 'bout no tape. I waz at the office with Rickey Dee that day she got killed—all day."

"You think the cops are going to take your word or Rickey Dee's word about where you were?"

"Hey, we waz with the Immigration people all day. Cops'll believe Immigration, don' you know."

Bruno smirked. When I had walked up to his poolside, Rickey Dee had thought at first I was with Immigration. He had said they had been with them the day before. Bruno knew he had me there.

He followed me with his eyes as I walked back to the bed. I sat next to the phone and started dialing.

"Enjoy the movie." I punched the remote control and turned up the volume.

Bruno had told Lola about one murder; he would have told her about both of them if he had done it. And she was so scared she would have spilled anything she knew. So I was still on the hook for Barb's murder. The last thing I needed was to get tangled up in this mess. I called Josh at home.

"Hello?" I heard loud music and a lot of laughing and shouting.

"Josh?" I talked out of Bruno's earshot.

"I can't hear you," he shouted. "Let me go to another phone."

A few seconds later another phone picked up. "Okay, you can hang it up now." There was a click as somebody hung up the other phone and the line became quiet. "Hello, this is Josh Hallman."

"This is Jack."

"Why are you whispering?"

"I don't want a certain person in this room to hear me."

"My, God, are you at some orgy?"

"That's the television. There's a skin flick playing," I said. "I've got the guy who killed Toulouse. It's Bruno Hebert, Rickey Dee McCoy's foreman. He also killed Nate, the manager of the Comus, the one I told you about."

"Where are you?"

"I'm at the Crescent City Courts out on Old 90."

"Where is this Bruno?"

"He's naked and cuffed to the foot of the bed I'm sitting on. He's down on the floor."

"You're in a hot pillow joint with a naked man handcuffed to bed and a porno flick on TV?" he said. "And they call *me* trange."

"Josh, listen. He confessed to killing Toulouse, and he did it n front of me. There's also another witness. It's the girl he was offing when I broke in on them. He's told her everything and he's ready to talk."

"Sounds good."

"Oh, yeah, he did it all right. He has a medallion in his possession that belonged to Toulouse. And his car is in the parking ot, the same car he used to dump Toulouse's body. I'm sure orensics can come up with something there."

"I take back everything I said about you meddling in the case. This is wonderful."

"There's a problem," I said, "He didn't kill Barb. I'm still on he hook."

"How do you know?"

"I'll explain it later. Right now I need to get the cops to come ick him up, and I don't need to be here when they arrive. Can you call them?"

"Yeah." Josh sounded weary. "I'll call them. I'll try to think of some reason they can hold him."

"How about murder?"

"Are you going to be around to give a statement?"

"I can't. I'm doing some things they don't like for people out on bond to be doing."

"This hooker you mentioned. Where is she?"

"I let her go and she naturally hauled ass. She's scared to death and looking for a place to hide. Her name's Lola. Call Candy Dixon at the Gator; she'll know where to find her."

"It might take all night to track her down. They won't hold Bruno on a phone tip alone."

I set the receiver down and walked over to Bruno's clothes, which were draped over a chair by the closet. I reached into his pants pocket and pulled out a clear plastic Baggie. There was at east an ounce of powdered cocaine.

"He's got enough flake in his pants pocket to do a ten-year stretch."

"That'll do it," Josh said. "I'll tell the cops that they'll get th
details on the murder tomorrow. Come by my office in the morn
ing. I can tell you about that second patrol car while you're there.

"That what?"

"You remember I told you that the niece of the lady across the
street saw a police car drive up to Miss Novak's apartment an
then drive away?"

"I remember."

"According to the niece, an unmarked car with one man in i
drove up a few minutes after you left. The driver was wearing
white shirt and a tie, but this niece says she knows it was a cop.

"How does she know that?"

"She said she could tell from his shoes. Cop shoes, she calle
them. Black, round toes, black rubber heels. Cop shoes. Also, h
had a pistol in a holster and a set of handcuffs on his belt."

"Good thing she saw those shoes," I said. "What did he loo
like?"

"He was big, she said, 'wide.' Big arms, big chest. Said he wa
a white man who had black hair. She didn't get a real good loo
at his face. I called NOPD to see who it was. They said they neve
dispatched any car there other than the squad car they sent t
investigate the murder. There wasn't any unmarked car, at leas
not one that reported in."

"Does your report say what the car looked like?"

"She said it was a four-door sedan with black-wall tires. N
markings. Had a radio antenna mounted on the trunk."

My heart sank.

"What color was this car?" I asked.

THIRTY-TWO

olor?" Josh said. "I'm not sure. Let me check."

My heart pounded as I listened to the rustle of papers on e other end of the line. God, it just couldn't be dark green.

"The niece said the car was blue."

I started breathing again.

"Josh, did she say blue, dark blue, light blue, whatever?"

"She described it as baby blue."

Bruno leaned his neck around and looked over his shoulder. ley! We need to talk."

"Josh," I whispered, "Call Lt. Cotton Broussard with NOPD d tell him where I am. Tell him to get here as as soon as he n."

"I don't like the sound of this. What are you planning to do?"

"I'm going to haul in the guy who killed Barb. But a team of uad cars would ruin everything. Call Cotton Broussard, all ;ht? Tell him it's Room 269, in the rear of the motel. And tell m I've got to have him here in fifteen minutes." I hung up.

I stepped to the chest of drawers and leaned back against them. ou want to talk, Bruno? What about?"

"About a deal. Look, about Toulouse, that waz buzinezz. He az stealing from the corporation."

"The corporation?"

"That's what Rickey Dee call it. Toulouse supposed to drive a :truck, mon. Nothin' more. He started skimming and selling on s own."

"And so Rickey Dee told you to take him out?"

"You can't start lettin' your own guys rip you off. You sta
that, you lose control. Like Mouton."

"So you were trying to frame Mouton with the voodoo stuff?

"Hey, we knew Mouton would beat that rap. We just hass
him some."

"Is that why you shot up the Comus?"

"Hey, Mouton own the Comus. We shot it up and took ou
one of his men. Then we say it waz because Mouton waz the dud
who killed Toulouse." Bruno tossed his head back and laughed

"That's pretty funny stuff."

"Hey, that Rickey Dee a smart dude."

The phone rang, a bubbling trill that sounded as if it wer
underwater. The red, marble-sized dome of the message ligh
flickered during each ring. I sat on the bed and rested my hea
against the headboard.

"Yeah?" I imitated Bruno's rasp.

"Jack?" Josh said. "Why are you talking like that?"

"Did you find Cotton?"

"He's on his way. He said he can be there in ten minutes."

"You told him to hurry?"

"Jack, as I explained in our initial conversation, I am a profes
sional. I carefully explained the gravity of the situation to Lieu
tenant Broussard. He was on his way to assist you as we wer
speaking. You're not going to do something stu——"

I hung up to avoid the lecture. Of course I was doing somethin
stupid. I was out of smart options. If I didn't get Wade over
Louisiana that very night, I'd be in Angola before another chanc
came along.

"Bruno, before we talk deal, let's talk about Barb. You tell m
who took her out and we'll talk deal."

"Hey, Rickey Dee's tinkin' you did it. Takin' out that girl wa
like spittin' in Rickey Dee's face. She waz his squeeze. If you outte
her, you pizzed off Rickey Dee real bad."

The phone rang. I scooped it up before the first ring ended.

"Josh?"

"S'ain't no Josh. S'the front desk." Dirty Charlie was knee-dee
into a young bottle of Kentucky Tavern. "S'about time to chec

t. That party of five I tol' ya 'bout s'gonna get here in forty-
e minutes."

He hung up without waiting for an answer. Forty-five minutes
uld be plenty of time if I could get through to Wade in the
xt few minutes. I called the sheriff's office in Bay Saint Louis,
t the line was busy. I kept the receiver to my ear and pressed
wn on the disconnect button.

"Hey," Bruno said, "how about this for a deal? They got you
murder one, *copain*. What if I told you about some world-
ss weight comin' in from Colombia. Three hundred kees. Be
re at three o'clock. Cops let you walk for a bust like that."

"Why don't you tell the cops yourself? I'll bet they'd be real
terested in hearing that."

"Aw, come on, mon. I don't need to land in no New Orleans
ckup. You let me walk, I tell you when it's coming. Then they
you walk."

"You use it. Maybe the cops will deal with you. You need it
orse than I do." I picked up the phone.

"They kill me in the New Orleans jail. Mouton have my azz in
n minutes."

"You want a deal, I'll give you a deal. Instead of turning you
er to the New Orleans police, I'm going to call the sheriff in
ay Saint Louis."

I let my finger off the disconnect and punched in the numbers.
runo glanced back toward me over his shoulder. The start of a
nile formed at the corners of his lips. He caught himself, held
ck the smile, and put his head down on his knees.

"Iz you choice."

The dispatcher for the sheriff's office answered the phone. I
d known her for years. Wade was on late patrol and she would
t me through to his car phone. I asked if it was a secure line
d she said it was.

"This is Wade." It was a fuzzy connection.

"I got something for you."

"This Delmas? Whadda you want?"

"I got the man who killed Toulouse Caron. He's waiting for
u to come pick him up. We're in New Orleans."

Bruno tilted his head to hear me.

"Who is it?" Wade asked.

"Bruno Hebert. Works for Coastliner."

"Call NOPD. That's a New Orleans case."

I whispered into the phone, low enough so Bruno could hear. "Wade, you better get over here. He also says he knows w‍ killed Barb Novak."

There was a pause. "You're trying to save your ass. He'd s‍ anything to get loose. That is, if you've really got him."

"Oh, I've got him all right. In handcuffs. Aren't you curio‍ about who he says killed the girl?"

"If he says it's anybody but you, he's lying."

"He says it's you, sheriff. You come and get him, and we c‍ pin both murders on him. We'll both walk. If he goes to N‍ Orleans lockup, he's afraid Mouton'll kill him. If you don't cor‍ over here, he'll give the cops your name to stay out of jail. I‍ said he would."

"That lying sack of shit don't know what he's talking about‍

"I got an eyewitness who saw you go into Barb Novak's apa‍ ment right after I left. And I know all about the payoffs you we‍ taking from Rickey Dee."

"You're crazy, Delmas."

"You come pick Bruno up. He tries to escape on the ride hon‍ he gets shot, and we both swear he confessed. If you don't wa‍ to do that, I'll let him nail your ass. I'm trying to help both‍ us."

He didn't say anything for a long time. "This smells like a setu‍ Delmas. How do I know you've even got him?"

"Hey, Bruno," I said, "the sheriff doesn't believe you're he‍ Looks like I'm going to have to send you to New Orleans locku‍ Sure hope Mouton doesn't find out you're there."

"Hey, Wade! Get you azz over here! They kill me over here‍

"You hear that? We're at Crescent City Courts on Chef Me‍ teur. You get here in thirty minutes or he goes to the cops. We‍ in room 269 in the back. No sirens or lights, got it?"

"Yeah. I'm on my way," he said. "Delmas, if you're trying‍ set me up, I swear I'll . . ."

I hung up the phone.

THIRTY-THREE

ngie . . ."

"Jack! You're all right."

"Yeah. Listen, I need you to bring my gun over here. Quick."

"What's wrong?"

"I've got Bruno handcuffed to the bed. Lola ran away, and the
eriff from Bay Saint Louis is coming. I need a gun. Please
urry."

She sighed. "Why did I even ask? Where is the gun?"

"It's in the toolbox of my pickup. That square key fits it.
here's a false bottom on the right-hand side, right behind where
e passenger sits. It's in there."

"Is it loaded?"

"Yeah. Don't waste any time okay? Just drive over here and
ing it to me. Fast, Angie—you hear?"

"Okay, okay! Where's the square key?"

I had the damn ring of keys in my pocket. "I've got it. Drive
1 over here—quick!" I hung up the phone. I had to keep the
1e clear in case Josh or Cotton called.

It took Angie forever to get there. I heard a car door slam in
e parking lot, then the slap of rubber-soled shoes as someone
n up the concrete steps. There was a knock on the door.

"Jack, are you in there?"

I moved the chair propped against the door and opened it.
ngie stepped to the threshold. Her jaw dropped as she saw Bruno
atching the screen. I grasped her arm and moved her out to the
alkway.

"You might not be able to get them zipped, but couldn't you at least put some pants on him?"

"I don't want to get that close to him."

"And wasn't that two people having sex on TV?"

"It's keeping him occupied. Where the hell have you been?"

"I forgot which room Candy said they'd be in, and you hung up before I could ask you. I had to look around for lights and guess where you were."

"Damn!"

"Hey! Just excuse me all to hell! How was I supposed to know which room it was?"

"I'm mad at myself," I said, "not at you. Here's the key. Run downstairs and bring me that gun, okay?"

She started running downstairs and called back to me over her shoulder. "I'll be back in a minute. I've got to drive back to the Alamo."

I saw her Chevy at the end of the building. "Why didn't you just bring the truck?"

She stopped and turned at the bottom of the stairs. "Because you had the keys, genius!"

They can make you so mad.

I went inside, propped the door shut, and sat on the chest of drawers.

"Whoa! Look at that. Thoze are the biggest knockers I ever zaw."

"Tell me about that big shipment coming in."

"You change your mind about that deal, mon?"

"If you tell me something and I let you go, how do I know you're not lying to me?"

"You talk like you don't trust me, *copain*."

"Would Rickey Dee be there at this drug deal?"

"Of course."

Even if everything worked and I nailed Wade that night, would still be tough to drag Rickey Dee in on Barb's murder. But if I couldn't bust that redneck for murder, at least I might be able to set him up for a big drug bust. That could even be better. Murderers get paroled; drug dealers do hard time.

"How's the shipment coming in?" I asked.

"Could be a truck. We got lots of them."

"Could be a lot of things. If you want to walk, you'd better tell me."

"Hey, did you see that?" Bruno's high was nearly gone. He was leaning back, not quite as wired, watching the movie.

I dug out the plastic bag of cocaine and the short straw from Bruno's pocket. I picked up a water glass from the dresser and sat on the side of the bed close to him. I turned the glass upside down, poured out a little powder on the bottom, and formed a line with the long blade of my pocket knife.

"Might as well enjoy this while we wait."

The corner of his mouth turned up in a trace of a smile. "Good tinking."

I held the glass to his face, and the straw to the end of the line of cocaine. I put the straw up to his nose and moved the glass along as he snorted.

"Is that enough?"

"Iz fine."

He turned back to watch the show; he was really into the movie, and his eyes widened.

"You need another line?"

"A little one. Iz good stuff. Never been on the street."

I prepared another line, a shorter one, and held the straw in place. He blew out a big breath, straight down—didn't want to disturb the line—tilted his head to the straw, and inhaled the line in one long, implosive snort. He sniffed four or five quick times, sucked in a lungfull of air, held his breath, then slowly exhaled with a low groan.

"Good stuff?"

"The best," he whispered.

"You sell this?"

"Got a load on the way."

Bruno's eyes grew and his lips curled into a smile as he stared at the now-empty blue glow that came on the TV after the movie.

"You'll cut what's coming in tonight, won't you? Cut it eight or ten times—right?"

"Soon as it comes in. Three o'clock." He let out a puff of air that made his lips flap. "Gotta cut it. Straight stuff kill people. Don' need that hassle."

"Do you cut it?"

He laughed.

"Does the crew at the ice house? I'll bet you're the boss man there, and they cut it. You the boss man, Bruno?"

"Boss mon . . ." He grinned and closed his eyes, leaning his head back against the foot rail.

"Yeah, boss mon," I said. "You run the show, don't you? Where do you cut it? In the icehouse?"

"In the factory."

"That big man, the one with the muscles . . ."

"That Roberto. We call him Bobby."

"Does he cut the stuff?"

"We all cut it."

"Do you unload it?"

"Naw, mon." He laughed. "I da boss mon."

"I'll bet Bobby unloads it. I'll bet he can pick up a load."

Bruno breathed out a raspy laugh. Everything was becoming real funny to him.

"Does he get down into the boat or does he stay up on the dock?"

"Bobby do both. He one strong dude."

"Will he be there tonight?"

"He'll be there."

Words rolled down onto the blue field on the television screen, like movie credits at the theater. "Next feature in three minutes— Please stand by." Bruno gazed up at the screen, his glassy eyes transfixed on the rolling script, which counted down in fifteen-second intervals to the beginning of the next film, which was titled *Tough Love.*

I planted the toe of my shoe on the floor and bobbed my heel up and down. Where the hell was Cotton? I glanced at my watch. Twenty minutes had passed, Wade was coming, and I didn't even want to think about Dirty Charlie's party of five. I scooted to the phone and tapped in Josh's number. Punched it in too fast and got a wrong number. Hit the button to kill the line. Tried again.

"HELLO?" Someone shouted into the phone over the noise and the music.

"Josh Hallman, please."

It took a long, few seconds. "HELLO? JACK?" Josh was yelling. "HOLD ON."

Soon he picked up another line, but no one hung up the phone in the party room, so we screamed at each other.

"YOU HEAR ME, JACK? IS BROUSSARD THERE YET?"

"NOT YET!"

"CAN'T HEAR YOU!"

"I SAID 'NOT YET!' "

Somebody hung up the phone in the other room, and the line quieted down.

"Oh my, that's better," Josh said. "I can hear you now. Is the movie still on?"

"It's a different one. Apparently they play all night."

"Sounds divine."

"Bruno seems to be enjoining it."

"Did you ever say if Lieutenant Broussard made it yet?"

I heard heavy steps on the concrete outside the room.

"He just got here. I'll call you later." I hung up the phone.

As I stepped across the room, the door burst open. The chair propping it up slammed against the wall. Wade held Angie in front of him like a shield. He covered her mouth with one hand and held a gun to her head with the other.

"Let her go, Wade," I said.

It was my gun he was holding to her temple. I smelled her fear. She shouted into the sheriff's big hand. He was in full uniform and his 9 mm was holstered to his side.

"Sheriff! Hey! Arrest me!" Bruno had a big smile.

"Let her go," I said. "All I'm doing is handing over a murderer. I'm giving you a break here."

Wade laughed. "You got that right. I can't believe how stupid you are, Delmas."

"Hey, get me outta thiz place, mon. Hurry up!"

"You and I can work things out here," I said. "She doesn't have anything to do with this. Let her go."

Angie yelled into the palm of his hand.

"Shut up and take off these cuffs!" Bruno shouted. "My arms are killing me."

"Yeah, major-league stupid," Wade said. "You gift wrap not only yourself, but that Haitian snitch on the floor over there, too."

"Who you call a snitch, mon?" Anger flashed across Bruno's face. He strained against the cuffs, glaring at Wade.

"Sherlock Holmes here told me all about your little story, Bruno. I don't know how you found out, but you've become a loose end. You know how I feel about loose ends."

"Are you crazy?" Bruno was puzzled. "What you mean 'found out'? Found out what?"

Wade turned back to me. "Yeah, Delmas, this is a better setup than what you gave me last time."

"You mean Barb Novak?" I asked.

Angie's eyes flashed to the side, like she was trying to look around into his face. Her screams died in his big hand.

"Like when you waited for me to leave and then went in and killed her? Is that what you mean, Sheriff?"

"A great setup, Delmas. That coke whore knew too much for her own good."

"You killed the girl?" Bruno's mouth dropped open. "You outted Rickey Dee's girl?"

Wade glanced at Bruno then at me. "He didn't know?"

"Nobody knew for sure until you just admitted it," I said.

"Hey, Rickey Dee will have your azz, big time! That was stupid! You know he said he didn't want nobody touchin' her. He'll have your azz in a . . ."

Wade shot Bruno in midsentence. The explosion flashed from the barrel; the blast rang through the room. Wade screamed and jerked his hand high into the air. Shook it violently, flinging blood against the wall from where Angie had nearly bitten his finger off. She scrambled toward the door.

I leapt at him as he reached for her. Body blocked him into the low chest of drawers along the wall. Stepped back and lowered my shoulder to ram him.

I lunged, he rolled, and I scraped his side. He pushed up, my gun still in his hand. I chopped down at his wrist, and the gun fell. Wade dropped to his hands and knees, reaching for it.

Kicked him in the rib cage. Like kicking a mattress. Snatched him up by the collar and slammed my fist into his jaw. His head jolted to the side, but he grabbed my arm and took me down on the bed.

He jerked loose, jumped up, and reached for his gun. I rolled across the bed and dove to the floor. Wade raised his revolver and drew a bead down on me.

"DROP IT! POLICE!" The door flew open. Cotton planted and aimed at Wade, both hands on his pistol. Wade swung his gun around.

Cotton popped two caps into Wade before he got set. It knocked him against the wall. He slid down to the floor and fell over on his side.

Cotton stood in place, hands down at his side. "Oh, God. I shot a cop."

"He didn't respond," I said. "He was drawing down on you."

"Oh, sweet Jesus," Cotton said.

Bruno had taken a hit in the rib cage but was still breathing, his chin slumped down on his chest. I uncuffed him, laid him flat, and put a pillow under his head. Wade was still down on the floor, eyes open and breathing hard. He raised a hand to his side, to where he had been hit.

I dashed to Wade's revolver. My own pistol, the one he had held on Angie, was two feet from it. I grabbed both and put one in each pocket of my jeans.

Wade blinked his eyes and winced as he pushed up and rested his elbows on the floor.

Cotton snapped to life and held up his gun, aiming it at Wade. "Don't move!"

Wade looked up at Cotton. "You're in some deep shit, my friend."

"I told you to drop it. You drew down on me." Cotton was pale; his voice quiet and uncertain.

"He's wearing a vest," I said. "That's what I felt when I kicked him. I've got to call an ambulance for this other one."

I knelt beside Bruno. The bullet had entered his right side, not much blood, but I couldn't apply a compress because the puncture wound was at the side of his chest. I stripped the light blanket off the bed and covered him. I dialed 911 for an ambulance. They kept me on the line until I heard the howl of several sirens, far off but growing closer.

THIRTY-FOUR

W hat's that he's calling you? Is it Cotton? Hey, Cotton, you boys at NOPD have some procedure that calls for shooting uniformed officers?"

"Shut up, Wade," I said, "we've got you now."

Wade feigned a puzzled look. "What you talking about?" He rested his back against the wall.

"You killed Barb Novak and admitted it," I said.

"Cotton, did you hear me say that?" he asked. Cotton stood as still as a street mime, his gun trained on Wade.

"All I was trying to do was track down a known drug dealer, and I walked in on a murder. Then a New Orleans cop walks in and shoots me. And here I am in full uniform."

Cotton didn't have a drop of blood in his face. A beading of sweat formed above his eyebrows. "Sweet Jesus," he whispered.

"Cotton, don't worry about it," I said. "We'll nail his ass."

"Yeah, don't worry about it." Wade said. "I'm sure my old friend Captain Guidry will understand. Guidry's head of Internal Affairs nowadays, isn't he?"

"Holy shit!" Cotton could barely be heard. The gun was about to drop out of his hands.

A siren screamed outside as it turned off the street into the parking lot. Through the open door came rhythmic flashes of red light. Red lights meant ambulance. I walked to the balcony and called out to them as they hurried to unload the stretcher.

An EMT bounced up the steps two at a time. He ran by me into the room and placed the oxygen mask on Bruno. Two others, one with a stretcher and the other with an IV plasma unit, followed close behind. Up toward the road, Dirty Charlie stood in the parking lot by the office, looking in our direction.

They started the IV, lifted Bruno onto the stretcher, and were walking him out when another pair of sirens turned off the highway. Two police cruisers raced through the lot to the back of the hotel and screeched to simultaneous stops near the ambulance. The syncopated flashes, red from the ambulance, blue from the police cars, washed the side of the building. One young cop hopped out of the nearest squad car and pulled out his revolver. He looked up at me as I leaned on the walkway railing and kept his eye on me as he jogged up the stairs.

"They're inside," I said. "You've got a murder suspect in there, gift-wrapped."

The other cops, older ones, trudged up the steps. If the paramedics were inside and some guy was standing around outside, the shooting was over. One of them motioned me inside with his head, so I walked with them into the room.

Inside, the young cop patted down Artis Wade. Wade was standing with both palms against the wall. Cotton sat on the side of the bed. He tilted forward like a man trying to catch his breath after a punch to the gut. I walked over and sat beside him.

"What took you so long?" I said.

"Some fool jacknifed a tractor trailer on the I-10 bridge," he said, wiping his face with his palm. "Looks like we both got our ass in a crack now, Cap,"

"We're all right, Cotton. He's the one who killed Barb Novak."

"You sure?"

"Before you got here, he admitted it."

"Sounds like your word against his, Cap."

"Two other people heard it. That guy in there who got shot . . ."

"That sheriff said that guy was a drug dealer," Cotton said. "His story might not mean too much."

"Barb Novak's sister was in there, too. She heard him."

"Where is she?"

"When Wade shot Bruno, she broke and ran."

"She's prob'ly scared to death," he said. "You think she'll testify?"

"No doubt about it."

Cotton dropped his head forward and propped his forearms on his knees. "Well, that's good. But I still got me some problems. I shot a cop while I was on an unauthorized call—and now he says he's buddies with the director of Internal Affairs." He kept looking down, tapping the fingertips of both hands against each other. "Looks like I can kiss captain good-bye."

I couldn't face Cotton anymore just then. I could have called other cops closer to the scene, and they would have been here waiting on Wade when he arrived. I tried to tell myself if I had done that, Wade wouldn't have confessed, that he would have walked. But I had put an old friend in a bad spot. I stood and walked to the television set and turned it off.

"Hey, who turned off the show?" One of the cops said.

"Yeah, it was just getting to the good part," another said.

The cops laughed the way cops do, and kept writing on their report pads.

One officer stood beside Cotton, while another one began talking to Wade. A third policeman, the young one who had first jumped out of the squad car, walked over to me.

"Over there," he said. "Against the wall."

"What are you doing?"

"Department procedure. Put your hands on the wall."

I spread my feet apart and planted my palms against the wall shoulder high. A little late for a pat down, especially with me having two revolvers sticking out of my pockets, but from what I had seen of NOPD procedure, no great surprise. About the time he finished the pat down, one of the cops began taking photos of the room from several angles.

"Have a seat," the young cop said.

Each person—Cotton, Wade, me—was in his own section of the room. When the questions started, they would see if the stories matched. They handled the case by the book—at least roughly by the book—since a cop had taken a bullet and that meant Internal Affairs was surely on the way.

Over by the bathroom, an older cop, pad in hand, talked to Wade. The old cop was squat and gray-headed, with thick arms and an enormous belly. Could have been fifty, could have been sixty-five. Rugged face, deep lines, big pores—looked like he hadn't had a good laugh since the last Dirty Harry movie.

Cotton stayed on the edge of the bed, his head down. They hadn't started questioning him yet. A dark-headed cop about my age took Cotton's revolver, labeled it, placed it in a plastic bag, and clamped the bag with a blue evidence tag. He picked up my gun by the barrel and reached in his hip pocket for another evidence tag.

"Okay. I need your name." The young cop positioned his pen and looked down at the notepad.

"Delmas. Jack Delmas."

He started with the top lines and worked down. He wrote with a wrinkled-brow effort. It was slow going through address, date of birth, height, weight, and the other characteristics that made me an identifiable entity to the New Orleans Criminal Justice Computer System. Under OTHER IDENTIFYING MARKS, he was making note of the inch-long white scar at the base of my left jaw when Internal Affairs walked in.

There were two of them, both in dark business suits and tassel loafers. They walked toward Cotton, who hadn't even looked up. When they stood in front of him, he raised his head. They nodded at him in recognition but didn't shake hands. One sat on the bed beside Cotton, an arm's length away. The other one set a chair backward and sat with his crossed arms resting on the chair back.

The young cop and I had nearly finished with the background questions when the older cop walked over and put his hand on the young cop's shoulder.

"Go help Loftin mark some of this stuff," he said.

"Yes, sir."

The young cop handed his pad and its incomplete report to the older cop and walked over to Wade, who was standing and removing his bulletproof vest. The old cop looked at the fragment of a report and grimaced. He blew a hard breath through his nose, shook his head, and tossed the pad on the bed.

"All right, Delmas. Stand up. We'll finish the questions downtown." He reached back for his handcuffs.

"What are you doing? I'm not under arrest."

"I'm trying to straighten out a damn mess. But in the meantime I'm taking you downtown for questioning."

"For what?"

"Suspicion of aggravated assault."

"What aggravated assault? I didn't attack anybody."

"I'm talking about the guy they just carried outta here on a stretcher."

"You mean you're taking *me* in? That sheriff you were just talking to, *he's* the one you need to arrest. He killed Barb Novak. He was about to shoot me too until Lieutenant Broussard got here."

"Yeah, well, he tells a different story. And your gun's been fired. His hasn't. Stand up."

I stood and he grasped my wrist. He cuffed it, turned me around, and cuffed the other one. "The sheriff tells me you're out on bond on a murder charge. That right, Delmas?"

"Yeah," I said. "But . . ."

"We're through marking the stuff, Sarge." It was the young cop who had interviewed me.

"Be sure to run that vest through Ballistics," the old cop said. "Tell him he can probably get it back when he comes in tomorrow. Oh, and his name is *Sheriff* Wade, ok?"

I could have sworn that Wade smiled at me just before he walked out the door. Looked like a smile.

Why not? I thought. How many people can you find who'll take two felony raps for you?

THIRTY-FIVE

Y ou're letting him go?" I said. "He killed a woman and confessed. Hell, he shot Bruno over there. And he was about to
shoot me too . . ."

He grabbed the back of my left arm above the elbow. "We'll
take your full statement downtown."

"I've got a witness who heard him."

"Officer Broussard told me about that. We'll find her after we
take your statement."

"Sergeant, if you let him go, he'll track her down and kill her.
He'll kill her tonight."

He pulled back on my arm, turning me around so we were face
to face. He looked straight into my eyes and lowered his voice.
"Listen, Delmas. I'm only saying this because I don't want to have
to listen to this bullshit all the way downtown. We can't book
him on anything. All the evidence backs his story, and Lieutenant
Broussard didn't see anything to contradict it."

"The sheriff's a murderer . . ."

"Listen up. He's coming back tomorrow, and you'll get a
chance to tell your story. Right now, this is all I can do."

The young cop walked over to us. "We got his vest. I'll run it
over to Ballistics tonight. When's he coming back?"

"He's supposed to be at Headquarters tomorrow afternoon at
two o'clock," the old cop said. "Tell those jerkoffs at Ballistics to
try to get it back by then. And tell 'em to send it to Internal Affairs.
Guidry wants to talk to the sheriff personally."

"You think he'll show?"

"Who knows?" The old cop shrugged. "He probably will. He and the director are supposed to be big buddies. It was Guidry hisself who said to release him tonight, so it ain't my problem."

He pushed forward against my arm and we took a couple of steps toward the door. I looked over my shoulder. "You let him go, he'll kill that girl. If he can't get to her, he'll run."

"There's nothing I can do, Delmas. If your story pans out, we know where we can get him."

"She'll be dead by then."

"Delmas, there's nothing I . . ."

"Hey, Sarge! Wait up a second." The dark-haired cop who had first talked to Cotton walked over to us. "I just got off the phone to headquarters. That black guy the EMT's were hauling off when we got here, he died on the way to the hospital."

The sergeant grunted. "When they dig the slugs out of him, call Ballistics. Tell them we got two pistols they need to run a match on." He pushed forward again, and we stepped through the door.

You've turned any stay in the New Orleans jail—however short—into a death sentence. You hear me, Jack? A death sentence.

Once out on the walkway, the sergeant stopped and called back to the dark-haired cop, "Hey, Loftin, come out here for a second; I almost forgot something."

Loftin stepped up to the open doorway. "Yeah, Sarge?"

"I need a witness. Got to do this one right. Delmas, you have the right to remain silent. Anything you say can and will be used . . ."

The old sergeant went through the Miranda litany. The air was humid and had never cooled off from the scorching day and sweat popped out all over my back, neck, and shoulders. I looked out over the motel's parking lot. We were at the corner of the building and up high, so I could see both the side and rear lots.

Somebody had killed the lights on the squad cars below so the parking area on the side was dark except for a dim glow from the highway and one sputtering mercury vapor light. The rear of the lot was even darker. There was a Dumpster back there, set against the fragrant ligustrum hedge that encircled the motel.

Beside the Dumpster, in its shadow, sat the yellow Chevy Lumina, its nose pointing out. The brake lights flashed for a split second and lit up the hedge behind it.

The sergeant zipped through my constitutional rights, Loftin stepped back into the room, and we started forward, around the corner, along the walkway at the rear end of the building, and down the steps to the lot below. I was in front and the old cop was one step behind, his hand gripping my arm above the elbow. He had the wheeze of a fat man and was heavy on his feet, each step landed with a thud.

The radios in the squad cars crackled through the hot and heavy air as dispatchers called to cars throughout the city. The highway noise rose and fell as big trucks went by. The motor idle of the Chevrolet wasn't even noticed.

At the bottom step the sergeant lost his balance, just enough so he loosened his hold on my arm for a second. I planted my left foot a step ahead, shifted my weight forward, and broke his grasp. I spun around and kicked him square in the gut with the side of my foot. His breath blasted out of his lungs, and he groaned as he landed on his back on the sidewalk.

I bolted down the rear wall of the building. The Chevy leaped out of its place. Feet out to the side, hands cuffed behind me, I ran like an ostrich to the corner of the building.

Angie got there just as I did. She threw open the passenger door. I jumped in head first, she gunned it, and we zipped down the side parking lot and onto the highway.

"What the hell are you doing?" she said.

"Run over to the Alamo. We've got to switch cars."

We bounced into the Alamo Plaza parking lot and raced to my truck. Angie jumped out, got both of us into my truck, and raced out to the highway.

"Slow down," I said. "They're not after a pickup truck."

"Why are you in handcuffs?"

Out the rear window of the cab I saw the red-and-blue light bars and wigwag headlights of two police cruisers coming out o Crescent City Courts. One went up the highway; one went down

I laid my head on the seat below the line of the rear windshield

Blue light swept the cab of my truck as a cruiser passed us, speeding down the road in pursuit of a yellow car that an old sergeant who'd just had the breath knocked out of him may have seen for an instant while flat on his back. They didn't know what they were looking for or which way it had gone. We would be out of the city in fifteen minutes.

"How on earth did you know I'd be coming out of there like that?" I said.

"I didn't. You still haven't told me why you're in handcuffs."

"You were just sitting in your car?"

"I was waiting to see what happened. When that sheriff shot Bruno and I ran out, I drove to the room and got my gun. I didn't know what else to do. When I got back, there was already another car there."

"That would have been Cotton."

"And it wasn't a minute or two later when an ambulance drove up. I saw you up on the walkway and I knew you were all right. Then the rest of the cops got there. I didn't want to go in 'cause I knew there'd be a dead body, or maybe two."

"Where were you parked all this time? I didn't see you until he was about to walk me down those stairs."

"Same place, right by that Dumpster. You didn't notice me the first time you stepped outside because of all the sirens and flashing lights. When those police cars drove up, I lay down on the seat."

"Did you see Wade come out?"

"Yeah. I got on the floorboard. When I saw you coming down the stairs with that policeman, all I planned to do was follow to wherever he was taking you. When you knocked him down and ran, I was as surprised as he was. Why in the world did you do that?"

"If I'm put in jail, Mouton will have me killed. Might be a prisoner; might be a guard. But he'd get me. He's already got a contract out. I'd be easy money for somebody."

"But why were they going to put you in jail?"

"Let's get these cuffs off. Pull into that Texaco station."

I pushed my manacled hands around, trying to reach into my pocket for the key to the cuffs I had used on Bruno. Handcuff keys are like skate keys; one size fits all. I stretched my arms forward and a sharp pain sliced through my stomach. I caught a short breath and Angie heard it.

"Are you okay?" she said.

"Yeah. But my stomach's still sore."

"You ought to go to the doctor."

"My schedule's a little full right now."

Angie pulled in to the gas station and drove to the side, out of the glare of the big yellow lights over the pumps. She fished the key out of my pocket and it worked.

"Now we go to Bay Saint Louis," I said. "Let me drive; we're taking the back road."

"Why are we going there?"

"Bruno was trying to work a deal with me so I'd let him go. He said there was a big cocaine run going down tonight."

"So?"

"So, I'm betting Artis Wade will be there. It looks like catching him in the middle of a drug run is the only way we're ever going to nail him. And if we don't nail him tonight, I go to jail."

"Why would Wade be there?"

"Because he doesn't know that Bruno told me anything about it."

"What the hell are you talking about?"

"Look, Angie, I'm not sure Artis Wade is going to be there, but he's getting paid to protect them. And if he's planning to run, one last payoff in cash would come in handy."

"When is this supposed to happen?" she asked.

"Bruno said three o'clock."

"Where?"

"At the icehouse."

"Well, if Wade's there when a drug shipment's coming in, he won't be alone."

"I'll get some help."

"In the next three hours, with the cops after you? I don't know much about drug smugglers, but I assume they'll be as well-armed as your average Israeli commando squad."

"Probably."

"That son of a bitch is gonna get away."

"No, he won't."

That's what I said. But I had no idea what we were going to do to stop him.

As we drove along, the hot air blew her hair and it danced around her head. She didn't speak for the next two or three miles as she stared out the window into the dark, summer night.

"Have you calmed down yet?" she asked.

"Yeah."

"You want to tell me what's going on?"

I told her the story to the point where they let Wade go.

"He said I shot Bruno, and it was my gun. He claimed he was only trying to save Bruno from me."

"And they *believed* him?"

"Nobody could contradict him. Bruno was unconscious, Cotton didn't see what he did, we didn't know where you were. That's the reason I broke and ran. It was the word of a sheriff in uniform against that of a guy out on bond on a murder charge."

"I could tell them."

"That'll come later. We've got to keep you alive until then."

"What do you mean?"

"You're the only witness they might believe who heard Wade admit to killing Barb and Toulouse. Wade doesn't like loose ends, remember?"

We drove on and the lights thinned out, and soon there were no more stores and houses. New Orleans pushes the edges of the swamps; there's no gradual change. The cane, the vines, and the bulrushes stake their claim at the border of the last yard of the last house.

"When did you know it was Wade who killed Barb?" She was looking out the window.

"I called Josh Hallman from the Crescent City Courts. He told me the other day that a plainclothes cop in an unmarked car had gone into Barb's apartment right after I left. Then he drove off before the other squad cars got there. Josh checked and NOPD had never dispatched that first car. A woman from across the street said the unmarked car was baby blue. I figured it had to be Wade."

"But why would Rickey Dee send Wade to kill Barb?"

"He didn't. He expected Wade to bring her back to Bay Saint Louis. I'm sure Barb had no idea that Wade would kill her, and Wade himself probably didn't plan to. But when he got there, he must have seen that I was in her apartment so he waited. He figured it was a perfect time to get rid of Barb and pin it on me."

"You don't think Rickey Dee ordered her killed?"

"You remember when Bruno started screaming at Wade after Wade admitted killing Barb?" I said. "You remember what he said?"

"He said, 'Rickey Dee will have your ass.' "

"Right. Bruno was totally surprised when he learned that Wade had done it. Wade knew he'd tell Rickey Dee, so Bruno had to go," I said. "Wade killed Barb on his own. I'm sure of that. Rickey Dee still doesn't know that Wade did it."

"I still don't see why he killed her."

"Same reason he killed Bruno. Same reason he'd kill you. Bruno knew too much, so did Barb. And now, so do you."

"What did Barb know?"

"You've got to understand the whole story. Wade's got social aspirations that take a hell of a lot of money."

"*Social* aspirations?"

"And political aspirations . . ."

"In *Bay Saint Louis*, for God's sake?"

"It may not seem like Manhattan, unless you grew up in Crawfish Corners. Believe me, Angie, living in a house on the beach and playing a few rounds of golf with the right people at Diamondhead on a regular basis are things Artis Wade would kill for. And he's mean enough to take out anything and anybody standing in his way."

"Was Barb in his way?"

"He thought she knew enough to send him to prison. That cuts out tee times at Diamondhead."

"But what did she know?"

"She told me that one day she and Toulouse wanted to surprise

Rickey Dee, and they burst into his office. He was paying Wade off with a thick stack of bills at the time, and they saw it."

"That's it? He killed her because of that? Everybody knew that! Hell, I was only in Bay Saint Louis a couple of days and even I heard that Wade was on the take."

"Some people might have believed it, but Barb could have testified to it," I said. "Truth is that Barb didn't even know who Wade was. She only knew he was some big, dark-haired guy giving Rickey Dee some kind of protection. Even if she knew it was him, she would have never thought of turning him in. That would have been the same as turning Rickey Dee in. But Wade doesn't leave any loose ends, remember?"

Angie raised her feet onto the seat, wrapped her arms around her legs, and pulled them in close. She closed her eyes and laid her forehead on her knees.

We left the canebrakes and the moon was full, sending moonlight shimmering on the saltwater bays beyond the marsh off to the right. We zipped by the fish camps, set up high on spindly poles, and the shrimp boats snugged against piers along the reedy banks.

It was low tide and the exposed swamp mud spread a rotten-egg smell over the savannah as we crossed the Pearl River Bridge onto higher, solid ground in Mississippi. We clipped along through the forests of tall, skinny pines and soon ran into the four-lane highway that took us into town. It was midnight when we reached Bay Saint Louis.

I stopped at the Junior Food Mart to call Roger. He wasn't on duty so I called him at home. The phone rang three times. I heard him knock the phone off the hook and roll it around the top of the nightstand before he picked it up.

"H'lo?" His voice had a phlegmy coat from interrupted sleep.

"It's Jack. Look, man, something's up."

He cleared his throat and coughed.

"Rickey Dee's got a drug shipment coming in tonight by boat. They're landing at Coastliner Ice at three o'clock."

"Where are you?"

"Here in town. You got some deputies you can trust?"

"Yeah, two or three."

"Artis Wade will probably be there."

"What do you mean?"

"He's been taking payoffs from Rickey Dee for protection."

The phone was silent.

"Roger?"

"You sure about this, Jack? And I mean *damn* sure?"

"No doubt about it."

Silence.

"These guys you plan to call," I said, "you trust them enough to handle that?"

He hesitated. "Yeah, these three I can trust."

"Let's meet in an hour at the back end of Buccaneer Park. Tell them to wear dark clothes—and bring all the firepower they've got."

THIRTY-SIX

A swarm of moths and a few grasshoppers circled the forty-watt bulb glowing above the back door of my house. Other than that, the place was dark. We killed the headlights just before we left the road and pulled deep into a stand of scrub pines two lots down.

Angie stayed in the truck with orders to leave if anyone drove up. I ran through the pines and across the vacant lots to the back steps. The dark clothes I had used to sneak over to Crescent City Courts helped because the moon was dazzling.

Stale air assaulted my nostrils when I opened the door; the place had been closed up for several hot days. Thick shafts of light from the big moon poured through the windows, enough light for me to move around without flipping on a lamp. I padded through the kitchen and living room to my bedroom up front.

A warm and steady southeasterly breeze was whipping in from the Gulf, and the limbs of the live oak outside my bedroom window were swaying, running shadows up and down the wall behind my bed. In the closet, propped in the rear corner, was the AK-47 I keep as a boarding gun for long, solo sails. The rifle still smelled of 3-in-1 oil from its last cleaning. Although I keep it loaded, I shoved an extra clip under my belt. That gave me sixty rounds. It would be over, one way or another, before I used all of that. From my nightstand I retrieved my .357 and its holster. I belted on the holster and laced the bottom cord around my thigh.

The wind had cleared any haze on the Gulf, and I could see out my window clear to the horizon. Four shrimp boats, two close in and two out near the Intercoastal, rolled and pitched in the three-foot seas. All four had white overhead dragging lights glowing; they were pulling nets. With so few boats and such a strong moon, we would be able to see the drug runners at least nine miles out.

Angie threw the passenger door open for me. "Did you get everything?" she said.

"All I can handle." I laid the AK-47 in the space behind the seat. "We need to go to Buccaneer State Park about a half-mile down the road. Don't turn the lights on yet."

She started the truck. "Well, what did you think?"

"About what?"

"Didn't the place look nice?"

"Huh? . . . Oh, yeah, real nice . . ."

She turned and laid her arm on the top of the seat to back up. "It was a wreck when I got there. And that *bathroom* . . ."

"Yeah. It looked good. Thanks." I glanced down the road.

"You didn't notice."

"Yes, I did. It looked great." I swear, sometimes they can make you so mad.

There were no cars coming and no one walking along the bench. Angie pulled out of the driveway, flipped on the low beams, and headed toward the park. It was 12:45.

Fifteen minutes later, headlights flashed at us from the road as a Jeep and a big Ford sedan skirted around the chain across the entranceway to the park. Roger's Jeep, an open-air type with a roll bar, was in front. The Ford was a big hog about ten years old. There were three men in it. Mike Brabston was driving, his big arm hanging out the window on the driver's side. They drove past us fifty yards, far into the pines behind the picnic tables. Mike and the other two deputies got out and started unloading their rifles from the trunk.

Roger was still sitting in the Jeep when I walked up. "How'd you find out about this?" he asked.

"Bruno Hebert. You know who he is, or was . . ."

"Was?"

"Bruno got killed tonight. Artis Wade shot him."

"Wade *shot* him? You sure?"

"I wasn't ten feet away."

"Damn!" Roger looked toward the road and wiped his hand across his mouth.

Mike Brabston, Randy Lucas, and Tommy Necaise walked toward us, and when they got close Roger stepped forward. "Thanks for coming, guys," he said.

"I hope there's something to come for." It was Randy. Randy's always been a smartass.

"Jack here believes there's a drug run coming in tonight down at Coastliner Ice."

"What makes you think that?" Randy said.

"Bruno Herbert told me," I said.

Mike hadn't spoken until then. "You mean that big Haitian who works there?"

"Yeah," I said. "He told me about it tonight, right before Artis Wade shot him."

The deputies glanced at each other.

"Wade killed Bruno a few hours ago in New Orleans," I said.

I told them the whole story. Nobody asked even one question. They knew it was true. When I stopped talking, the only sounds were the waves on the shore across the street and the wind through the pines above us. It was a full minute before anyone spoke.

"I can't believe this," Mike said.

"We can talk about it later," Roger said. "The shipment's due in less than two hours."

"How many people will be there?" asked Mike.

"Only a guess," I said. "Five or six of Rickey Dee's men. Probably three or four on the boat. Plus Wade. I'd say ten or twelve, total."

"And we've got five." Randy said.

"Maybe not," Roger said. "I called Chief French at Gulfport Coast Guard and told him what we heard was going down. He said they couldn't authorize sending a force because the local cops haven't requested it."

"Who do they think you are?" Randy said.

"I ain't the sheriff," Roger said. "Besides, we're operating on a rumor. We don't even know for sure that this is the right place." He looked at me. "That right, Jack?"

"Well, Bruno never exactly *said* it would be here. But where else could it be?"

"Coastliner's got a plant on the water in New Orleans," he said, "and one in Grand Isle."

A hollow feeling started in the pit of my stomach and rose to my throat. I hadn't even thought about the other Coastliner Ice plants. Hadn't considered the possibility that the shipment could be somewhere else. I opened my mouth, but couldn't think of anything to say. All the deputies, including Roger, stared at me.

"Well, that's just great!" Randy shifted his weight from one foot to the other, put his hands in his back pockets, and spit off to the side. The new deputy I didn't know shook his head from side to side.

"Hold on," Roger said. "If this *is* true, it's our best chance—hell, our only chance—to bust Coastliner. We've got to at least check it out."

"And what are we gonna do if it's true?" Randy said. "We gonna take on the Haitian National Guard over there? I've got a twelve-gauge automatic, six shots. One of their Uzis can pop out five times that in two seconds."

"Would you hold on a minute?" Roger said. "I told you about the coast guard . . ."

Randy snorted.

"French couldn't send a force, but he said the New Orleans base has three helicopters on night maneuvers, and they're scheduled to leave Mobile on their way back to home base about the time the shipment's supposed to get here."

"They gonna wave at us when they pass over?" Randy said.

"The chief wasn't real happy about it," Roger said, "but he said he'd delay their flyover until I radioed into the Gulfport base. If the shipment comes in, the 'copters will give us backup."

"Now you're talkin'." It was the first time Tommy had said anything. "Them Jayhawks can set down in Rickey Dee's lap."

"Yeah," said Mike, "a Jayhawk'll pin their ass down so tight all we'll have to do is slap the cuffs on 'em."

Randy nodded. "That'd do it." He looked at me. "If the damn boat shows up and this is the right place."

A heat from anger and embarrassment rose up my neck. I took a step forward and balled my right hand into a fist. We both stood still and silent and locked in one of those schoolyard stare downs that usually mounts until the first punch is thrown.

"Hey!" Roger shouted. "We ain't got time for this noise. Let's go set up."

Randy held his glare for a second before he turned toward the car. Roger grabbed my arm above the elbow and steered me toward his Jeep.

"You think this thing will go down?" he said.

"Bruno definitely said there was a run coming in at three and that they would be unloading from a boat."

"But it could be somewhere else?"

"It could be."

He reached under the driver's seat of the Jeep, pulled out a flat, round can of polish, and tossed it to me. "Here, put this on."

Roger went back toward the Ford and I walked to my truck. Angie was slumped low in the seat; nobody had noticed her. I laid my arms on the roof above the passenger-side door, but when I bent forward a pain shot through my gut so I straightened up and squatted down to where my face was at window level.

"We're going in. You stay here, OK?"

"Do you think there'll be a lot of shooting?" Her voice just above a whisper.

"Not if we handle it right. But it's not going to be safe there. You stay here. You hear?"

"I can take care of myself."

"Why do we always have this same argument? These guys are trained in things like this. I am, too. You're not. One wrong move and you can get us all killed. I know you want to go, but it's not fair to these other guys. You're staying here."

"I could help."

It was a feeble last shot.

We trotted along Beach Boulevard, keeping an eye out for headlights. The stretch from Buccaneer Park to where the pavement runs out is a wide concave arc laid out like a contour map, from which you can see cars a mile away, but there were none at that late hour.

We fanned out at the gate across the icehouse's driveway. Mik took the middle area between the drive and the north flank Tommy stayed near the driveway; and Randy went down to th beach. Roger and I set out through the trees toward the north edge of the parking lot. The trees were spaced far apart, but the palmettos and sawgrass were tall and thick, and they blocked our view of the icehouse as we pushed through the woods. We found a good spot to set up beside a squatty live oak at the edge of the clearing.

"Well, look over there," Roger whispered. He pointed toward the icehouse. A light-colored Crown Victoria was parked beside Rickey Dee's Jaguar. "That's Wade's car."

"Hell of a time to be buying ice," I said. The knot in my stomach loosened up a touch.

Roger put his hand on my shoulder. "The other guys already know this. Don't shoot unless you absolutely got to. We threw this operation together pretty fast and we ain't got a hint of authorization. Even if we get something, who knows what piss-ant technicality we could get caught on. If we kill somebody and they throw the whole bust out, we're all in deep shit. Understand?"

"I got you."

"And one more thing. If it comes to a fight, I've got Rickey Dee, and you've got Wade. You're the only one here who's not on the force."

"What does that mean?"

"They were uncomfortable with the idea of going after Wade."

"Hell, Roger, he's as dirty as they come."

"You were in the army. You were in the same squad with some real horse's butts, right? Every group has 'em. But you still were on the same team, right?"

I nodded. "Okay, he's mine."

We didn't see anybody at the icehouse. There were two other cars parked in front of the loading dock, an old Mustang and white sedan, looked like a Buick. Out on the Gulf I saw the red and-green running lights of a boat, probably a fifty-footer, five six miles out, heading for the channel to the icehouse.

"Out there," I said. "That boat looks like it's heading in. Keep in sight and see if it turns."

Ten minutes later the running lights went out.

"Bingo!" Roger said.

In the moonlight the silhouette of the trawler was sharp and ear. She chugged at top speed, eight or nine knots, toward num-r one, the last lighted buoy at the end of the channel. She'd be the dock in half an hour.

Roger held up his VHF "There she is, boys. That trawler out ound number-one buoy. She just cut her running lights. Over."

Roger stooped and stepped through the palmettos toward an l drum at the edge of the woods twenty feet from the bank of e bayou. The wind was holding steady and the waves were eaking on the beach, so I couldn't hear him stepping through e bush even at thirty feet; there was no way they could hear ything upwind at the icehouse.

Soon Artis Wade came around the corner of the building. He tched his thumbs in his belt and rocked back and forth on his es, looking out over the lot. The white oyster shells glowed like snowy field on a clear December night. He surveyed the open ea for a minute or two. Then he walked to the steps at the edge the loading dock, sat against the handrail, and lit a cigarette.

The boat was at full throttle and riding deep, pushing up a onstrous wake. Fifteen minutes out and anxious to get in to the ck.

A second man walked around the corner from behind the ice-use. He said something to Wade, and they both went back ound to the boat docking area. To my right, Roger's dark form ided across the bright field to Wade's car, which was parked osest to him. He crouched behind the shield it provided and ve me a hand signal—arm extended, palm down, pushing down ward the ground—telling me to stay put. He jammed his knife to the side of Wade's rear tire. The car slumped to that side. He awled around and flattened Wade's other rear tire.

Randy jogged in a crouch along the beach, advancing a hun-ed feet, taking cover behind a clump of sea oats. Neither mmy nor Mike moved; they had nothing to use as a screen.

Wade stayed behind the building for a long time. He was st
there when the boat entered Bayou Pitasa and disappeared fro
view behind the icehouse. I smelled the diesel exhaust on the wir
and heard the hum of the engines as the boat docked. Then tl
smell and the sound stopped. They had killed the engines, whi
meant they were already docked and tied.

Wade walked back around the corner to the front of the buil
ing. He must not have felt like unloading. He took up the san
position, leaned back against the handrail, and lit another cig
rette.

Behind Wade's car, Roger sank to one knee, bent down lo
and held the radio up to his mouth. Without a radio I had to ta
my cues from the movements of the others, a half-step later. N
one moved. Maybe he was calling in the Coast Guard chopper

Wade finished his cigarette and flipped the butt out into tl
lot. A whiff of the smoke blew across the field. The only soun
were the steady roll of waves breaking on the beach and the ro
of the wind.

From behind me, a soft drone rose as it came toward me.
could see down Beach Boulevard for miles through a clearing
the trees. Back where the road rounds a point and goes out
sight, up in the sky just above the treetops, I saw three bright, ti
lights. Three Jayhawks, coming fast.

Flying into the wind, they were almost on top of me before
could clearly hear the bubbling sound of the blades. They flipp
on their searchlights when they were directly overhead, and o
of them hit squarely on Artis Wade. Without a sound, with r
attempt to warn the men at the back of the icehouse, Wade r
down the steps and jumped in his car.

Randy ran up from the beach, Tommy and Mike burst out
the trees straight across the field, and Roger sprinted to the ed
of the building to stop anybody coming around the corner.

Wade threw his car into reverse and bounced back a few fe
on the flat tires. He jumped out and ran away from the icehou

A 'copter trained a spotlight on him and hovered low, t
downward blast of wind from its blades kicking up a stingi
cloud of dust and sand. Wade ran, pumping as hard as he cou
across the wide, shelled lot, toward the woods. I sprinted in l

rection, and he bolted off away from me toward the trees. The
copper drifted toward the icehouse and ran its spotlight up and
down the bank of the bayou.

Wade kept running and never looked around. But he was fat
and slow, and I caught him fifty feet before the woods. I slammed
into his side with a flying tackle and we slid along the shells,
scraping my knees and forearms.

I got to my knees and took a swing at his face. He blocked with
his forearm. He struggled to his feet and took two steps toward
the woods, still wanting to run. I pushed up and lunged for his
arm. I caught his wrist and held on. He dragged me three steps
before he broke my grasp. I fell to the ground. His momentum
carried him another couple of steps. I rolled to the side, fumbling
for my .357. He planted his feet and squared his shoulders back
toward me. He pulled his revolver and drew down on me.

I heard the blast, saw the stream of fire from the barrel. A spray
of shell and sand kicked up and hit my face. I reversed my roll
and drew out my gun. On my back, I saw an upside-down image
of Artis Wade, two beefy hands on a pistol, his eyes squinting
down the barrel. I rolled, trying to get my pistol up to shoot.

A gunshot flashed from the woods. Then another. Wade
wheeled around and pumped a round into the trees, fire explod-
ing out of the barrel. He shot a second round. I extended my arms
I rolled onto my stomach. I took quick aim at Wade's chest
and popped two slugs into him. He fell backward, hitting the
ground so hard I heard the thud.

I lay for half a minute with the .357 in firing position, aiming
along the ground at his limp body twenty feet away. He never
moved.

I pushed up from the ground, keeping Wade in my sights. I
got to my feet and stepped toward him, my pistol trained at his
torso. A dark stain of blood soaked into the sand and white shells,
outlining his left shoulder. I knelt at his side and felt his neck for
a pulse.

Artis Wade was dead.

Two copters had landed in front of the icehouse and the third
one hovered above the roofline behind the building, training a
searchlight down on the boat. Tommy held a rifle on two guys,

who leaned spread-eagle against the front wall while Mike frisked
and cuffed them. The Coast Guard boarding teams rounded the
icehouse with their M-16s.

I raced toward the woods to where the shots had come from.
At the edge of the lot, where the shells touched the grass, Angie
lay face down, the pistol still in her hand.

THIRTY-SEVEN

t had not been a pretty day. The sky was gray and so was the water, and we dodged pesky thunderheads all afternoon. But we stayed to the inside of the island, protected from the winds ut of the south and west, so at least it was calm.

Wade's second shot had caught Angie just below the ribs on er left side. It was a hot round and it had zipped through her leanly, but it nicked just enough soft tissue to send her into shock nd cause some major bleeding inside. Thank God the sheriff's epartment had shifted to 9 mm's the year before. The .45s they sed to carry would have taken her out.

Angie wasn't ready for sailing, too much movement and work or someone just released from a two-week stay in the hospital. o we took Neal's cabin cruiser, and she slept below in a side unk when we rode out.

For most of the day I steered while Neal and Kathy sat in the vo deck chairs, trolling for mackerel with artificial lures. Drop shing with cut bait was too messy for Kathy and too much trou-le for Neal. He set out four lines, two of them spread wide with ie outriggers, and the other two propped in the holders attached o the front of the chairs. We had good luck along the trough etween the leeward shore of Cat Island and a shallow bar half a iile out that parallels the coastline for a nautical mile. In three asses we pulled in a dozen good-size Kings.

I sat up top and piloted the boat from the flying bridge. Angie ad joined me earlier and I let her steer some. She was getting ronger, but, as usual, she pushed herself too hard and had sink-ig spells and I told her to go below and rest.

Angie was flying back to Michigan the next day, leaving out o
Lakefront in New Orleans on a ten o'clock flight. I was to begin
a job in Biloxi for Bayou Casualty the day after that. It was the
same job they had wanted me to start a few weeks earlier, before
I was arrested and booked for murder. There had been yet another
fire since then. They wanted me to investigate that one, too.

Angie had been below an hour when Neal climbed up to see i
I wanted a turn at trolling. In the two weeks since the bust, I had
been questioned by the sheriff's department, the state narcs, the
DEA, NOPD, the Coast Guard, Immigration, and the PI licensing
bureaus of both Louisiana and Mississippi. And even though
had managed to bust Rickey Dee McCoy for them, and agreed to
testify at his trial, the FBI had still made sure that everybody else
was through with me before they dropped the interstate flight
charges. After all that, I was enjoying the solitude of the upper
deck. I told him I'd stay there for a while.

"What have you heard from Josh?" I asked.

"He got a copy of the order dismissing your assault on a law
enforcement officer charge. He's putting it in the mail today."

Neal reached into the forty-quart Igloo and sloshed around
until he came up with two Budweisers.

"Here's to Big Jim," he said.

"One measley beer? If Big Jim Brannan were here right now
he'd take that as an insult."

"You're right," he said. "The next three are to Big Jim."

We touched the cans against each other. I looked out toward
the horizon and my mind returned to one fishing trip I'd take
with Big Jim. We had taken his boat, gotten into a school of
redfish off Chandeleur, and filled two ice chests. During the two
hours we worked the school, I had never seen a grown man show
such unabashed and contagious joy.

"Yeah, you nailed Mouton good," Neal said.

The flashing screen on the depth finder caught my eye, and
blinked back into the present.

"How about Cotton?" I asked. "Is Internal Affairs still giving
him a hard time?"

"Josh told me that when Cotton gave the chief your videotape
the boys from Internal Affairs just disappeared. He seemed sur

that Cotton's going to make captain when the next promotion list comes out."

"I hope he's not mad at me for putting him in a jam like I did."

"Apparently, all is forgiven. Josh said Cotton and Janelle are planning to invite you down to their camp in the next few weeks."

"Janelle's planning to be there?"

"That's what he said."

He sat on the padded bench beside me until an outrigger clip snapped and the drag on one of the reels sang as some big King, or maybe a Bonita, ran Kathy's line straight out and she called up for some help. He stood and stepped back to the ladder. "I'm going back down," he said. "I'll check on Angie."

Another hour passed and the day was nearly over. We were making our last pass along the shore when Angie climbed the ladder and sat beside me on the bench under the canopy of the flying bridge. She rested her head on my shoulder.

"Feeling better?" I asked.

"Uh-huh. I'm fine," she said. "How about you? Is your stomach still bothering you?"

I hadn't noticed any pains for at least a week and until then I had forgotten about it. "It quit hurting a few days ago. Just went away."

"You think it was Maurice's friend?"

"Olivia? No, she didn't have anything to do with it."

"So you don't believe you had a hex on you?"

"I do not."

"Well, why did you get her to come to your house four or five times and sprinkle magic powder around your room?"

"Who told . . ."

"Kathy."

"I did it to get Maurice off my back. OK?"

"Uh-huh."

"Shut up, woman."

She put her head back on my shoulder. I reached my arm around her and soon she nodded off once more. A few minutes later a forty-foot Hatteras crossed our bow, and when we hit the wake it woke her up.

"I guess we'd better head in," I said. "You've got to get packed."

We reeled in the lines and pulled in the outriggers. Neal and Kathy leaned back in the deck chairs and propped their feet on the stern rail as I swung around to run back along the trough to the narrow pass that would take us to deeper water.

"You're welcome to stay down here as long as you want," I said.

"No, I've got to go back home. It's sad for me down here. And Mom and Dad need me right now."

We drew even with a rusted old barge on the shoreline, that had washed up there some years earlier during a storm, and since that time has served as my landmark for the end of the shallow bar and the pass that would lead us to deeper water. I turned due north until we got into ten feet of water and then I set on a west-northwesterly heading. We would reach the mouth of the bay in an hour and a half, and the dock around sunset. I pushed the throttle forward, but only a little past trolling speed.

"When will you come back down?" I asked.

"I can't say. It's going to take some time."

"Maybe I can go up to Michigan."

She started to say something but hesitated. She was silent for a few seconds as she decided whether she should say what was on her mind. "I think I need to spend some time away from here," she said.

"Am I part of 'here'?"

"I . . . just need some time . . ."

"I understand."

And I did. She had too many emotions to confront and rearrange for me to push anything just then.

So did I.

The sky darkened and the wind grew cold. The smell and feel of rain was in the air. Kathy tossed up a light blanket and Angie covered herself. She laid her head across my lap as the gentle rocking of the boat and the hum of the diesel put her to sleep once more.

When we neared the channel marker, about to cross the Marieanne Pass, I spotted an open boat, a runabout, a mile or so to the west. I put the binoculars on it and saw a teenaged boy, bare chested and wearing swim trunks, waving his arms. A girl who was with him sat on the passenger's seat, her feet pulled in close, hugging her knees for warmth.

We made a swing over and brought them on board. They had run out of gas. Kathy took them below and found them some warm clothes, while Neal secured the tow line to the runabout's anchor cleat. Angie slept through it all.

By the time we got underway, nightfall was near and the lights of the channel markers along the Intercoastal came on. Off to the west, toward New Orleans, lightning beyond the horizon sometimes lit up the sky and a deep, slow rumble would roll across the Gulf. It was going to be rough out on the open water that night.

But we were in the channel, headed toward the familiar lights on shore which were guiding us home, back to the safe and quiet harbor of Bay Saint Louis.

Read on for an excerpt from
Martin Hegwood's latest book

A GREEN-EYED HURRICANE

Available in hardcover from
St. Martin's Minotaur

ONE

When I was growing up, Mr. Cass laughed a lot. That was years before he became a sad and solitary old man. Some people in Biloxi grew to hate him, and I'll admit those people had their reasons. But I was the one, not one of those enemies, who lay awake in my camphouse those steamy July nights with the sheets clinging to me, tossing and sweating even under the ceiling fan and the air conditioner. I was the one he had trusted. I was the one who let him down.

Casper Perinovich was like a second father to me. He and his wife Marie had one child, Mike, my best boyhood friend. Every summer vacation I visited for two weeks in the Perinovich home in Biloxi, thirty miles east along the Mississippi Gulf Coast from our home in Bay Saint Louis.

Mr. Cass was still living in that same house that cloudless summer day when I drove to Point Cadet, the eastern end of the peninsula on which Biloxi sits. The white glare off the sand and crushed oyster shells in the driveways and on the shoulders of the tip of Howard Avenue made my eyes water. Waves of heat squiggled from the sun-softened asphalt, and sunlight danced like sequins on the broad inlet of the Mississippi Sound at the end of the street. The pungent ammonia smell from Acme Shrimp Company, running hard at the height of the season, blew in from up Back Bay.

As the founder, owner, and only employee of Jack Delmas Investigations, Incorporated, I was working two arson investigations on the Point for Bayou Casualty Insurance Company out of New Orleans. I handle most of their work on the Mississippi Gulf Coast at fifty dollars per hour plus expenses. I live in Bay Saint Louis and it's cheaper for them to hire me at an hourly rate than to send out an in-house guy. It's also a hell of a lot more effective, since the Mississippi Coast is my turf. I promised my mother and father I would stop by to visit Perinovich since the fires were close to his house. I stopped by on Thursday, my last day on the last case.

The sign said BEWARE OF DOG, so I stopped outside the gate and whistled. Not a dog or even a cat in sight. Got halfway between the gate and the front steps when five sharp barks echoed as if from an empty room, and the monster came barreling out from under the porch and trapped me.

I froze where I stood. The dog laid its ears back and made short lunges at my throat, pulling up only inches from my face. I smelled the dog's hot breath through two inches of pink gums and three inches of ivory fangs. My heart went into overdrive, and I had to force myself to breathe.

Eye contact can trigger an attack, so I caught only glimpses of the dog's face, its blazing yellow eyes. The fur bristled and its back arched higher than my waist. It let loose with a series of ear-splitting barks. I know dogs; these were no idle barks.

"Mr. Cass!" I screamed. "Help! It's me, Jack Delmas!"

The screen door creaked open. The dog backed away, still snarling and still snapping. Perinovich tottered through the screen door, shifting his weight from side to side as he walked to the front of the porch. With an underhand toss, he flipped a Milk Bone in a high arc. The dog snatched it in mid-flight. Sounded like finger bones crunching. It stopped growling at me and turned its amber eyes to Perinovich. Even started wagging its tail. Cass tossed a second dog biscuit, and the monster chomped it on its downward flight.

"Dat's all you get, Sweetie," he said. "Get on 'round back." Perinovich swept his arm toward the side of the house, and the wolf trotted to the corner of the house and crawled back to the cool shade and soft dirt under the porch.

"Jack! Good to see you, son."

"What was *that*?" My hands trembled as the adrenaline worked its way down to my fingers.

"I figure German shepherd mostly. Some people say he's a wolf. It's them yellow eyes. He might have a little coyote in him, but he ain't a wolf. How's ya mama 'n them?"

"I think my heart's about to jump out of my chest."

"Woulda got out here sooner, but I was hoping maybe Sweetie had cornered that pain in the ass Bobby Weldon."

Perinovich padded to the left front door, as if each step hurt and held it open for me. He had shrunk since the last time I was there, but even at seventy-eight years old he was still solid. I hadn't seen Mr. Cass for nearly three years, and felt guilty about it. But there had never been a good time. When I called him earlier that day, he invited me to go night shrimping. My brother Neal, the lawyer, was running for the state senate and needed some shrimp for a fund-raiser he was holding in a few days. It was good that my fire investigation ended on Thursday. It's big time bad luck to start a shrimping trip on a Friday.

"I got Sweetie to keep dem Vietnam gangs off my property, but she works just as good on Weldon. He come around here twice a week before I got my dog. 'Bout to worry the hell out of me to sell this prop'ty to him."

When my heart geared back down, I felt light-headed. I was wet with sweat, so I balanced on the edge of the couch and held my face toward the oscillating fan. The breeze from the fan felt almost frosty against my skin and drew the smell of fresh brewed tea from the kitchen.

"Guess you heard 'bout the casino," he said, "the one dey tryin' to put in here on the Point. Weldon ain't admitting dat's why he wants to buy me out, but it's gotta be. He got too much money backing him for it to be anything else."

I had indeed heard about the new casino. I was five days into a pair of arson investigations, fires number four and five on Point Cadet since the first of the year. That's eight times the normal rate, so the computers kicked out the order to investigate. There had been a lot of talk about the casino that week.

"You look a little hot," Cass said. "I got some tea cooling back in the kitchen." He had the barrel chest and bull neck of a lifetime shrimper. He still had more black in his hair than gray, but his skin had started to hang on his frame. "So what you doing on the Point? You investigatin' some big crime or something?"

"We've had some fires."

"We?"

"Bayou Casualty out of New Orleans. I do investigation for them sometimes. They pay me by the hour plus expenses."

"You think somebody set dem fires?"

"The company thinks it's unusual to have so many."

"I ain't trying to knock you outta work," he said, "but I can tell your Bayou-whatever company what the problem is. The casinos done jacked the price of land up sky-high. Don't even want the houses, just the land. So the folks, they sell the land and torch the house to collect the insurance. Dat casino money, it's making crooks out of a lot of folks."

"Is it the casinos' fault that they put a lot of money into circulation, Mr. Cass?"

"Didn't say it was their fault. They just supply the temptation. The folks around here're taking it from there. I could use a glass of tea. You want one?"

He stepped into the kitchen. The living room still had the touch of Marie, Perinovich's wife. It had been thirty years since that great tragedy had claimed her life. Faded lace doilies were spread on the arms of the overstuffed couch and matching chair. In the corner, a half-written letter was turned into the carriage of the black Royal manual typewriter. Earth tone lamps flanked the ends of the couch, like props from the set of the *Mary Tyler Moore Show*. It sent me back to when I came over from Bay St. Louis to spend the night with their son, Mike, who died with his mother. It felt as if Mike were going to walk into the room at any minute.

"You take yours with lemon, don't you?" he said. "Sure you do. I remember."

"You writing another letter to the editor?"

"I got the goods on him this time, Jack. That crook Bernie Pettus and that whole bunch. I'm about to bust it wide open."

"You might ought to go to the district attorney before you put it in the paper."

"Tried that thirty years ago," he said. "Found out you got to

make it public first. Then there ain't no way for a DA to bury it.
He handed me the glass, up to the brim with sweet lemon tea and
dripping with condensation.

"What kind of evidence do you have?"

He shook his head. "Got it in yesterday from up at Jackson.
It's a public record, all anybody's gotta do is know where to look.
I can't tell you about it just yet."

"Does it have anything to do with the new casino?"

"What I'm talking about ain't got nothing to do with casinos.
But you can bet Bernie's got his fingers in that thing somehow.
Too damn much money floating around for him to stay away
from it. I'm talking about something that's gonna get the feds
down here."

"Put your stuff in a safe place, Mr. Cass."

On the sideboard along the opposite wall sat three framed pictures. One was a family shot, Casper, Marie, and Mike, at Mike's
sixth grade graduation, just three months before he and his mama
died. He wore that smile of devilment, as Mama called it, that he
got when he and I were about to embark on some adventure
which he had dreamed up. The second frame held a picture of
Jesus in a pink robe pointing to the sacred heart on his chest. At
the base of the picture, two tiny flames glimmered in squatty, red
votive candle-holders. The other picture was of Sheila, Perinovich's niece. Her black hair was cut in a page boy and she was
holding her son who looked to be about two years old.

"What do you hear from Sheila?" I asked.

"She's doing great. Got her own hotel down in Miami and
raking in the cash. She asked about you the last time we talked."

"Her own hotel?"

"Got it in her divorce." He shook his head. "You young people
nowadays just don't stay together."

"I tried, Mr. Cass. I sure didn't want Sandy to go back to Memphis."

"I ain't gettin' on you. It's a different world nowadays."

I had lost touch with Sheila, but I thought of her often. Any
man who spent any time around Sheila would have a hard time
forgetting her. We dated one summer, the summer before I left

for Ole Miss. Three hundred miles at that stage of life was enough to kill the romance.

"Sheila's boy, he's about to graduate down at the University of Miami," he said. "Marine biology. Maybe he can come up here and tell me how to find them shrimp." He held his gaze on the portrait. "Sheila, she's real busy with that hotel."

He touched her image lightly as if he were stroking her hair, and looked as if he had gone inside the picture. When I was around Mr. Cass, I got the feeling that he took such trips fairly often.

"Mighty good tea," I said.

He turned and stepped toward his chair. "You ready to get some shrimp?"

"Maybe I ought to just buy some from you," I said. "Neal needs about thirty pounds for this fund-raiser he's having."

"I heard about dat. State senate, isn't it? Maybe I can call the shrimp a donation." He reached back and gripped both arms of his padded armchair and eased himself down.

"I'm not asking you to give me any shrimp," I said. "This is how you make your living."

"You ain't heard? I'm the richest man in Biloxi. I just go out shrimping for the fun of it."

"You don't have to take me. I'll get in your way.

"I don't sell shrimp to any Delmas. You got to work for 'em. And as far as you getting in the way? You're a Delmas, son. The Delmases fished along this coast two hundred years before us Yugoslavians even got here. Your daddy, he's still the best I ever saw. I swear, he can smell where dem shrimp are. It's in your blood, boy, whether you know it or not."

So I decided to go. It was a Thursday and clear weather was predicted. What could possibly go wrong?

A COLD DAY
IN PARADISE

STEVE HAMILTON

Other than the bullet lodged less than a centimeter from his heart, former Detroit police officer Alex McKnight thought he had put the nightmare of his partner's death and his own near-fatal injury behind him. After all, Maximilian Rose, convicted of the crimes, has been locked in the state pen for years. But in the small town of Paradise, Michigan, where McKnight has traded his badge for a cozy cabin in the woods, a murderer with Rose's unmistakable trademarks appears to be back to his killing ways. And it seems as if it will be a frozen day in hell before McKnight can unravel the cold truth from a deadly deception in a town that's anything but Paradise.

"When a prize-winning crime reporter tries his hand at mystery writing, what do you get? You get a real winner. Don't miss it."
—Tony Hillerman

Jitter Joint

Howard Swindle

SOON TO BE A MAJOR MOTION PICTURE STARRING SYLVESTER STALLONE!

Jeb Quinlin has been issued an ultimatum by his boss and his wife: dry out or get out. So he hits his favorite bar for a last fifth of Wild Turkey and reluctantly enters detox. Once inside, Jeb is forced to confront his years of alcoholism with the help of Librium, hard-core therapy, and AA meetings. But someone is taking the words of the Big Book too far, as rehab patients begin to die mysteriously, each tagged with one of AA's Twelve Steps. Now Jeb is on a sobering hunt for the Twelve-Step killer, a twisted psychopath who's taking the battle with the bottle to horrifying new heights...

AVAILABLE WHEREVER BOOKS ARE SOLD FROM ST. MARTIN'S PAPERBACKS

JJ 3/00

From the acclaimed author of *Flat Lake in Winter*
comes a gripping legal drama that's
"just like Grisham."*

FELONY MURDER
Joseph T. Klempner

A small-time lawyer in private practice, Dean Abernathy has a big case on his hands. His homeless client has confessed to killing the police commissioner, claiming it was an accident. But Dean thinks there's more to this case than anyone's admitting. And with the help of a gutsy single mom, he's about to discover that behind the notorious blue wall of police silence stands a conspiracy so menacing, that the deeper he gets into it, the more he realizes he'll be lucky to get out alive…

"A book you can't put down…A winner."
—Edwin Torres, State Supreme Court Justice and author of *Carlito's Way*

"[A] tautly woven legal drama."
—*Booklist*

Kirkus Reviews

FM 2/00